SECRET SUBMISSION

MASTERS OF MARQUIS
BOOK 8

GOLDEN ANGEL

THE LETTER

Dear Mistress Julie,

I want to apologize for any fright or distress I might have inadvertently caused you. I don't think I have, but just in case. I didn't mean to worry you when I sent the gift to your house.

If you'd like to know who I am, I am willing to meet.

I haven't revealed myself before because I've been unsure of what you would think. Of what everyone would think. But I'm tired of hiding.

I'll be at Marquis next Friday in a booth by myself. I'll have a bouquet of roses for you. If you would be open to joining me, I would love to try serving you for the evening. If not, I understand. I hope, at the very least, that I've given you some pleasure over the past year.

Yours, ever in admiration.

1

JULIE

It was a normal Friday night. At least, that's what she had to convince everyone around her. Her friend and co-teacher, Law. Freddy and Morgan, who were working at the front desk of Marquis this evening. Master Patrick and Lexie, who were performing a Shibari scene for the evening's entertainment.

One of the things she liked about Marquis was how theatrical everything was. She enjoyed watching a good, honest scene at Stronghold, but there was something beautiful about the way Marquis became a performance. It added an extra dollop of something to the voyeuristic experience.

And she did love a good Shibari scene. Master Patrick, who owned both the Stronghold and Marquis kink clubs, had been working on his technique over the past year, and he was enjoying making Lexie fly with more and more intricate knots and arrangements. Julie enjoyed watching it happen.

She'd always been more of a voyeur than an exhibitionist.

"Are you staying to watch the show?" Law asked as he got to his feet in the office they shared. He ran his hand over his bald head, the way he sometimes did when he was thinking. They co-taught the introduction classes for new members of the clubs, and they'd been doing it together for a while, so she knew him pretty well. She enjoyed teaching the classes with him, but when it came to the topic of the secret admirer who had been sending her gifts for months, he became a bit of an annoyance. She was glad he was headed home to his submissive and girlfriend, Iris, rather than staying for the evening.

"Yeah." She smiled at him as normally as she could. *What does my normal smile look like?* "You know I enjoy the Shibari shows."

He nodded, smiling back at her, tugging his dress shirt down to adjust it over his chest. Was he smiling normally? Had he noticed something was up?

The last thing she wanted was Law up her ass all evening when she was finally going to find out who her secret admirer was. For the longest time, she hadn't cared. It had almost been nice not to know, but now that they'd offered to reveal themselves, she *had* to know.

Her mother had always cautioned her about her curiosity when she was younger.

Curiosity killed the cat.

Julie still remembered the feeling when she was twelve years old and discovered the rest of the saying... *but satisfaction brought it back.* She'd taken great satisfaction in informing her mother, who had not enjoyed being corrected but had mostly taken it with good grace.

Her admirer had been sending her gifts for just over a year now. Always her favorite things. Always—until recently—delivered to Marquis when she was working. Which was what had set Law off in the first place. Some of those deliveries had happened when it wouldn't have been common knowledge she was present at Marquis. They never arrived during classes.

He'd been convinced she'd had a stalker, but as the months had gone on with no contact other than gifts and notes, always delivered by a third party, Julie had relaxed. Right up until she'd gotten a gift at her house because she hadn't been at Marquis on the 'one-year anniversary' of when the gifts had first started. At least, that's what the note had said, explaining why it had been sent to her house.

Law had nearly hit the roof.

She'd been more disturbed than she'd let on to him, mostly because she hated admitting he might be right. But, again, nothing had happened after that. No one had appeared at her house or started calling her or doing anything that might be construed as escalation.

One might argue that coming to Marquis to reveal themselves was an escalation, but they were leaving it entirely up to her whether or not to join them. Julie couldn't make the decision until she knew who they were, and having Law breathing down her neck was going to be counterproductive to all that. Plus, she didn't want him barging in to scare them away or scold them. Then she'd have to kick his ass, which could damage their coworker relationship.

"Have a good night," he said, giving her a little wave before walking out the door.

Julie breathed a sigh of relief. He definitely didn't know something was up, or he'd never have left like that.

Glancing at the clock, she felt a flutter in her stomach. People would be starting to arrive, those who were eating before the show started. Would her secret admirer be one of them? Or would they just show up for the show?

Dinner would make sense if they wanted her to join them. On the other hand, maybe they wouldn't want to sit there eating alone if she didn't. Maybe they'd show up at the last minute, just in case she didn't come.

The phone in her office rang, and she picked it up.

"Are you going to come over to watch on the security cameras with me or not?" Olivia demanded as soon as Julie picked up, rather than greeting her. Another Domme, Olivia, was the manager of Marquis and the only one who knew about the secret admirer's latest note. Julie hadn't even told Camille, the third member of their little coterie. Not because she didn't trust Camille, but Camille's submissive *was* Freddy, who worked at Marquis, and although he could be tight-lipped, too...

The fewer people who knew, the better. If she didn't go to meet her secret admirer, she didn't want anyone to know she'd rejected them. They'd brought her a lot of joy over the past year, and she didn't want to hurt them, even if she decided not to accept their offer of service.

"I'm coming. I was just giving Law a minute to clear out."

"He's gone, now come over!"

Julie laughed softly as she put down the phone. There were very few people she allowed to boss her around anymore, but Olivia was one of them—sometimes. Mostly because she was technically Julie's boss. In this case, she'd allow it because Olivia was demanding something she wanted to do, anyway.

Getting to her feet, she smoothed her hands over the black skirt she was wearing, even though it didn't really need it. She'd dressed carefully today in a skirt she could easily move in and pull up if she wanted to and a button-down silky jewel-tone blue blouse. Just a little dressier than she might normally be. Nothing to set anyone's alarm bells ringing—as Law's evidently had not.

Lifting her chin, she stepped out into the lobby and gave Freddy and Morgan a little wave. They were preoccupied with talking intently about something, but they both waved back. She had to laugh at herself. This was what main character syndrome felt like— thinking everyone was paying attention to her when they were wrapped up in their own lives.

With her day job of being a therapist, she was pretty familiar with the symptoms, though she didn't often experience them herself. It was very interesting to realize she felt like everyone was looking at her and paying far more attention to her than they actually were. Law had gone about his day as usual and left to go home. Freddy and Morgan were having their own discussion.

No one was as interested in her life as she was.

Which really helped her relax as she crossed over to Olivia's door. She knocked at the same time she turned the handle, opening the door to cross the threshold. Olivia looked up as Julie came in, grinning widely. She loved being in the know, and she'd promised not to even tell her fiancé about the admirer being revealed.

"You look nice," Olivia said, casting a scrutinizing eye over Julie.

"Thanks." Julie automatically reached up to smooth her hair back, even though it didn't need it. She'd put the long, silky mass back into a bun and added two decorative chopsticks to it. They were pretty and good for sensation play.

She'd also found they were good for stabbing impertinent Doms, who assumed she was submissive just because she was Asian. Painful but not harmful, as long as she wasn't wielding them with too much force. Thankfully, not something she'd had to worry about since coming to Stronghold and Marquis. The vast majority of members knew better than to stereotype, and the ones who didn't quickly learned their lesson. Still, it was better to be safe than sorry, and since she didn't know what to expect from her secret admirer, having some kind of self-defense weapon on hand seemed smart.

At just barely five feet tall and petite in every way, she was used to everyone being bigger than her and, therefore, assuming they were stronger. Sometimes, they were even right, though many underestimated her. The first time she'd met Olivia had been at a Jujitsu class, and she'd rocked the other woman's world, despite Olivia's experience with other martial arts. That was how they'd become friends.

Walking around the desk, she sat down in the chair Olivia had obviously pulled up for her. Olivia didn't even glance at her—the redhead was practically sitting on the edge of her seat, her eyes glued to the screens, watching everyone who was approaching the building from the members' entrance.

Marquis was set up as a restaurant in front, with the kink club on the second floor. Members came through a separate, hidden entrance. Some of them dined in the regular restaurant beforehand, though most preferred to come to the second floor's more private surrounds for their meal. Groups were the most likely to eat downstairs, then split up once they reached the second floor, though the booths upstairs would also accommodate parties up to six or eight.

"Anyone with roses so far?" Julie asked, even though she already knew the answer was no. Otherwise, Olivia would have called to tell her, even if Law had been in the office.

"Nope." Olivia didn't look surprised or offended Julie had asked.

She knew Julie was nervous. "No one with flowers at all. So far, I've seen Master Eric and Steve and Master Roman and Glory."

No one unexpected, then. There were no solo reservations for the evening, which was what made everything more curious. Several reservations had been made under assumed names, which wasn't unusual. Some of the members were more secretive than others. As long as they showed up with their Member ID, they were allowed in, even if they'd made the reservation under a different name.

There were also a few reservations for groups that had been made under a single name. So, it was hard to tell just from the reservations who her admirer might be, unfortunately.

"Oh, isn't that Noelle... and she's alone and carrying flowers?" Olivia's shocked and slightly panicked tone matched Julie's reaction as her jaw dropped open.

If it was Noelle, that would explain the reticence to come forward, but... Julie would not have pegged the woman for a secret admirer type. Everything she'd seen Noelle do, from very early on since she joined the club, was followed by a wake of noise and drama. She was very good at getting others on her side, very good at playing the victim, and very good at knowing exactly what to say and how to twist words and actions to her own advantage. Julie didn't feel comfortable diagnosing her, but there were a lot of narcissistic markers in her behavior.

She also hadn't presented as anything other than straight in the club. Most recently, she'd been dating a Dom named Damian, though she had heard they'd broken up, which was why Julie had assumed Noelle hadn't been around as much. Things had been significantly less dramatic with her absence.

On the other hand, if she had been hiding part of her sexuality—if she'd been in love with her old roommate Iris—that would explain so much of her—

"Oh! She just stopped. Carolyn and Amy are coming up behind her. She's giving the flowers to... Oh, that's right, it's Amy's birthday." Olivia flopped back in her chair, putting her hand on her heart.

"Okay, that was way more stressful than I thought it would be. I'm not sure I can take this."

Relief poured through Julie as well. She hadn't needed Olivia's play-by-play since her eyes had been glued to the screen, but in some ways, it had been nice to have someone else panicking over it, too. She couldn't imagine rejecting Noelle going well. It also helped build some of her own confidence back—if Noelle had been her secret admirer, that would have been an entire facet of her personality Julie had completely missed.

"Wait, why is Amy here for her birthday? Where's her fiancé?" Although she tried not to get involved unless asked, she'd been keeping her eye on Amy for a while now. The fact that her partner had never come to Stronghold or Marquis and had never shown any interest in that side of Amy's life had both surprised and worried her.

"Hmm." Olivia leaned forward, frowning at the screen as they watched the three women go inside. "I don't know."

And if Olivia didn't know, chances were that no one around the club knew. Julie huffed. It wasn't her business to get involved in. She should stay out of it. She had enough going on. But it made her feel itchy.

"Oh! Oh!" Olivia bounced in her seat again, pointing at the screen.

Julie stared at where she was pointing, the man looking much smaller on the screen than he did in real life. He was dressed in his usual leather pants and vest, but it looked like his short hair had been gelled and styled. He was holding a large bouquet of what were clearly roses... and even over the security camera feed, she could tell how nervous he felt.

She also immediately understood why he'd been hesitant to approach her before.

"Oh, my..." Olivia murmured, all the ramifications apparently hitting her at the same time. She turned her head to look at Julie. "What are you going to do?"

Still staring at the screen, Julie slowly shook her head.

"I don't know."

2

CONNOR

This was a mistake.

No, it's not. Just try it. If she doesn't come out, then maybe that's the sign that everyone was right.

"Connor, hey!" Morgan perked up when she saw him, and her greeting made Freddy look up and smile at him. Okay, well, that was that. He had to go in now. If he turned around and walked back down the stairs without going in, everyone would wonder why. He forced himself to start walking to the desk as Morgan glanced down at the computer screen in front of her. "Did you have a reservation?"

"I'm in there as Master C." He cleared his throat, flexing his fingers around the bouquet of flowers, wishing he'd chosen a less obvious way to indicate who he was to Mistress Julie. But flowers were romantic, and other people sometimes brought flowers with them to Marquis. So, they weren't entirely out of place, just because he'd never done it before.

"And you're meeting someone?" Freddy asked, his sharp blue gaze going from the flowers Connor was holding over to the computer screen. Well, that answered one of Connor's unspoken questions. He'd wondered if Julie would tell her friends about her secret admirer revealing themselves tonight. He'd wondered if he was walking right into a hailstorm of gossip.

If Freddy didn't know and didn't see any significance in the flowers, then Camille probably didn't know. If neither of them knew, it was likely that nobody did. He relaxed. Not all the way, but a little knot of tension worked itself loose from between his shoulders and flittered away.

If nothing else, at least he wasn't the subject of everyone's attention tonight.

"Yes." Much better to say yes than he wasn't sure. If she didn't show, people would just assume some submissive showed him up. Which was fine. Eventually, they might find out that it was Mistress Julie, but she seemed like a private person, so they might not.

He hoped not.

Revealing himself like this was making a big ball of anxiety churn in his gut. He'd never meant to take it this far. He'd just liked sending her things and knowing it made her happy. He'd wanted her to know she was admired. It wasn't until he'd decided that he had to stop that he'd started thinking about seeing if maybe...

Maybe...

"Great. Well, right this way," Freddy said cheerfully, picking up the menus for the evening. He was dressed in a dark pink suit that clashed with Morgan's red hair. Next to him, she was wearing a simple black dress that showed off her curves and looked both classy enough to eat out in but sexy enough that she'd fit right in with the other club members.

As Freddy led him into the main dining area of Marquis, Connor couldn't help eyeing the other man curiously. Freddy was flamboyant, as demonstrated by his pink suit, and submissive, but he also had a reputation as an absolutely ruthless lawyer, and he wasn't afraid to go toe-to-toe with any of the dominants in the club if he needed to protect another submissive. Yet despite his ruthlessness and his aggressive protectiveness, no one questioned whether or not he was a submissive.

"Have a great evening," Freddy said, putting the menus on the table of one of the booths. He'd put them on the far side of the stage, which took up the center of the room, with all the booths arrayed around it in a semi-circle. Whatever curiosity he had about who Connor was meeting, he kept to himself. Though Connor would be willing to bet, he and Morgan would be discussing it as soon as he got back to the front desk.

Sighing, Connor put the roses down on the table, wondering again if this was a mistake.

He was already here, so he might as well sit down and see if she showed up. Or maybe Law would show up to drag him out and kick him out of the club. Connor sat down and scrubbed his hand over his face, as though he could wipe away the visual. While he might tower over Law, he'd let the other man kick him out if that's what it came down to. Especially if he'd made Mistress Julie uncomfortable, which was the last thing he wanted to do.

He was aware that she was half his size. He was aware of how ludicrous they'd look as a couple with her dominating him. No one would expect that. Everyone—from the moment they'd met him and he'd expressed an interest in kink—had assumed he was a Dom. And he'd assumed they were right. After all, he hadn't known much about kink other than it made him feel... things.

It wasn't until he'd been through the classes and really started to pay attention to what he was the most drawn to that he realized he wasn't the same as the other Doms. He wasn't the same as his friends. And no matter how hard he tried, he couldn't make himself feel the same way they did.

He didn't want to be the one ordering someone else around. He didn't want to be the one tying someone else up. He didn't want to be the one administering the flogging.

At the same time, who wanted a submissive who looked like a Dom? And how could he tell all of his friends they were wrong about him? That he wasn't like them?

He wasn't sure he could.

Tapping his fingers against the table, he barely looked at the menu before Annette, one of the club subs he'd scened with before, came over to get his drink order.

"Hi, Master Connor. Do you want to order a drink now or wait till your date gets here?" She smiled down at him, but just the use of the honorific made him want to flinch. What would everyone think if they told him he wasn't a Master? Wasn't a Dom? Would they feel like he'd lied to them?

Would she be angry that she'd scened with him, and he'd deceived her?

"Not a date," he corrected automatically. Just in case. Though it really wasn't a date, even if she showed up. She might come just to turn him down. Which would be fine. Well, not fine exactly, but definitely within her rights. "Um... I'll have a beer, please. Whatever is on tap."

At his size, one beer barely affected him. Not that he was expecting Mistress Julie to jump into scening with him. Shit. Did he *want* her to jump into scening with him?

"Okay, great." Annette shot him a curious look before walking away. Some of his internal panic must have shown on his face.

Bracing his elbows on the table, Connor pressed the heels of his hands against his eye sockets, taking several deep breaths as he tried to calm himself down. This was feeling more and more like a mistake every second. Why hadn't he thought through all the possible repercussions before walking in here?

Because I was so focused on Mistress Julie, I forgot to think about everyone else.

Maybe not forgot so much as pushed it out of his mind. He'd wanted to roll the dice and see what happened if he revealed himself. See if the fantasies he had in his head matched up with reality.

He should go.

Dropping his hands, he lifted his head... and found himself looking at the woman herself, standing on the other side of the table. She looked stunning in a blue shirt and black skirt, her long hair pulled back up away from her face in a bun, with two sticks that had little dangly decorations hanging from them stuck through it. With him sitting down in the booth, they were about the same height. Her gaze pierced him as she tilted her head, as though she was wondering what he was doing there... or maybe just wondering why he appeared to be having a meltdown.

He felt a moment of panic.

She did realize he was there to meet her, right?

Or would it be better if she didn't, and he could just pretend all of this never happened?

"Hello, Connor," she said in that low, cool voice that made shivers dance over his skin. The voice she used when she was scening with a sub, which always made him wish *he* was the sub. The voice that had made him really start questioning everything he thought he wanted when it came to kink.

"Mistress Julie." Unfortunately, he didn't sound nearly as calm or cool as she did. He kind of sounded as if he was being strangled.

She reached out, resting one finger atop the cellophane on the roses.

"Are these for me?" Her dark eyes bored into him. It was the moment of truth. He could lie and say no and get up and run. He fully believed she would never tell anyone, never humiliate him that way. There was compassion in her expression, as though she under-stood how hard this was for him. As if she recognized how much he was struggling.

He cleared his throat, placing his hands flat on the table, the hard wood cool beneath his palms.

"Yes."

---

*J*ULIE

Connor looked ready to bolt.

With his hands flat on the table, his shoulders hunched as if he was trying to make himself smaller than he was, and the panic in his expression when he realized she was standing there, she wondered if she should have come inside. He had been about to run; she was sure of it.

Part of her wondered if it would be better if he did.

While she believed he was very possibly submissive, or perhaps switchy, if he wasn't ready to accept that side of himself, then he wasn't ready. Sometimes, a crush was just a crush. Sometimes, reality didn't match up with expectations.

What she could do was talk to him and help him figure out what he wanted.

"Thank you, they're beautiful," she said simply, sliding into the booth. She smiled at him, her voice flipping from her Domme voice to the one she usually used in the office with her clients. "We can just talk."

"Um. Right." He cleared his throat again, and Julie couldn't help but smile.

They hadn't spent much time together after the introduction class he'd taken, though she'd seen him watching nearly all of her demonstrations since then. Something she hadn't realized was significant until right now. After all, he was hardly the only Dom to attend as many demonstrations as possible, adding to their knowledge base.

However, as far as she knew, Connor rarely used what he learned. He was a softer Dom, and the submissives loved that about him. Especially the ones who needed some coddling and caretaking, which was what most of them went to him for. He was their gentle giant, their big teddy bear, and they teased and bratted, knowing he'd just laugh and enjoy their antics.

Thankfully, for a segue, Annette appeared at their table with a tall glass of beer for Connor. Her eyes widened when she realized it was Julie sitting there, with the flowers in front of her, then comprehension settled onto her expression.

"Hello, Mistress Julie. Can I get you something to drink?" she asked as she slid the glass of amber liquid in front of Connor.

"Water and a dirty martini, please."

"Sure thing. I'll be right back." Annette flounced off, and Julie looked over at Connor with some bemusement.

"Did you tell her I was coming?" she asked.

He shook his head.

"I just told her this wasn't a date." The hesitation in his voice made it clear he wasn't sure how she would take that. Julie wasn't offended since he hadn't known whether she was going to show up to meet him. She didn't blame him for trying to save face in case she didn't.

Even now, Annette likely thought they were just two dominants having dinner to talk shop and watch the performance. That's what the gossip train would say. Olivia wouldn't correct anyone's misconceptions unless Julie asked her to.

"Well, that takes some of the pressure off," she said with a smile. Connor managed a half-smile back at her, a bit of the tension leaving his shoulders. "So, is Shibari something you're interested in?"

She could have gone straight into questioning him about why he'd wanted to meet her, what he wanted out of tonight, but she was pretty sure that would put his back up. Right now, she wanted to get him more relaxed, get the conversation flowing a little more naturally, then she'd be able to make her way around to that once he wasn't so anxious.

"I'm not sure." He shrugged and held up his hand, laughing in a self-deprecating manner. "My fingers are too big for delicate knots most of the time."

"Mine aren't." Julie held up her own hand with her very delicate fingers. They were petite, just like the rest of her. She winked. "I bet you'd be surprised if you tried, though. Patrick doesn't exactly have small fingers."

Connor's shoulders went down a little more, and he chuckled as he took a sip of beer. The air of tension hadn't completely dissipated, but it was lessening.

"That's true. Though my hands are bigger than his." He eyed her, as if he was wondering if she was going to say something about big hands and what that meant.

Julie smiled back at him serenely. She was sure he'd heard all the jokes before.

She liked to be different.

"Well, you won't know until you try. You can do some really beautiful things with Shibari." It was the right thing to say.

Connor relaxed even more, smiling back at her.

How had she never noticed the eager-to-please expression on his face? Had he been hiding it, or had she just passed right over it because it wasn't expected?

What else had she missed about him?

3

JULIE

Connor Bright was an attractive man. It was something she'd noticed before, but she hadn't really thought about whether she was attracted to him because she hadn't realized he was an option. Sitting next to him, talking to him, really taking the time to look at him...

Yeah.

She was attracted.

There was something exhilarating about the idea of dominating him, too. He was so much bigger than her—taller, broader, stronger—and he wanted to submit to her. Such a large, strong man on his knees for her... and he'd probably be nearly as tall as her, even when he was on his knees. Like her own personal mountain to climb and play with.

As they chatted, their dinners arrived, and he slowly relaxed—until Annette came to clear their plates, and tension started leaking back into his frame. Julie paused to take a sip of her drink. This was usually the point in a session with a client where they were working themselves up to admit something or say why they were really there.

Averting his gaze, looking down at where his big hands were wrapped around the base of his glass, he cleared his throat.

Julie waited.

"So, um. I hope I didn't bother you with all the gifts."

"You didn't. It was clear you put a lot of care into them. I was flattered." She had no problem admitting that. Chances were, he'd already heard that from Law, anyway. She had no doubt that Law had shared *his* concerns about her admirer with his friends. The fact that Connor was one of those friends made it more amusing in some ways.

The more she thought about it, the more likely she thought it was Law's fault that her secret admirer had often known when she was at the club. What was more natural than talking to his friends about when he had a meeting? And, of course, she would be there...

She couldn't wait to rub his face in it.

As long as Connor didn't mind, of course.

But she really wanted to.

"Even the one sent to your house?" His tension ratcheted up another level.

Julie hesitated, because she didn't want him to feel bad, but she also didn't want to lie to him.

"That one... surprised me more. It worried me a little. But I wasn't scared, just... concerned," she said carefully, watching his reaction. He winced, which made her feel a little bad, but it was the truth. "After nothing else happened, I wasn't as concerned anymore."

"That's good." He rubbed his finger across his glass, the condensation making a kind of soft squealing sound. "I'm sorry about that. I didn't think about how it would be different from sending it here. I just..."

Reaching out, Julie put her hand over his when his voice trailed off, causing him to look at her. She smiled sympathetically. Poor guy. He hadn't thought, but he'd clearly learned and accepted the feedback, and that was just as important to her. Maybe even more so.

"I understand. Thank you for the apology." She smiled at him. "Now, do you want to talk about why you chose to reveal yourself?"

She was still in shrink mode, but she felt her axis shift when his expression did. The anxiety had mostly cleared, leaving behind a kind of hunger that called to something deep inside her. The look in his eyes had turned pleading and eager, just the kind of look she liked to see on a sub.

"I... felt like I shouldn't keep sending things when I wasn't sure if it bothered you or not. And I... I wanted to know. I guess. If there was any chance..." He was stumbling over his words, frustration starting to show on his face, as he couldn't quite seem to get his meaning out clearly.

"Have you tried submitting to anyone else?" She was pretty sure of the answer, but she wanted to be positive. Connor shook his head, confirming her suspicion. "What makes you think you want to try submitting?"

She kept her hand on his as he sighed, tilting his head back to look up into the darkness of the ceiling. The shadows were strong up there, most of the light coming from the sconces on the wall behind them and the dim lights that were currently up on the stage in the center of the room. They would be darkening soon, heralding the beginning of the show and ending their chance to talk.

"I can't stop thinking about what it would be like to be on the receiving end. I know I'm kinky. I enjoyed the Dom class, but when I'm in the club, I don't get a lot of enjoyment out of being the one in charge. I do like making the subs feel good. I enjoy that. I like being able to give them what they need. But it feels like something is missing for me. And every time I watched you do a demonstration, I didn't want to be in your spot. I wanted to be in your sub's."

The admission must have been hard for him. It came out in a rush, his voice low. The booths were designed to help keep conversation and sounds as private as possible, but some still escaped. Yet he couldn't hold it back any longer, even knowing there was a chance someone could overhear him.

Julie rubbed his hand, a kind of physical reward for his bravery in speaking, and when her head dropped down to look at their hands and he smiled, she knew he felt it.

"That makes sense." It did. Connor was a helpful person. She'd noticed that about him. Everyone assumed he was a service Dom or even verging on a Daddy Dom who just didn't take the title. He liked to caretake. He probably got some of that fulfilled by taking care of the submissives, but if he still felt like he was missing something, and he kept picturing himself in their place... It was very possible he'd figured out the absent component but was still hesitant. She understood that, too. "What did you hope for tonight?"

With a short laugh, Connor spread his hands, which shifted her hand on his. Rather than move it away, she let it rest in his palm. Partly because she didn't want him to think she was pulling away and partly because she didn't truly want to stop touching him yet. He needed the contact, she wanted to give him support, and she rather liked touching him.

It felt like now that she'd been given permission to notice him, she couldn't stop. She did like what she saw. And the fact that he'd seen *her*, that he'd been sending her the most thoughtful gifts she'd ever received in her life for the past year... But she also didn't want to throw herself into something that he might quickly back out of. It was clear he wasn't sure about what he wanted, and she understood that.

After all, how could he know if he really liked it if he hadn't tried it?

"I hoped you would show up. I didn't really think past that." He was looking at her with big, hopeful, puppy dog eyes. The kind of eyes that begged for her to take control and lead him down the path he wanted to walk.

Annette came up to the table, and Connor quickly pulled his hand away from Julie's, which stung a bit. She knew he was protecting both of them, but she'd been enjoying that contact, and she hadn't given him permission to end it.

That was either a warning sign for her to be wary of - or something they'd have to work on. Since they weren't officially doing anything yet, she decided to put the matter to the side for now.

"Would you like any dessert? Show should be starting in about ten minutes." Annette smiled brightly, her gaze flitting back and forth between them, leaving Julie to think that she might have noticed the handholding, despite Connor's efforts. However, handholding wasn't necessarily indicative of anything romantic. Friends could hold hands, so she might not think much of it, though Connor snatching his away would raise more suspicion that something was going on than if he'd left it.

Julie glanced at Connor, who looked back at her.

"Any objection to chocolate cake?" she asked. It seemed like an innocuous choice. Connor shook his head, and she turned back to Annette. "Chocolate cake to share, please."

Interesting. Despite pulling his hand away, he'd still taken her lead with a witness there. Now that she thought about it, when he was around other Doms, he tended to take their lead. Sometimes, he would go do his own thing, but mostly, he went along with what the others wanted to do.

Considering his closest friends were Doms—well, Q was a switch, but he was also a newer friend for Connor—it made a lot of sense that he'd gone along with being a Dom for a while. She also suspected it was part of why he'd kept his confusion and conflicting desires a secret from them. Which meant starting anything could be a lot more complicated. Julie had promised herself she was never going to let herself feel like anyone's dirty little secret ever again.

"Would you like to try some submission tonight?" If they tried tonight, she could keep it from going too far. Even though she was definitely attracted to him, that didn't necessarily have to mean it would lead somewhere. He'd never tried before. It might be that he backed off afterward. It might be that he realized it was what he really wanted.

As much as she liked making plans, sometimes she couldn't jump ahead too far into the future.

One step at a time.

That meant offering to give him a chance to try things tonight, then seeing where that led. Maybe nowhere. Maybe somewhere interesting. She needed to squash the impulse to try to travel all the paths before she even knew which way he would leap.

He might not even take her up on this offer.

In fact, for a moment, she thought he wouldn't. He hesitated, unsure, despite the hunger in his eyes... then he nodded.

"Good." Julie scooted a little closer to him, her voice going a little lower. This time, rather than putting her hand in his, she put her hand on his thigh. Felt his tension ratchet up as he sucked in a breath, as if he hadn't been expecting it.

Rather than trying to jump into the future, attempting to figure out what could happen after tonight, her brain finally got into gear, trying to decide exactly how she wanted this evening to go.

CONNOR

Would he like to try?

Yes. Absolutely. That was what he'd really wanted to ask for but hadn't been able to bring himself to. He hadn't wanted her to feel pressured. Or obligated. Though so far, she seemed like she was... interested? Maybe not as interested in him as he was in her. After all, he'd been sending her gifts for the past year.

Maybe she felt like she owed him for that.

He was struggling with her easy acceptance that he wanted to submit. Shouldn't she be... angry? Disappointed?

He didn't know.

Her acceptance left him breathless and feeling vulnerable, as well as excited. His cock was definitely excited. The second she touched him, all the blood in his body rushed straight to his groin and made his pants extremely uncomfortable. Yet he liked it. That was one of the things he'd liked the most about watching her scenes—the hard-on that he would get that he couldn't do anything about while he watched.

Then he'd do a little self-torture by not getting off until he got home and could close his eyes, imagining himself as her sub, with her low, sultry voice telling him to cum for her.

Yeah, he fucking wanted to try.

When Annette appeared at the other side of the table with their cake, he also felt like scrunching down and hiding. Not that he could. He'd always been too big for that, no matter how hard he'd tried. He'd had horrible back pain in high school from making the attempt to be smaller. Now, he always stood tall for the sake of his spine and muscles, but right now, he wished he could.

She didn't seem to see anything wrong, though, which set him at some ease. Julie's hand still felt like a brand on his thigh, but if Annette realized Julie was touching him, she didn't show any sign of it.

"Here you go, enjoy! You've got about five minutes before the show starts." She smiled serenely. "Do you want to leave the curtains open?"

"Draw the sheers, please," Julie said. It was a request, but it was also an order, and it made both his heart and his cock jump.

Once all the lights went down for the show, the sheers would make it nearly impossible to see into the booth. It could mean nothing other than they didn't want to be seen by those on stage or that they wanted a little extra privacy to be unobserved. A lot of people used the sheers without doing anything extracurricular behind them.

It also opened up a lot of opportunities, especially for someone who was feeling uncertain. Someone who was going against everything everyone thought of him and trying something new. Someone who didn't want to be observed while they explored the other side of kink.

"Sure thing." Annette was cheerful as she drew the sheers and moved on to the next table.

Once the curtains dropped, their view of the stage became a little fuzzier, but they could still see clearly through them, at least that far. The booths on the other side of the room were almost completely obscured, though. Julie gave his thigh another little squeeze when he started to reach for the fork.

"Stop. Put your hands on the table, palms down flat." Her voice was still low, meant for his ears only, but the short order made his pulse race. His cock pushed against the front of his leathers, as if it was trying to break free.

Connor put his hands on the table, spreading his fingers out, his breath coming a little faster as he obeyed. Knowing exactly where to put his hands, knowing exactly what she wanted him to do... it felt like relief.

"Good boy," she murmured, reaching out with her other hand to pick up the fork. His balls tightened.

Fuck, he liked that. Almost too much. He'd fantasized about her calling him 'good boy,' but it was so much better in reality.

Scooping up a forkful of chocolate cake, she lifted it to his lips, and Connor froze, nearly going cross-eyed as he tried to stare at it.

"Open," she ordered, and he did, even though it felt weird. Not wrong, just... weird. He'd always imagined him serving her, not the other way around, but if this was what she wanted...

Stop thinking and just do what you're told.

Which was somehow incredibly freeing.

And the chocolate tasted delicious.

4

———————

By the time the lights started to dim, signaling the start of the show, Mistress Julie was feeding him the second to last bite of cake. Being fed while he was immobile—not that anything was holding him in place other than her command—was an entirely new experience for him. It was also something he never would have thought to do as a Dom.

Which made him wonder, again, if he'd been failing the subs he'd scened with.

On the other hand, he'd never had a meal with any of the subs he'd scened with. Maybe if he had, he would have thought of feeding them, but... probably not. He was self-aware enough to know that. Still, at least he wouldn't have disappointed any of them since there had been a lack of opportunity.

"You're thinking too hard," Mistress Julie said, rapping the back of his knuckles with the spoon. It didn't hurt that much, but the sting was enough to jolt him back to the present and her very enjoyable company.

"Sorry." He gave her a sheepish smile. "Sometimes, it's hard to turn my brain off."

"Which isn't necessarily a bad thing, but right now, I'd rather you were focused on feeling instead of thinking." She smiled back at him, and he caught it right before the lights completely went dark.

Music started to throb through the room and the lights on the stage lit up, bright and focused on that one area. With the sheers drawn, it would now be next-to-impossible to see into their booth, even from the stage. If anyone even wanted to make the attempt.

Fingers slid into his hair, and Connor almost groaned as she tugged gently on his scalp.

"Under the table, Connor. I want you to start at my ankles and work your way up to dessert."

Oh, fuck.

His dick hadn't gone down while she was feeding him, but somehow, he was even harder than before.

And he had to get under the table?

He wasn't sure he would fit, but if that's where she wanted him, he was going to try his best to make it work. Especially because there was a prize at the end of the effort. He hadn't imagined she would be willing to go nearly this far, but now that he knew it was possible, he was eager to take it there.

Taking a deep breath, he began to sink down, twisting slightly to fit his bulk under the table and turning to face her. One hand was still in his hair, and he heard the muffled clink of silverware against glass, letting him know that she was eating the last bite of cake.

While he was under the table about to eat her.

Why that felt so deliciously exciting, he didn't know, but it sent an unexpected thrill through him.

Shifting back, he felt her let go of his hair with reluctance, but he needed the room to maneuver if he was going to start at her ankles. It was nearly pitch black under the table, only the faintest hint of light coming from the stage. He was missing the entire show, and he didn't care at all.

Sliding his hands down her legs, he lifted one and pressed a kiss to her ankle, sliding his tongue over her smooth skin. He began moving his mouth with slow, hot kisses up to her knee, then he switched to the other side. It wasn't easy. He was bent over uncomfortably, he felt completely squished, he couldn't see what he was doing, and the throbbing music made it hard to tell if she was reacting or not, yet...

Yet he was already happier than he'd ever been when he was in charge of a scene.

Despite all that, his dick was throbbing in time with the music, and he didn't care one whit about the discomfort. He just wanted to make Mistress Julie happy with him. This felt... good. Right. He'd been given a mission, and all he had to do was accomplish it.

All the thoughts that had been swirling around his mind disappeared as he focused on moving his mouth up her legs, his hands caressing at the same time. As he reached the edge of her skirt, her fingers slid back into his hair, and she pulled up the hem of her skirt with the other hand. Her body slid forward, legs parting, though he was still cramped because of his broad shoulders and did not fit easily between her legs.

His back and head bumped the underside of the table, but he didn't care.

Breathing in the sweet scent of her arousal, he was focused on one thing and one thing only—his promised dessert. Not that he rushed things. This was about *her* pleasure.

His mouth moved over her inner thighs, getting closer and closer until he was able to finally taste her. She tasted as good as she smelled. Connor groaned, pushing his head forward, his shoulders moving her legs wider. He bumped the underside of the table again and ignored the thud as he finally reached the promised land. Over the music, he could hear her moan as his tongue slipped between her folds, the sweet flavor of woman coating his taste buds.

Fuck, he liked hearing her moan because of him.

Eagerly, he pressed inward, not caring about the humid air that was hard to breathe. Who needed air anyway? He just needed *this*. He felt more alive, more engaged, more free than in any scene he'd ever done.

Burying his mouth in her pussy, he feasted.

Though she was trying to keep quiet, to preserve some semblance of secrecy about what she and Connor were doing—just in case the occupants on the booths on either side of them were paying any attention—it wasn't easy. Partly because she wanted him to know he was doing a good job and partly because he really was doing a *very good job.*

It was very distracting.

As good a show as Patrick was putting on, wrapping Lexie in a rope dress and preparing to lift her into the air, Julie was having trouble watching it. She was far more interested in the massive man kneeling at her feet, eating her out like a starving man, who kept banging into the table and not pausing in his efforts. It was a good thing the tables were bolted to the floor, or he probably would have shifted the whole thing.

Julie shuddered, moaning again as his tongue laved over a particularly sensitive spot. One hand gripped his hair, the other gripped the table. She was too short to truly be able to lean back against the back of the booth—the seats were made particularly wide for a reason—but she was leaning back as much as she could to give Connor as much access to her pussy as possible. Her thighs trembled slightly at the stretch necessary to accommodate his shoulders.

If she could have put them over his shoulders, she would have, but being in the booth only allowed for certain positions. Especially with as big as he was.

"Oh, fuck..." she moaned as he shifted, managing to get his mouth even more firmly on her pussy, sucking her clit between his lips. Her insides clenched in response, quivering as her orgasm slid closer to its peak.

On the stage, Patrick was lifting Lexie into the air, an expression of utter bliss on her face as she flew. The music was swelling as he lifted a crop and began to work her over while she hung in the center of the stage like a work of art. Her cries at the sting and the moans of pleasure blended in with the music, as did all the sounds coming from the booths around them.

No one would be able to tell what sound came from where.

Which meant she could let go of her own worries about revealing too much. Gripping Connor's hair tighter, she ground her pussy against his mouth, crying out when he seemed to realize how close she was, and sucked her clit back between his lips. His tongue flicked against the tiny bud, the suction pulling at her in waves. She cried out again, her thighs tightening around his shoulders as hot bliss exploded inside her.

Muscles quivering, she gasped and moaned as she rode his mouth, clutching his head tightly against her as the waves of pleasure crashed over her. Her body buzzed from the heady sensations, his mouth and tongue working until she was nearly limp.

Only then did she tug on his hair, moving him away from her, giving her the space to catch her breath. He went with reluctance she could feel, even though she couldn't see his face.

Still using his hair to guide him, she pulled him back out from under the table.

The lighting wasn't great, but it was good enough to see the light shine around his lips from her juices, the way his hair was properly mussed. The sheepish expression was back on his face as he reached up to wipe his mouth clean.

Damn, he looked good, sheepish and pleased with himself, while her body was still humming from the orgasm. He deserved a reward.

"Sit next to me and watch the show," she said, releasing her grip on his hair now that he was out. The music and sounds from Lexie, as well as everyone else watching, were loud enough that she was no longer worried at all about being heard. "Hands back on the table."

Which meant she could touch him as much as she wanted while he was back to sitting still.

He got into position, but he wasn't watching the show; he was watching her. Julie decided not to chastise him. Eventually, he wasn't going to be able to see what she was doing, anyway.

Getting up on her knees, she knelt beside him on the booth, so she was facing him. One hand went over his arm so she could run her fingernails across his chest, teasing his nipples, while the other went to free his cock from his pants.

He'd been in her class, and she'd seen him at the club, so she knew he was well-endowed, but it was one thing to know and another to wrap her fingers around the thick, hard shaft. Connor made a noise, almost like a whimper, as she did so, and Julie smiled at the feeling of power that went through her.

There was nothing quite like making a grown man whimper to turn her on even more.

<u>CONNOR</u>

Thinking?

Who needed thoughts?

All the thoughts had completely flown out of his head. He'd been completely focused on Mistress Julie's pleasure, and now he wasn't able to think about a thing other than what she was doing to him. How she was touching him. How fucking good it felt when her hand wrapped around his cock, even as her nails dragged a stinging trail across his chest.

He could still taste her on his tongue, breathing in her essence with every panting breath he took as she slid her hand up his cock and back down again. His fingers tried to curl against the table before he could force them flat again, letting out a guttural groan. He'd never been in a position *not* to be able to touch the woman he was with.

He hated it.

But he loved it even more.

The hand on his chest moved away, to his regret, but she was still slowly stroking his cock, so it wasn't like he could complain.

On the stage, Patrick had covered Lexie with little red marks from the end of the crop that stood out starkly against her pale skin. They'd been centered on her breasts, her ass, her thighs. She was panting, mouth hanging open, and he spun her in place to turn her so he could step between her thighs and place his mouth on her pussy.

Connor groaned, licking his lips as he was reminded of how good Mistress Julie's pussy had tasted.

Her fingers caught his hair, this time at the back of his neck, tugging his head back as he groaned. Hot breath wafted over the sensitive shell of his ear, her fingers tightening almost painfully around his cock.

"Did you like being on your knees for me, Connor?" she whispered in his ear. Her tongue flicked against his earlobe.

If he'd been standing, he would have ended up on his knees again. He could feel them buckle even though he was sitting down.

"Yes." He could barely say the word through his groan as her teeth dragged across his earlobe, right after her tongue. The slight sting and pull went straight to his cock, which she was stroking harder and faster as the music swelled. Lexie's cries on the stage were becoming louder.

"You did because you're a good boy, aren't you?"

He couldn't respond because as soon as she asked the question, she sucked his earlobe into her mouth, pulling on it, her hand moving up and down on his cock. He lost control of his voice. All of his focus was on his tightening balls because he wasn't sure if he was allowed to come or not.

As if she knew, she released his earlobe just long enough to whisper:

"Come for me, good boy."

Fuck.

The effect was instantaneous. Even before she sucked his earlobe back into her mouth, his cum was spurting out, arching high and splashing across the table onto his hands. Her hand kept moving, milking his cock as droplets of cum slid down, lubricating his shaft and intensifying his pleasure.

It felt like his toes were curling in his shoes, like every particle of his being had centered in his groin and was pouring out of him.

The most intense orgasm of his life, and it had just happened in her hand.

Connor panted for breath as Mistress Julie nipped his ear again before pulling away and picking up a napkin to clean off her hand. Breathing hard, Connor stared straight ahead, almost afraid to look at her. He wasn't sure if he had just embarrassed himself or not.

He felt like he should be embarrassed, but on the other hand, she'd called him a good boy.

I'm a good boy.

So, maybe he didn't need to be embarrassed at all.

The music crashed in a final tumult, then the lights on the stage went out, but only for a moment before coming back up to a brightness where some helpers could come out to assist Patrick in getting Lexie down. The two of them disappeared off stage with the helpers, Lexie still mostly bound in rope.

"Would you like me to clean you, or would you prefer to clean yourself?" Mistress Julie asked, bringing his focus back to their booth.

"Myself," he said, then immediately regretted it. Sort of. He knew he would feel awkward having her clean him off, but part of him wished she would. It was too late, though. She was already handing a new napkin over, and there was no way he was going to change his answer and ask her to do it now.

She stroked his hair while he did it, which made it better. He tucked himself back into his pants, blushing furiously as he did so. By the time they were done, the stage was cleared, and dim lights had come on throughout the booths. Many of them had emptied, their occupants having moved to the hotel rooms in the back hall.

There were a few others still present in their booths, either finishing their own pleasure or just talking. Those who had their sheers drawn were obscured from view, which reassured him that he and Mistress Julie still were, too.

"So," she said, putting her hand on his thigh again. This time, it felt reassuring rather than sexual. "We should talk about what comes next."

5

_J_ULIE

Damn, that had been... intense. Far more so than she'd expected it to be. She was doing her best to keep her head on straight, even though her body and hormones were humming. Keeping her guard up usually wasn't that difficult, but right now, she was desperately trying to shore up her walls. She hadn't been sure if Connor would be able to truly let go, but he had and in spectacular fashion.

Did she want more with him?

Absolutely.

Did she think it was a good idea?

She wasn't sure.

A lot depended on how he reacted. Whether or not he could deal with submitting rather than being the one in charge. Just because he was submissive didn't mean he'd be ready to submit. Letting go like that could be scary. It put him in a very vulnerable position. One he might not want to stay in.

The fact he'd jumped right to taking care of himself at the end of the scene indicated he might already be trying to regain control over the situation. It could mean something, or it could mean nothing.

Don't jump to conclusions.

He might not want me.

But she wanted him to still want her.

Since he was still staring silently at her, rather than stammering or trying to excuse himself, she took the lead.

"I enjoyed that." It was always best to begin with a compliment. She smiled at him, so he knew she meant it. Her pussy was still humming from the aftereffects, though her stomach felt like it was roiling with anxiety. While it made her feel vulnerable to admit her enjoyment, he'd already made himself vulnerable to her, so it was only fair she returned the favor on some level. Especially since she was about to ask him to expose his emotions after being physically exposed. "Did you?"

It was hard not to let the need, the want, seep into that question, but she also didn't want to influence his answer.

Connor took a deep breath, dropping his gaze away from hers. Ashamed? Or just struggling to admit the truth because being so open was difficult? It could be either or both.

"Yes. I enjoyed it," he replied quietly. He lifted his head so he could look at her. "I would want to do it again."

Her smile widened.

"Good. Now, the next question is how you want to approach it. Scening again would mean seeing each other again. We could do it privately or at the club. I do understand the club would be more difficult for you." The idea of having to hide what she was doing twinged a little, especially since it would also curtail the amount she'd be able to talk to her friends. Connor had a right to privacy, though, especially as he made the transition.

"I don't mind telling people. I'm going to tell my friends, anyway. But... do we have to scene publicly?" The pained expression on his face tightened her chest.

It wasn't that he was ashamed of her, otherwise he wouldn't be willing to tell his friends, but just knowing he wanted it hidden brought up some triggers. She was self-aware enough to understand they had nothing to do with him and everything to do with her ex.

Connor wasn't asking for anything unreasonable. In fact, he was offering quite a bit more than he had to.

"Absolutely not. Plenty of people don't scene publicly. That's what the private rooms are for." Though some did prefer to keep the doors and curtains on those rooms open, for voyeurs, Julie was perfectly happy to close them. She usually did so because she preferred privacy since most of the submissives she'd scened with didn't care.

"So, are we dating?" he asked.

Something inside her settled. That was more than she'd hoped for, but the truth was, she would like to get to know him better.

"Well, why don't we try a few dates and see how we feel." She patted his leg. "But we can scene together, regardless. There's certainly chemistry here, and if you'd like to explore submission, I am happy to be your guide."

"That sounds good to me." He relaxed completely, which helped her to relax, too. "I... I've liked you for a while."

"Oh, really?" she asked teasingly. "All the gifts you've been sending hadn't clued me in." She laughed as he blushed a beet red. He truly was incredibly cute, which wasn't normally an attribute she would think to describe for a man his size. "Trust me, I enjoyed all of it. Especially since Law was throwing such a fit. I assume you want to be the one to tell him you're my secret admirer?"

"I would rather he hear it from me," Connor admitted, giving her a sheepish look, seeming to understand that she'd be disappointed she wouldn't be able to be the one to do the big reveal. "So I can explain... everything."

Which was only fair. She and Law were friends, but not like he and Connor were. Besides, her desire was motivated by wanting to rub it in Law's face that not only had he been overreacting to the secret admirer thing but that the danger had been so lacking, it was actually one of his best friends.

"Just tell me one thing... was he part of the reason you knew when to send the gifts?"

The sheepish expression on his face grew even more so, but there was also a glint of mischievousness in his eyes. Oh, there was a little bit of a brat hiding in Connor's hulking exterior. That was good to know. Something to watch out for in the future.

The future being something she was suddenly very excited about. She wanted to know what made him tick. What he liked and didn't like. Where his boundaries were. All things that were going to need to be explored. She would definitely be pulling his file from the Dom class to go over what his responses had been.

Of course, it wouldn't be as thorough as if he'd taken the submission introduction course, but Master Patrick insisted the Doms experience as much of what a submissive went through physically as they could—everything from implements to plugs. The idea of pegging Connor...

Don't jump ahead of yourself. You've barely taken the first baby step with him. That might not be something he's into at all.

Though she didn't remember him protesting the plug the way some Doms did. Yes, she was definitely going to need to go back through his file.

Connor coughed.

"I, uh... yes." He shrugged. "Law would tell us what was going on at work, then I'd know where you were."

"I knew it." She pumped her fist in the air as the feeling of triumph suffused her. That made him laugh, which made her like him even more. There had been far too many times with her ex where he hadn't liked her shows of exuberance, even telling her that being occasionally silly diminished her and made him not want to submit to her. John had had a very specific idea of how a Domme should act, at least, a Domme he was willing to submit to. Though, no matter how poised and proper she'd been, he still hadn't wanted anyone to know he was submitting to her, so she wasn't sure why it had mattered. Or why she was thinking about him now.

She pushed him straight out of her thoughts as she grinned at Connor.

"You know Law is going to explode, right? Would you mind videotaping?"

That made him laugh again.

"I'm pretty sure that won't help at all." Connor shook his head, but that mischievous glint was still in his eyes.

"I'm not trying to help; I'm trying to be entertained."

She really, really liked making him laugh. She wished she could have kept entertaining him all night, but they both had to get going. The dining room needed to be cleaned.

Connor walked her out to her car. She thought about pulling him down for a kiss goodnight but decided against it. They exchanged numbers so they could try for another date and agreed to meet the next Friday for another scene.

One of the perks of working at Marquis, she happened to know there was a room free and was able to reserve it. Since she was teaching the classes, she could reserve an overnight for free whenever she wanted. A perk she'd never taken advantage of before, but it made sense now.

Of the two sister clubs, Marquis was far more private. If they were at Stronghold, eyes would be on them from the moment they walked through the door. Also, if they stayed at Marquis, it wouldn't feel quite so much like she had to hide what she was doing with him. Privacy was part of the package, not something that had to be deliberately set into place... which would be easier on her than feeling like he didn't want to be seen with her.

She wasn't sure where this would lead, if anywhere, but she was looking forward to finding out.

***

<u>CONNOR</u>

"You look happy."

Blinking, Connor gave himself a little shake. His mind had wandered off again in between clients, going back to the night before with Mistress Julie. The woman looking up at him now was a little taller than Mistress Julie and a little curvier, but she had a very similar expression. Searching, scrutinizing.

He'd been working with Sandra for about three years now, and he was used to the tiny whirlwind, also known as his work wife. She was happily married, and he got along well with her husband Marcus, but at work, she bossed him around as if he was a henpecked husband. In fact, he was pretty sure she didn't boss Marcus around nearly as much as she did him.

"What?" he asked, sidling away from her intense stare.

"I said that you look happy." Her gaze narrowed.

Damn, she really looked like Mistress Julie when she did that. Not that he'd ever want to say that out loud. He didn't think all Asian people looked alike; it was just true that these two *particular* Asian women looked alike. The main difference was that he was attracted to Mistress Julie whereas he could acknowledge that Sandra was an attractive woman, but he'd never been attracted *to* her.

"Doesn't he look happy, Aubrey?"

From behind the front desk, Aubrey looked up from whatever paperwork he was doing and inspected Connor's expression. He seemed to be having a good day today, which Connor was happy to see. He had a chronic condition called Arnold Chiari disease that sometimes gave him terrible headaches, but he liked being at the front desk of A2Z Physical Therapy and getting to interact with everyone coming in and out. The patients and all the PTs loved him.

"I look the way I always do," Connor insisted, rubbing his hand over his face, as if he could rub away whatever it was they were seeing. Sandra was nosy as hell, and she was going to want all the details if he gave her an inch.

"No, she's right. You look extra happy," Aubrey said, tilting his head and grinning up at them. His hazel eyes sparkled with mischief. "You're normally more... stoic."

"I don't know what either of you are talking about." Except that he did. He was happy because Mistress Julie had not only shown up, but she'd sat with him. Showed him what was possible.

He was still nervous as hell about telling his friends, but... maybe he could practice now. Sandra and Aubrey didn't know the details about the kink stuff, so they couldn't be mad at him for hiding anything from them. Both of them were staring at him now, letting the silence draw out, waiting for him to fill it. He sighed.

"I had... a date last night."

"And it went well!" Sandra squealed, bouncing up and down as she clapped her hands. "It went well, right? You wouldn't look happy if it didn't go well. What's her name? How old is she? Where'd you go?"

"No, no, and no." Connor pointed his finger at her. "I do not need you looking her up online."

"Just a first name then." Sandra smiled innocently at him, but he knew better than to believe that. He knew exactly why she wanted some of those details.

So did Aubrey.

"Don't trust her, man. She found Riley's new boyfriend with nothing more than knowing his name was 'John.' I still don't know how she did it." Aubrey shook his head. "Do you know how many Johns there are in the world?"

"You're forgetting the part where I also saved her from dating a man with a wife and two kids he forgot to tell her about." Sandra put her hands on her hips, sniffing with annoyance at their lack of appreciation.

"She's not married, and she doesn't have kids," Connor said firmly.

Sandra's eyes lit up.

"You already knew her from somewhere. Okay, I can work with that."

"Sandra!"

She was already bustling away, reaching into her pocket to grab her phone, probably looking for some corner where she could start internet sleuthing. Connor sighed. Aubrey shook his head.

"You gotta choose... either information blackout, or you might as well just tell her everything. You know she's going to take this as a challenge now." Shaking his head again, Aubrey got back to his paperwork. "Also, you need to get ready. Your first appointment is Mrs. Mavity."

It wasn't just that he needed to prepare his station; he also needed to get ready to have his butt pinched. Mrs. Mavity was five feet of sassy grandma, and she'd had no hesitation about telling him how much she liked his butt during her first appointment with him. She had asked permission before pinching first, and he'd automatically said 'yes' without thinking about it, and it had made her so happy that he hadn't been able to bring himself to change his answer during any of the sessions since.

Sandra had offered to tell her, but really... she was only there for ten sessions. He could stand having his butt pinched ten times. It really did make her happy, and she only had two more sessions to go.

Sighing—far more concerned about what Sandra was doing with her phone than he was about Mrs. Mavity's butt-pinching propensities—he headed over to his station. Sandra was at hers, head down, finger gliding over her screen. When she saw him out of the corner of her eye, she looked up, gave him a little finger wave, and went right back to looking at her screen.

"I'm not going to tell you anything more unless you stop looking," he called to her.

"I don't need you to," she called back without looking up.

Well, he'd tried.

Strangely, he felt a little better about telling his friends tonight. Sandra and Aubrey were excited for him. Maybe the others would be, too, even though he'd have to admit that he wasn't who they thought he was.

Well, Law might not be excited, but Mistress Julie was excited about Law not being excited, so that was good enough for him. He knew she'd be telling Olivia and Camille at brunch today, so that meant he needed to tell his friends when he saw them tonight. He'd much rather they find out from him than from club gossip.

6

JULIE

Walking into her upcoming interrogation—brunch, but she knew what it was actually going to be today—Julie was unsurprised to see Olivia already sitting there expectantly. The vibrant redhead was dressed incredibly casually, wearing a three-quarter-length sleeve Star Wars t-shirt and jeans. Her fiancé's influence, no doubt. Camille was already there as well, in a colorful blouse that only someone with her coloring could pull off, her expression confused but interested. She'd taken out her braids since the last time Julie saw her and had her hair pulled back from her face, the tightly wound curls now a large pouf on the back of her head. Damn, Julie would kill to have that kind of volume.

"I hear you have some news for us, but Olivia won't say what it's about," Camille said with bemusement after Julie had greeted each of them and sat down.

"That's because it's Julie's secret to tell," Olivia said, putting a slight emphasis on the word 'secret.' Cute.

The server appeared to fill Julie's water glass and take her drink order before silently gliding away, giving her a moment to get her bearings.

She was a little surprised Olivia hadn't already spilled the tea but was appreciative. She was *not* surprised that Olivia had been torturing Camille with hints since she knew Julie would be there to tell her the whole deal, eventually.

"Well, I found out who my secret admirer is last night," Julie admitted, a smile coming unbidden to her lips as just saying the words threw her mind back to the events of the prior evening. The realization that Connor was her secret admirer, joining him in the booth, and the absolutely lovely way he'd submitted to her.

"Oh, really?" Camille's eyebrows shot up, and she leaned forward with interest. "You can't just stop there, woman. Who was it? Is it?"

Leaning forward, Julie dropped her voice a little lower, even though there wasn't any real need to. No one at this restaurant knew her or Connor or anyone else, but for some reason, it felt right to keep it quieter.

"Connor."

"What?!"

So much for quieter. Camille practically shrieked the word, jumping in her seat and slapping her hand down on the table at the same time, which cracked Olivia up so that she started cackling like a hyena. The server had just returned with Julie's bellini and was giving them all a rather skeptical look. She smiled up at him.

"Thank you."

"Of course. Are you ready to order?"

Ordering gave Camille a chance to come to terms with the new world order—really, Julie couldn't blame her for her response. She hoped it wasn't too indicative of how people would react when they found out, though. Connor was already on edge about that. She didn't think anyone would really be upset with him, but she understood where the fear was coming from.

They put in their orders. By the time they were done, Camille was past her initial reaction, a contemplative look in her dark eyes.

"So... Connor is a sub. You know..."

"We might have realized it if we'd been looking at his behavior and not him," Olivia said, finishing her sentence for her.

"Exactly." Camille shook her head. "I can't believe we all missed it."

"Well, we also believe people when they say what they want and what they are. There was no real reason to look deeper when he was so certain that he was a Dom." Julie had been thinking about that all night, especially since she'd been the instructor for his class. "He doesn't make a bad one, though I think that's partly because he's dedicated to giving people what they need. So, when a submissive needed something from him, he was able to top her in order to fulfill that need."

"That makes so much sense." Camille tapped her finger against the table. "Freddy is going to be so mad he didn't realize."

Olivia chuckled.

"I think a lot of people are going to be mad they didn't know." The redhead rubbed her hands together gleefully. "When does Law find out?"

"Tonight. Connor is going to tell him." Julie shot her a look. "And no one is going to give Law a hard time because I don't want him giving Connor a hard time."

"Aw, you're no fun," Olivia complained.

"That's not what Connor said last night," Julie retorted with a smirk.

"Wait, wait, wait, I'm behind." Camille put her hands up in a 'stop' gesture. "I got the who but not the how—how did you find out Connor is your secret admirer?"

It took until their food got there to catch her up on the final note and Connor's appearance, then both of the other women on what happened after she joined him in the booth. Not that she went into too much detail, but they were also Dommes, and she wanted their opinions.

Some of what she was doing with Connor was uncharted territory, just because she'd never been with a submissive who entered the lifestyle thinking he was a Dom before. Camille and Olivia listened, their reactions mirroring each other's as she went into the night.

"So, you're dating now?" Camille was the first to speak once Julie was done, she and Olivia glancing at each other in surprise. "Not that I'm against it, understand, but it just seems kind of fast."

"Well, we're not going straight into a committed relationship. We're getting to know each other first, which is what dating is for." Though, to be fair, it wasn't as though Julie dated much. She was far more used to scening with no commitment than dating... and, truth be told, she tended to be a serial monogamist more than someone who dated a bunch.

"That's true. I feel like the people around us just go from zero to full speed ahead very quickly, so that's what I'm used to." Olivia laughed. "On the other hand, all of them were in denial about how things would go in the beginning..."

"We're just dating."

"Okay." But she said it with a smirk.

As Julie narrowed her eyes, Camille pressed her lips together in obvious amusement.

"He just admitted he's submissive, and he hasn't even told his friends yet."

"Uh-huh." Olivia picked up her drink to take a sip. She was saying all the right things, but her tone indicated otherwise.

"Is it okay to tell Freddy?" Camille asked, cutting things off before they could devolve. Which was probably a good thing. Sometimes, she had to play the role of peacemaker, but she didn't seem to mind much.

"Yes, but ask him not to tell anyone else until tomorrow... and maybe check in before that." Just in case Connor didn't actually follow through with telling his friends.

Olivia frowned at her, as if reading her thoughts.

"He's going to tell them." She sounded very sure of it. Far more sure than Julie felt.

"I know he plans to, but..." Julie shrugged. She didn't want to set herself up for disappointment. Just in case. She could remember the number of times her ex had said he'd do something, only to never follow through. Not that he'd ever said he would tell anyone he submitted to her. That was a secret he would probably prefer to take to his grave since it didn't suit his idea of a 'real' man.

But Connor wasn't John, and logically, she knew she should give him the benefit of the doubt. Emotionally... it was a bit more of a struggle.

Hearing Olivia say it helped, though.

"I'll tell Freddy to wait, just in case. I'll still tell him tonight, though, because if anyone could help talk Connor through any doubts, it would be Freddy." Camille smiled proudly, and she wasn't wrong.

There was an unhappy, queasy feeling in the center of Julie's stomach at the idea of Connor needing to be talked through it. Which wasn't fair. She knew that. If he needed it, he needed it, and it wasn't a reflection on her or his feelings for her if he did. It was just something he needed.

Now, if only she could get her subconscious reactions on board with her logical thinking.

She was starting to think she had a few more leftover issues from her divorce than she'd realized.

***

CONNOR

Pulling up to Law's house, Connor stared at the exterior for a long moment. It was a nice house, one in which he normally felt quite welcome. He'd spent a lot of time in this house, yet the walk seemed to loom longer than normal. Something about it appeared far more threatening.

One bright spot in his day—Sandra had been completely stymied in her search. She hadn't been able to find anything about his mystery date, though that wasn't going to stop her from continuing to look. Whether or not she'd eventually find Julie... well, if he was lucky, by the time she did, he'd feel more comfortable talking about him and Julie.

If there was still a him and Julie.

She had texted him today to tell him that Olivia and Camille were cheering for him and that they'd both offered up their partners to talk to him if he wanted to. Which made him feel better. Freddy might be a lot smaller and slimmer than him, but he was known as a ruthless lawyer in the courtroom, and there were quite a few dominants who stepped gingerly around him, even in the club. It didn't matter that he was a sub. Olivia's fiancé, Luke, wasn't someone Connor knew personally, but he was a fairly big, muscular, Alpha-type-looking guy. He might know what it felt like to have people make assumptions about who he was in the scene, except that he'd come into it as Olivia's submissive from the beginning.

Connor sighed.

This wasn't getting him anywhere. He needed to get out of the car and go inside and tell his friends.

Julie had already told hers. He'd thanked her for letting him know about Freddy and Luke. He might reach out to them. Especially if things went poorly tonight.

He really hoped it didn't go poorly tonight.

A knock on his window made him jump, which made him hit his head because there was only about an inch of space between him and the roof of his car. Muffled laughter filtered through the closed door, and he ruefully rubbed where he'd hit his head as he looked out the window to see Asad and Morgan standing there.

"Doing okay there, buddy?" Asad asked, grinning widely. The two of them made an attractive couple—Asad with his tanned skin, black hair and eyes, and muscular frame, next to Morgan with her extremely pale skin and long red hair. She had bright green eyes that stood out against the pink and cream of her cheeks, and her hair and makeup were always done to perfection.

"I'm fine." He waved his hand at Asad, motioning him back—Morgan had already started to move out of the way—so he could get out of the car. She tugged on her boyfriend's hand, pulling him with her. "Just... thinking."

"Very deep thoughts, I saw," Asad teased. He was always joking around and teasing. It was how he showed he cared. Connor didn't mind because it meant Asad did most of the talking for him.

Actually...

"I was thinking about my date last night with Mistress Julie." Saying the words out loud made his chest clench, but it was easier to say them to Asad than just about anyone else. Even Q, who was a switch. Maybe because Asad never took anything too seriously—other than Morgan—so he was the least likely to be upset about Connor's deception.

Asad froze, blinking like a deer in headlights, as though he couldn't understand the words Connor had just said. Which made his anxiety ramp up again, but Morgan's expression lit up.

"That was a date? You're her secret admirer? Oh, Connor, that's lovely." Letting go of Asad's hand, she rushed forward to throw her arms around Connor. Since Morgan wasn't exactly free with her hugs, he appreciated the gesture as he hugged her back, doing his best not to crush her. It was a fast hug, because that was all Morgan did, but a much-appreciated one. She stepped back, brushing her hair back from her face as she turned to Asad. "Isn't that lovely?"

"You're her secret admirer?" Asad repeated blankly, rather than answering Morgan.

The little bit of ease that her hug had given Connor wasn't lasting very long, but he managed to nod. If Asad freaked out, he was just going to get in the car and drive away because if Asad freaked out, he couldn't imagine what everyone else's reaction was going to be. His nerves were ramping up as Morgan frowned and reached for Asad's hand again. He was about to get back in his car and flee when Asad suddenly broke out into a gleeful grin.

"Holy crap! Law is going to *freak!* This is amazing! Let's go tell him!"

"Asad!" Morgan called after him in exasperation as he bounded toward the front door, leaving her and Connor behind. He spun around to look at them.

"Come on! Hurry up!" He waved his hand impatiently.

The weight on Connor's shoulders lifted. Not all the way, but a lot of it. Asad wasn't mad. Even the prospect of needling Law wouldn't distract him if he'd been mad. He didn't get mad often, but when he did, he wasn't going to be goofing around and annoying his friends.

So, that was one person who wasn't upset with him. Two if he counted Morgan.

"The date went well?" she asked as they started walking toward Asad, who was impatiently hopping back and forth, still waving them on. Connor took shorter steps than usual... to keep up with Morgan, of course. Not because it would drive Asad nuts when he was trying to get them to hurry. Funny enough, Morgan was taking her time, too.

"I think so. She was surprised, I think, to find out that I was her secret admirer—"

"I bet," Morgan murmured.

"But we had a good evening. And she said she'd be interested in seeing me again, and not just at Marquis. I think we're going to date, and I'm going to... explore."

"I'm happy for you." She tilted her head to look up at him, smiling, and he could feel that she really meant it.

"I'm happy for you, too, but I'm even happier for me," Asad said gleefully, grabbing Morgan's hand now that she was in reach and pulling her along with him. She shot Connor an apologetic look over her shoulder. "Tonight is going to be so much more entertaining than I anticipated. Come on!" He got to the door and opened it, pulling Morgan in along with him, no knocking needed. Law tended to leave it unlocked when he knew people were coming over.

Taking a deep breath, Connor followed them.

7

———————

"Law! Law, Connor has something to tell us!" The gleeful note in Asad's voice made Connor smile and shake his head. At least he had one friend who would completely back him up. Following Asad and Morgan down the hall into the kitchen, he found Law there with Iris, Q, and Sam. *The gang's all here.*

He couldn't decide if that was better or worse.

Ripping off the band-aid with Asad had been impulsive, which wasn't like him, but it had been a relief. He'd been fairly certain how Asad would react, and it felt easier to tell just one of his friends instead of all of them. Having Morgan there had been helpful, too. The two of them had become close even before she'd gotten together with Asad, and he'd known she would accept him as he was.

He didn't know Sam or Iris as well. Though he liked both of them, his time with them was due to their being connected to Q and Law. Eventually, that might change, but they hadn't had enough time to get close or anything. A small part of him cared a little about what they thought, but not as much as he did about Law and Q.

Those were the two he didn't want to disappoint.

And as much as part of him enjoyed getting one over on Law, he also didn't want his friend mad at him. He would only be able to enjoy it if Law wasn't actually upset with him. It was the thought that Law might be truly angry that was making his stomach churn. Asad's glee was somewhat reassuring in that he didn't think Law was actually going to be angry, or else he wouldn't be looking forward to the reaction.

"Oh?" Law asked, raising one eyebrow as he looked up from where he was standing behind the counter. It looked like he and Iris were assembling food to go out on the grill. She was beside him, short and cheerful, smiling up at Connor as he came in. Law wasn't that much taller than her, but he packed a presence. Asad liked to joke that he was the Filipino Mr. Clean, and with his bald head and stern demeanor, he'd make a good one, though he'd have to shave his goatee.

Looking back and forth between Law and Connor, Asad made a little circle gesture with his hand. *Go on. Tell him.*

Connor's courage was failing him, especially with that look on Law's face.

"I had dinner with Mistress Julie last night." There. That was the truth, even if it wasn't everything.

Law frowned and looked over at Asad. He clearly realized something was up because of the way Asad was acting, but he hadn't caught on yet.

"It wasn't just dinner, though, was it?" Asad prodded, stepping over to put his hand on Connor's shoulder. Some of his glee had dissipated, as though he'd realized that something about this was making Connor nervous, so he was stepping in to help. "It was a *date*."

"A date?" Law blinked.

Beside him, Iris' eyes widened, and from over to the side, he heard Samantha's small gasp and Q's low murmur. They were picking up what Asad was putting down, but it appeared Law was a little slower on the uptake.

"With Mistress Julie? But..."

It felt like the air in the room stilled, everyone waiting with bated breath to see what Law would say next. His frown deepened.

"Are... are you the secret admirer?" Q asked after the longest moment in the world.

Connor kept his gaze on Law, mostly because he couldn't bring himself to look away as he answered.

"Yes."

Law's deep frown didn't budge, but he didn't turn to sudden anger either.

"Aw, that's so cute!" Iris brightened in a similar manner that Morgan had, putting her hands on her chest over her heart. "Oh my God, I would have never guessed! Wait... so you're submissive? Or a switch, like Q?"

It would be so easy to claim he was a switch, that he liked both sides of the coin, but after last night, he knew that wasn't true. While he could do both, the only side he really *wanted* to do was the bottom.

"I think I'm a sub," he said apologetically, his shoulders rounding inward.

"Welcome to the club!" Iris said, coming around the counter to hug him in very much the same way Morgan had, except Iris really liked hugs and didn't pull away quickly. Instead, she held him closely while she started chanting, "One of us, one of us!"

Connor burst out laughing.

At least the subs didn't have a problem with him. At least, not so far. He looked over at Law, who was still frowning fiercely, and his eyes had done that unfocused thing Asad's had done...

He met Connor's gaze, and his eyes narrowed even further.

"Have you figured it out yet, Law?" Asad asked, leaning over the counter to snatch up a strip of green pepper and crunching into it. "How the secret admirer always knew when to send the presents? Cuz *I* figured it out right away."

"You're the secret admirer." Law's voice was flat, demanding confirmation of what Connor had already admitted.

Iris stopped dancing, pulling away slightly from the hug, though she still kept her arms around Connor. Well, as much as she could, considering he was too big for her to be able to reach fully around him, even when she was snuggled up against him.

"Yes." Connor braced himself, but Law just stared at him.

His nostrils flared.

"Oooh, he's super mad," Iris said, though she didn't sound scared. If anything, she was taunting her boyfriend. "His nostrils only do that when he's super mad."

Law's angry gaze flipped to her, and Connor immediately shifted so he was slightly in front of her. Not that he thought Law would really hurt her, and he was pretty sure she was trying to draw her Dom's ire away from him, but he didn't need her to protect him. Subs stuck together, and she was trying to help, but he'd feel awful if she took a metaphorical hit meant for him.

"It's not a secret anymore, though, since she knows. And now, you know. And probably by tomorrow, everyone else will know since she told Olivia and Camille today, which means Freddy and Luke will know soon, too, if they don't already."

"Also, because Sam is texting all her friends right now," Q said dryly, interjecting and giving Connor a moment to take a breath. Once the words had started coming out, they had been surprisingly hard to stop.

"I am not! I mean, I am, but not about this." Sam looked up from where she was seated at the kitchen table, phone in her hand. "Noelle and Master Damian broke up. That's all that's being talked about, I swear. Though if I could tell them that I know who the secret admirer is, it might help to cheer her up to be one of the first to know."

"Sure, go for it," Connor said tiredly, waving his hand. At this point, the more people who knew already, the fewer people he had to tell himself. They could get it all talked out among themselves without talking to him about it, hopefully. The less he had to talk about it, the happier he'd be.

It was too much to hope that everyone would completely leave him and Julie alone, but he'd prefer not to have to answer questions. Plus, if it cheered someone up, great. Noelle could be difficult at the best of times, though he knew he was a little biased since when she was making difficulties, it was usually for Iris. There were plenty of people in the club who didn't have a problem with her, and she'd been doing a bang-up job of painting Iris in a bad light with those people.

He gave Iris a little squeeze, knowing it would be difficult to hear about Noelle. She completely respected that Sam was friends with her ex-friend and never complained about it, but he knew it made her antsy. Noelle had been a pretty shitty friend, from what he understood, and after joining Marquis, she'd done her best to make it appear the opposite. Recently, she'd even accused Iris and her friends of bullying her because they were ignoring her... which apparently, in her mind, they weren't allowed to do.

He knew part of the reason his brain was getting sidetracked with Iris' issues was because it was so much easier than focusing on his own.

Like the way Law had gone back to glaring at him.

"Why didn't you just tell us?" Law asked, sounding affronted.

Connor blinked. Maybe Law hadn't realized that he'd used things Law had told him to know when to send the gifts yet. That's what he expected Law to be the most upset about.

"That I was her secret admirer? I wasn't sure how you'd react. You seemed pissed that she had one." For a little while, he'd almost wondered if Law had a thing for Julie himself, but that hadn't fit. Eventually, he'd realized Law was just being really protective, but since Connor knew who the secret admirer was and that Julie was in no danger, it had been kind of fun watching Law fuming every time she'd gotten a gift.

There was no way in hell he was going to admit that to Law, though.

"That you had a... crush on her." Law stared at Connor like he was the one making no sense.

Connor was having a little trouble following Law's conversation leaps.

"Julie and Connor, sitting in a tree," Asad started singing.

"Morgan, can you shut him up?" Law tossed a piece of pepper at her as he spoke.

She caught it smoothly and shoved it in Asad's mouth. He

grinned, crunching down on it but also catching her wrist in his hand and holding her fingers in front of his mouth for him to nip at once the pepper was in his mouth.

Law was already hyperfocused back on Connor again.

"Why didn't you just tell us you were the secret admirer so I wouldn't be so worried?"

Oh. Right. That made sense.

"Because I wasn't sure how you'd take knowing that I'm a sub." There, he'd said it, out loud, to the people most important to him. No 'think.' No hedging. He'd said he was a sub. And it felt scary and good at the same time. It felt right.

"Why would I care that you're a sub?" Law threw his hands up in the air, one of them coming down to scrub over his bald head in frustration. "I mean, of course, I care because I care about you, but not in a bad way."

"Is it because everyone thought you were a Dom?" Q asked, his voice full of sympathetic understanding. Connor nodded, relieved that one of them got it. He should have realized Q would get it first—after all, he'd thought he was a Dom at first, then realized he was a switch. Of course, being a switch meant he was both. People hadn't been completely wrong about him like they were with Connor.

"I... I didn't want to tell you that you were wrong." He snuck a peek at Law. It was hard to tell what the other man was thinking. "Or that I wasn't like you. Or that I wasn't the person you thought I was."

"Oh, buddy, you're still the guy we thought you were." Asad released his hold on Morgan, coming over to nudge Iris out of the way. She went willingly, though she stood off to the side, looking over at Law, appearing to be ready to jump back to Connor's side if she felt it was necessary.

Asad patted Connor on the back of his shoulder.

"You're still like us. You're kinky. We serve our subs. You serve... well, your mistress. Okay, that's going to take some getting used to," he admitted. "But it doesn't really change who you are."

"If you have any questions, let me know," Q chimed in. "You can come join the cool club that these guys don't get to be a part of."

Frowning, Asad looked around Connor at Q.

"Cool club?"

"Yeah, you know..." Q grinned. "The pegging pack."

"Oh my God, that is not what you call yourselves." Sam put down her phone and shoved it away from her across the table with one hand, the other one coming up to cover her face as she groaned.

"Freddy came up with it," Q insisted, grinning wider, even as he reached over to take Sam's hand. "We're talking about getting t-shirts. Only people who have been pegged get one."

"I could get pegged if I wanted to." Asad frowned. "You don't have to be a sub to get pegged. And not all subs get pegged."

"Know a lot of Doms who have been pegged, do you?" Q asked, raising his eyebrow.

"That doesn't mean we couldn't be." Asad put his hands on his hips, looking highly affronted. "I did the course. I've been plugged."

"Plugged isn't pegged."

Behind the counter, Law groaned and leaned forward, elbows braced on the counter, as he buried his head in his hands. Giggling, Iris scooted back around to his side of the island and patted him on the shoulder.

"I'll peg you if you want, honey," she said.

His head jerked up so fast, Connor was almost worried Law was going to need his services. But he didn't seem to have hurt himself, or if he did, it was hidden under his epic glare.

"The fuck you will."

"What's wrong with getting pegged?"

"Nothing's wrong with it, but we're not doing it."

"What if it was something I really wanted to try?" Iris asked so earnestly, it seemed to stop Law in his tracks. His mouth snapped shut, and a muscle worked in his jaw where he was clenching his teeth.

Rather than answering her, he turned toward Q and Asad, who were still arguing over whether Asad would actually go through with getting pegged.

"Would you two shut up?" Law threw more pieces of pepper at

them, this time fast and hard enough that one of them bounced off of Asad's forehead, which made Morgan start cracking up.

Chuckling, Connor ambled over to the other side of the kitchen table, out of the firing line, and sat down. An odd feeling of contentment stole over him as he watched his friends bicker like they always did, as if nothing had changed.

Because it hadn't.

He still wondered what it would be like at the club when he was actually there with Mistress Julie or when people saw him submitting, but at least his closest friends had his back.

Whether or not Law had worked out that he'd played a part in Connor's ability to be Julie's secret admirer remained to be seen.

8

JULIE

"Oh my God, Law, leave me alone!" Apparently, finding out one of his best friends was submissive meant that all of Law's protective busybody ways had been transferred from her to Connor. She almost missed the days when he was freaking out about her secret admirer.

Sadly, she hadn't even gotten the joy of seeing his reaction, though she'd laughed over Connor's description of it—and laughed even harder when he'd told her about the pegging conversation. While it shouldn't be funny because there was nothing at all wrong with being pegged or enjoying anal sex as a dominant, something about the idea of Iris pegging Law had cracked her up.

"I'm just asking what your plans are for tonight," Law replied irritably, as if it were perfectly reasonable for one dominant to question another about an upcoming scene for no reason.

"And I told you to mind your business. Twice now." Putting her hands on her hips, she glared at him from across their desks, tapping her foot impatiently. Connor was going to be there soon, and she wanted to meet him for dinner—downstairs in Marquis' main restaurant tonight. They were going to eat there, then go straight up to the room she'd reserved for them, skipping the show.

"You can't blame me for being protective." Law bristled. "Connor has never submitted before. He's completely new to this. And he's... well, sometimes, he's not very good about speaking up for himself. If he was, he wouldn't have hidden the fact he's submissive for so long."

It bothered Law, Julie suddenly realized, that Connor had kept that a secret. It wasn't the secret admirer stuff, and Connor had already mentioned that Law didn't seem to care that he'd used things Law had told him to send her gifts—it bothered Law that his friend hadn't felt comfortable sharing his revelation. He didn't like thinking that he'd made Connor feel like he couldn't come to him.

So now, he was going overboard on the protectiveness, probably partially in a bid to show support to Connor. It was cute in a wildly frustrating way, which summed up Law as a person.

Julie decided to unbend. Just a little.

"We're going to have dinner, then I've reserved the shoe room." Also known as the foot fetish room. Julie didn't have much of a foot fetish, but she had a bit of a shoe one... at least, when it came to trying on very cute, very pretty, or very expensive shoes. Since she didn't know Connor's preferences, and it had been the only room open for tonight, it seemed like a good enough place to start.

The rest of the room was well equipped for anyone who wasn't into feet or shoes, including a queening throne if she felt so inclined. She'd also asked for one of the wooden frames she preferred when using the flogger to be moved into the room. Even though she hadn't known Connor was submissive, she hadn't been able to miss how often he'd shown up for her flogging demonstrations.

Was it because he wanted to be flogged?

She was going to find out tonight.

Law frowned.

"That's all you have planned? Shoes? I don't know if he's into that."

Oh, for Pete's sake.

She frowned back at him fiercely enough, he had the sense to look abashed, averting his gaze after a short moment.

"I'm sure I can figure out what a submissive is interested in on my own, thank you, Master Law." Heavy sarcasm laced her tone, making him shift uncomfortably. Especially when she called him Master Law since she wasn't doing it to be deferential—they'd become good friends, and using the honorific was a way of verbally distancing herself from him and reminding him that he *wasn't* above her.

"Sorry," he muttered again.

"The overprotective mother-henning has to stop. If you want to go mother hen someone, go find Iris." Not that Iris would take that well, either, but she'd respond by bratting, then Law could beat on her ass a little to get some of his anxiety out, and they'd both be happy. "Or I could go find Iris and give her some pointers about pegging."

Law gaped at her.

It was a bit of a low blow, but at least it had the desired effect.

The phone on her desk rang, and she immediately picked it up, grateful for the distraction.

"Hello?"

"Mistress Julie, your date is here." Freddy practically trilled the words, obviously happy to be able to say them. A smile immediately tried to appear on her lips, which wasn't going to help her intimidate Law, so she pushed it back.

"Thank you, Freddy, I'll be right out." Putting down the phone, she glared at Law, hands on her hips. "Connor is here. I'm going to my date. Any last words?"

The right answer was 'no.'

He hesitated for a moment before sighing.

"Go have fun. Take care of him, okay?"

"I'll make sure he has a great night," Julie said firmly. She really hoped that whatever happened between her and Connor didn't affect her friendship with Law. That was something she hadn't really considered when Connor had revealed himself. Although Connor had been worried about his friendship, she'd assumed Law would understand that he needed to keep his nose out of their business.

Obviously, she'd assumed wrong.

Sighing, she made her way out of the office, letting her smile bloom on her face as she stepped into the lobby of Marquis. Connor was standing by the front desk, talking with Freddy and Tori, another submissive who sometimes worked the desk. Both of them were beaming at him, and he appeared relaxed, though he was smiling rather than the one talking. Which wasn't surprising.

Tonight, he was wearing a nice pair of jeans that fit him like a glove and a button-down forest green shirt that looked like he might burst out of it if he flexed too hard. Julie appreciated the visual. The buttons weren't straining across his chest, but the shirt certainly wasn't loose, either.

It was a very different look from last week since they were eating downstairs rather than upstairs.

Julie was wearing one of her favorite date dresses, a bright emerald-green silk that cut low in front and had a slit up the front. The slit was really only visible when she walked, where it flirted around her thighs. With her hair pulled up high and back and her makeup on point, she felt sexy as hell, and when Connor looked up to see her coming toward him and his eyes widened, drinking in the sight of her, it felt like confirmation.

Lifting her chin, she sashayed right up to him and smiled. Did she have to tilt her head back to do so? Yes. Did she feel any less powerful? No. Not when the expression on his face was one of pure worship.

"Hello, Connor."

"Mistress." He said the word as though he savored it, filling her chest with warmth, his eyes still eating her up.

Yeah, whatever hard time Law gave her, she had a feeling Connor was going to be worth it.

Reaching out to take his hand, she slid her slim fingers through his giant ones. At some point, she would very much like to know what those fingers would feel like inside of her. Maybe even sometime tonight.

Hand securely tucked in his, Julie turned to smile serenely at Freddy and Tori, who were watching them with starry eyes. This was one of the reasons she'd decided to have their first evening together here at Marquis rather than at Stronghold.

"Thank you, Freddy. We'll be back up later." Turning away from the front desk, she only had to tug Connor's hand a little to get him moving. He gave Freddy and Tori a little wave as they went.

Julie didn't have to turn around to know the two were immediately bending their heads together to discuss her and Connor. She couldn't hear what they were saying, but she could hear the whispering. Amused, she led Connor down the stairs to the main dining room, where they entered through the back of the restaurant and made their way to the hostess stand.

The restaurant was packed, but thankfully, the acoustics were such that conversation was still possible without yelling. Julie had always appreciated the design of the restaurant—there were so many bare-bones places now where it was hard to actually talk if the tables were filled up because everyone's voices just echoed against the walls and ceiling.

Not that she and Connor were doing much talking yet. Other than greeting each other, they didn't say another word till they were seated at a corner booth. Julie detected Olivia's hand in the table selection, even though the Domme wasn't anywhere in sight.

The corner booth meant they were seated next to each other in a way, but they could also see each other. They could hold hands if they wanted to, while watching each other talk. It wasn't as awkward as sitting on the same side of the table and also far more intimate than sitting on opposite sides of the table.

"Have you eaten down here before?" she asked as they picked up their menus.

"Yes, but it's been a while. I've met Law here for dinner a few times." Connor looked down at the menu, seemingly a little nervous.

"I haven't," Julie admitted, which made him look up at her in surprise. "At least, not for dinner down here in the dining room. I've come to brunch, and I've been to the bar a few times around happy hour, but this is the first time I've actually eaten in the dining room."

"I would have thought you'd eat down here all the time."

"I think it's one of those things where you don't often do the things that are closest to you." She grinned at him. "Like living right outside DC, but never having been to the top of the Washington Monument."

"You've never been to the top of the Washington Monument?" It wasn't the first time that admission had garnered a slightly horrified reaction, and it made her laugh every time.

It also got the conversation rolling through the server coming to take their food and drink orders as they compared notes on what local features they'd never actually been to. While Connor had done the Washington Monument, he'd never been to the Cherry Blossom Festival—which was one of Julie's favorite things to do every year—and neither of them had gotten around to visiting the Spy Museum. However, Connor did admit that was because he'd never been particularly interested in spies. His favorite museum was the Air and Space Museum, while Julie preferred the art galleries. Though, she did admit that she liked the IMAX movies the Air and Space Museum showed.

It was the most she'd ever heard Connor talk in one sitting, in part because she didn't allow him to just sit back and listen to her. She wasn't a huge talker herself, though she could hold her own, and she wanted to know as much about him as he did about her. It was only fair.

Talking about all the places they'd been turned the conversation to their families, who had taken them to such places. By the time their food arrived, they were comparing notes once they found out they were both only children.

"I have a huge family. My mom is one of four, my dad is one of five, and all my aunts and uncles decided to have multiple kids. I was an only child in most ways, but not in others since I was always spending time with my cousins." She smiled at the memories since it was her cousins she'd gone down to visit the museums with.

"My mom was an only child sand so was my dad, so no cousins for me. I have some second cousins that I met a few times. Or... cousins once removed?" Connor shook his head. "We just called them my cousins, even though they weren't, really."

"Were you lonely?" Considering what an introvert he was, her heart ached at the idea of a lonely little boy.

"Sometimes, but not usually. Somehow, I always got adopted into a group of friends. Someone always took pity on me and pulled me in to hang out with them and their friends." He said it so matter-of-fact, but she couldn't help noticing that he didn't call them *his* group of friends. It was someone else's group of friends he got to hang out with —an important distinction that explained a lot about why he'd been so nervous to tell his friends about his crush on her.

Did he think they weren't really his friends, but actually someone else's who he also got to spend time with?

"Who brought you into your current group?" she asked. Maybe it was Law, and that was why he was so protective.

"Asad."

Well, there went that theory. But it was interesting. She wondered if knowing how protective Law was of him would help Connor realize that his friends valued him for him.

"Asad is definitely an extrovert. I feel like he's done that with quite a few of his friends." She smiled at him. "Olivia did something similar with me and Camille. She just decided we were going to be friends, and the next thing I knew, we're having regular lunches together."

He laughed, which made her smile widen.

"That's kind of how it was with me and Asad and Law. Then Q started hanging out with us, too."

"You know, Law was laying down the law with me before this evening," she said teasingly, making light of it, but she wanted him to know that Law had been concerned about him.

"Laying down the law?" He blinked, looking up in confusion.

"About you. He wanted to make sure that I treat you right."

Unfortunately, her joke didn't quite land the way she intended it to. Instead of laughing or being reassured about his friend, Connor frowned.

"He thought you would treat me badly? You'd never do that. He shouldn't have said that." The defensiveness in his voice surprised her. On one level, she was pleased because she was happy that

Connor would defend her; on another level, she really had been joking and didn't want to cause trouble between him and Law.

"He didn't really think that. He's just protective." She raised her eyebrow at him, smiling, trying to keep it light so he knew she wasn't bothered. "I believe you experienced a bit of that when I was getting notes from a secret admirer. And I certainly didn't need his protectiveness then, either."

That seemed to be a good comparison because Connor's shoulders immediately came down as he relaxed.

"Oh. Yeah, he does get a little overprotective."

"Of people he cares about? Absolutely." She wasn't sure if it was a direct hit, but she hoped it was. "He also seemed a little concerned because I reserved the shoe room for us tonight. It was the one that was open, but... just in case, do you have anything against shoes?"

Connor considered the question, chewing on his mouthful of steak as he did so. She took a bite of her own dinner while she waited for his answer.

"I don't think so," he said finally. "I've never really done much with shoes. Or feet. I don't have anything against them."

"Good." Speaking of feet, she slid one of hers over to rub against the inside of his calf. Connor blinked and tensed again, but this time, it was the good kind of tension. "Then we'll see where the night goes."

They could experiment with her feet and his fingers.

9

<u>Connor</u>

Dinner with Mistress Julie was good, and it made getting alone in a room with her even better. They'd been texting regularly for the past week, but it wasn't the same as sitting down and having a conversation over a meal.

He really did *like* her. Liked hearing her talk and, even more importantly, liked talking to her. Which wasn't something he always did a lot of. But she was easy to talk to, and somehow, she kept drawing the conversation out of him. The only part he hadn't liked was hearing how Law had given her a hard time.

Why Law would think that she wouldn't take care of him was beyond Connor. More than that, he felt uncomfortable knowing Law had tried to tell her what to do. He didn't really know what to do with that. Especially because he knew they were close friends as well, and he didn't want to cause trouble between them.

Even with Julie's reassurances, he still felt like he should say something to Law.

However, he had more important things to focus on right now.

He'd been in the shoe room before, but he hadn't ever used any of the equipment. Tonight, there was also a large square frame taking up space in the center of it. The walls were lined with shoes, and on one end of the room was a throne that was actually a queening chair. Connor felt a little shiver go down his spine as he looked at it.

He'd always wondered what it would be like to be under that chair.

Was that what Mistress Julie was planning tonight?

Did he hope so?

"I was thinking tonight we'd maybe play with some foot worship, just to see how you feel about it, and then move on to flogging and... see where the night goes," Mistress Julie said, her voice lilting up suggestively as she walked around in front of him, sauntering toward the throne.

The word 'flogging' made his skin tingle. Foot worship he wasn't so sure about, but he was willing to try. He had a feeling he'd like just about anything, as long as he was doing it with her.

She sighed as she sat down on the throne. For the first time, Connor noticed there was a basin full of water at the base of it, just off to the side.

"I love these heels, but they do not always love me back," she said as she lifted one dainty foot, examining the high heel almost mournfully. She looked up at him. "What do you think?"

Connor moved forward, feeling a little awkward, but she smiled as he moved, and that helped. He knelt at her feet, which felt more natural than he would have expected. Kneeling wasn't something he did often, but with where she was sitting and where he ended up, she was actually now looking down on him.

His cock stirred.

Yeah. He liked this position. At her feet.

However, he didn't think it was her feet that were doing it for him. It was just the simple act of kneeling down.

As if she could hear his thoughts, Mistress Julie reached out and ran her fingers through his hair. Connor sighed, closing his eyes and bending his head so she could touch it as much as she wanted. All the stress of the day felt like it was draining away, giving him a release of tension as a good massage would.

And all she'd done was have him kneel and touched his hair.

Nails slid down against the back of his neck and around his ear. With the way he was sitting, his legs were in front of him, bent, and he felt the heels of her shoes as she rested her feet on his thighs. He leaned forward between her legs, feeling her breasts touch the top of his head as she ran her nails down his neck and back up.

It was... peaceful. Despite his arousal. Which was something he never felt in the club. Normally, he was anxious, worried about what someone might need from him, what they might ask of him, that he might get something wrong, that he might disappoint his partner...

But Mistress Julie would tell him what she wanted from him. She would let him know if he was doing anything wrong. There were no expectations of him other than to do what she wanted, when she wanted it, and she would let him know what and when. Right now, she wanted to sit on the throne and stroke his hair with her feet resting on his thighs, and that was good enough for him. The longer they sat there, the more he relaxed.

Well, everything except his cock.

A part of him was enjoying being aroused and doing absolutely nothing with it.

He didn't know how long they sat there before she shifted again, her fingers sliding through his hair, then gripping rather than coming out. A shiver went down his spine, and his cock jerked against the inside of his pants as she tilted his head back to look at her. Her dark, liquid eyes were like pools of calm as her gaze met his, and he felt like sighing again, but it was too difficult with his head pulled back.

"My feet hurt, Connor. I want you to wash them and give them a massage." She smiled as she said it, so he knew she wasn't mad that they'd taken time to just sit.

The time had let him sink into a new headspace, and he felt oddly peaceful as he smiled back at her.

"Yes, Mistress."

Kink had always seemed to be about sex, and it wasn't that he wasn't aroused, but right now, he felt like it was less about the sex and more about serving her. About giving her what she wanted. Which was what he wanted. Knowing exactly what to do made him feel settled, sure of himself.

Easing the shoes off her feet, he placed them beside the basin, which he then carefully lifted up onto his lap, placing it between his thighs. The water sloshed a bit but didn't spill over. Beside the basin was a washcloth and a small bottle of soap. Once he had the basin on his lap and had put her feet in it, he reached down to pick up the cloth and soap.

Mistress Julie sighed happily as her feet soaked, her fingers playing with his hair again. The water must have been very hot when it was placed in here, because it was still warm, and he was sure it felt good on her feet. He hoped he could make it feel even better.

Wetting the cloth, he squirted some soap onto it and rubbed the sides of the cloth together to create a lather. It smelled like lavender, and inhaling it was putting him in almost a meditative state. Picking up one of Mistress Julie's feet, he started to scrub, working his fingers against the soles of her feet to massage as he did so.

Was he into feet? Not really. Was he aroused because he was getting to do something for Mistress Julie that made her moan?

Hell, yeah.

JULIE

Connor could give her a foot massage any day of the week. In fact, she was starting to think maybe she should demand it. His hands were huge, strong, and surprisingly gentle, though he seemed to have a knack for knowing exactly where to dig his fingers in to massage her soles. The slippery water and soap added to the experience, and he expertly washed and massaged her feet until she wanted to sink into a happy little melty puddle of contentment.

She was also squirming in her seat a little because she was enjoying his service. He was utterly intent, so focused on her feet, he didn't even glance up at her—and she didn't think it was because he was that into her feet. It had more to do with his determination to make her feel good, and he was using her feet to do so.

And it felt really damn good.

"Oh..." She sighed out the word as he hit a particularly sore spot.

Sometimes, when she was wearing her heels, she wondered who the real masochist was. They looked fantastic, but the older she got, the more of a number they did on her feet.

Opening her eyes, she looked down, watching him as he reverently handled her.

She wiggled her toes at him.

"Do you want to try kissing them?" It wasn't her thing, but it might be his. She could tell he was enjoying himself. Even if he wasn't into feet, he seemed to be the type who would be into body worship. It might not necessarily matter what part for that.

He tilted his head like he was considering it.

"Do you want me to?"

The uncertainty in his voice made her realize he needed a little more direction. He didn't sound necessarily interested, but he wasn't repelled, either.

"Why don't you try it and see what happens." It was more a suggestion than an order, in case he wanted to back out, but she didn't think he would. Connor tilted his head, lifting her foot up to his mouth. It was reminiscent of their first night together, with him under the table, yet entirely different.

Meeting her gaze, he kissed it right on the arch rather than the toe. With their eyes locked, there was something achingly intimate about the moment as he kissed her foot. Julie sucked in a breath as her insides quivered in response. His hot breath washed over her skin as he lifted his mouth away and moved it up toward her ankle, his lips coming down to press against the soft skin just underneath it.

Oh my.

Lifting her other foot, he turned his head to repeat the kisses, leaving the first foot resting lightly against his chest, his big hand still wrapped around her leg just above the ankle. Julie squirmed, pressing her thighs together at the unexpected tingles of pleasure that climbed up her legs.

She hadn't expected to enjoy this as much as she did.

Some of it was the physical sensation. The spots he was touching, kissing, were far more sensitive than she'd realized they would be. A big part of it was having a huge man at her feet, kissing them so worshipfully, his hands gently wrapped around her legs... not quite abasing himself for her, but certainly putting himself in her hands.

The heady thrill of power was exactly why domination had called to her.

"Kiss up my legs," she demanded, flexing her toes against his chest.

Connor's eyes lit up. He reached down to move the basin to the side out of his way, then started doing exactly what she'd requested.

Again, similar to their first date when he'd gone under the table, but entirely different. This time, she could watch him, and he had room to move. It was worth watching. She almost regretted not being able to the first time. At least she was getting a do-over where she got to play the part of voyeur.

He was just so damn big, yet so gentle. So eager to please.

His mouth moved up her legs with his hands, her skirt falling back as she spread her thighs, tilting her hips forward to meet him. Soft, sweet kisses up the inner skin of her thighs left a little path of pleasure before she lifted herself up so he could take off her underwear before draping her legs over his shoulders.

The fabric of her skirt fell back, pooling around her hips, exposing her from the waist down. This time, she could see the expression on his face before he buried it between her thighs. She could see the way his eyes lit up, the hunger that filled them.

"Good boy," she murmured as his mouth reached her pussy, leaning back on the throne to give him full access. Big hands cupped her bottom, pulling her forward a little more, her legs resting easily on his broad shoulders. Sliding her fingers into his hair, she held him in place as he started to feast, shuddering with the pleasure that bloomed so quickly thanks to his talented tongue. "Oh, yes..."

At some point, they might use the queening throne the way it was meant to be used, but right now, she was perfectly happy with what he was doing. Her toes curled, heels digging into his shoulders as his tongue moved, sliding through the slick folds, seeking out the nub of her clit. Julie cried out, moving her hips upward, her grip on his hair tightening as he explored her with his tongue.

"Oh, yes, just like that." She gasped, arching, as his tongue circled her clit, his grip on her bottom tightening. Fuck he had big hands. "Use your fingers."

It required shifting a little, but that didn't interrupt her pleasure. When one thick finger pushed into her pussy, his tongue lapping against her clit while he stretched her open, it was so worth it. Julie moaned, letting her head drop back as her pussy clenched around his finger.

Thrusting back and forth a few times, he kept up his oral assault as he added a second finger.

Huge.

His fingers were huge.

Thick, long, and curving inward to press against her G-spot.

The stretch was delicious, and he knew exactly how to use them. His tongue kept moving, teasing her, as he began to move his fingers back and forth inside her, twisting and pressing against that sensitive inner spot. She could feel her climax rising, higher and higher, the need pulsing through her as her muscles tensed, knees and toes curling in response.

"Oh, fuck... Connor... more..." she demanded, and he gave it to her.

Sucking her clit into his mouth, he thrust his fingers in, hitting her G-spot at the same time, and Julie went off like a rocket. Her pussy clamped down around the digits, squeezing and pulsing as she cried out with ecstatic abandon. Her clit throbbed against his tongue, waves of pleasure crashing over her as he sucked.

The rapture swirled around her, leaving her panting and quivering, on the verge of sensory overload.

"Stop," she ordered, patting the top of his head.

Immediately, he stopped, moving his mouth away, allowing her to slump and sigh with pleasure. Opening her eyes, she saw the concerned expression on his face as he slid his fingers from her.

"Very good boy," she said, and his expression cleared, tinged with relief. She stroked her fingers through his hair. "A little too good. Let me catch my breath, then I'll reward you with a flogging."

Connor sucked in a breath, but the smile that lit up his face made her want to hurry up and get him under her lash.

10

———————

Stripped down, standing under the wooden frame with his hands resting against the wooden beam going across the top of it, he couldn't decide if he wished he was cuffed to it or not. Hanging on gave him more freedom, and this was his first time going through a full flogger session as a submissive—he'd experienced multiple types during his class to become a Dom, but that hadn't included a full-on session. On the other hand, part of him wondered about being restricted.

"For standing up like this while we're here at Marquis, I'm not going to use cuffs." Julie smiled at him, as if it was no big deal that she'd just read his mind. Her dress had, sadly, fallen back into place, though she hadn't put her underwear back on. Putting one hand on his chest, she patted it reassuringly. "Just in case you get a little spacey. It would be difficult for me to get you down from them by myself. If you want to try cuffs, we can do that on the bed after this."

She laughed at his change in expression because he hadn't been able to stop himself from perking up.

Yes, he liked the idea of being cuffed and at her mercy. It wasn't often that he felt truly vulnerable. Even when he was kneeling at her feet, he knew that he was bigger and stronger than her—it was a choice. His choice. His gift of submission. That's what some of the people in the scene called it.

He liked the idea of finding out what it would be like to be vulnerable to her. To put even more of his trust in her.

"Thank you," he said, for both the offer of cuffs and because he realized she was thinking of him by not using them right now. If he went into subspace or something happened and he needed out of the cuffs immediately, it would be difficult for her to get him out of them by herself while he was standing. Even quick-release cuffs. She'd need a stepstool to get up to where his wrists were above his head, both to put the cuffs on and to take them off.

Curling his hands over the top of the beam, he rotated his shoulders, loosening up the muscles. Mistress Julie smiled and patted his chest again, rubbing her hand through the hair there. He'd wondered before tonight if he should shave—a lot of the male subs did—but it seemed like she liked touching his hair, and it didn't matter whether it was on his head or his chest.

He'd leave it unless she asked him to remove it.

"Did you have a favorite flogger during the class?" she asked, her hand still in place.

"The one with the knots," he said immediately. Sometimes, he'd dreamed about that flogger. It had felt like a massage, and he hadn't wanted it to end, but that wasn't something he'd been able to admit during the class. Not in front of the other Doms. Or Law.

Patting his chest one last time, Mistress Julie nodded and let her hand drop. Immediately, he missed her touch. His cock moved. No longer tightly confined by his pants, it made a huge tent out of his boxers. Not that she seemed to notice that his dick was straining toward her—she'd already turned to go to the floggers.

Which, of course, just made his dick even harder when she hefted the one in question in her hand.

The falls were a couple feet long with big knots at the end that gave them a 'thuddy' feel. He hoped it felt as good as he remembered. With one last little smile in his direction, Mistress Julie walked around behind him. His muscles tensed, knowing she was back there but unable to see what she was doing.

When she put her hand on his shoulder, he almost jumped in surprise.

"I'm going to start in a moment, then I'll stop regularly to check in since this is your first time. You can drop your hands down or say 'red' to stop me at any time unless you have another safeword you want to use."

"Beatles."

He felt her pause.

"Beetles? Like the insect?"

Connor felt his cheeks heat. This was what he got for trying to be clever when he was thinking of a safeword.

"Like the band," he mumbled. "You know... help, I need somebody?"

Mistress Julie cracked up, and his blush receded as warmth filled his chest. That was the reaction he'd been hoping for.

"That's one I haven't heard before." She chuckled again, and the warmth expanded to his whole body as a sense of pride filled him.

Was it that big a deal that he'd used a safeword she'd never heard? Probably not, but he liked knowing that he'd done something first with her when she was going to be his first for so many things.

"Beatles it is. Though my goal is to make sure you don't need to call for help."

"I'm sure I won't."

As far as he knew, Mistress Julie had never pushed anyone to their limit, much less past it. He didn't think she was suddenly going to start with him, but he knew that having the safeword made everyone feel better. It certainly had him when he'd been the one in charge. Maybe it was different for real Doms, but she had asked for one, and he knew most of his friends preferred having one.

A safeword wasn't a guarantee, especially if a submissive was stubborn or was too out of their head in the scene to truly be able to understand and consent to what was going on, but it was still a good thing to have. Especially when scening with a new partner, even one as experienced as Mistress Julie.

The little slap she gave his shoulder was slightly reproving.

"But you'll use it if you need it?" There was a hint of warning in her voice.

"Yes, Ma'am."

No, he didn't think he'd need it when this was literally his dream come true, and he had full trust in her to not push him too far, but he knew better than to argue with a dominant. Especially one about to flog him. She didn't need to hurt him to torture him. His dick and balls were already aching—he really, really, really hoped he was going to get an orgasm tonight, but he also knew better than to expect one, especially if he started behaving badly.

With the promise of being cuffed to the bed, he would much rather continue being her good boy.

She patted his shoulder and stepped away. His muscles tensed, and Connor rolled them again, forcing himself to relax. It was the anticipation making him tense, not fear.

As soon as the flogger thudded against his skin for the first time, all the tension fled in a rush, and his shoulders came down. The thud was just as good as he remembered, like tapping against his skin but harder and better. Connor closed his eyes, letting himself lean against the frame and enjoy the sensation as the leather falls came down again and again.

A moment later, Mistress Julie touched his back again.

"How are you doing, Connor?"

He didn't open his eyes. He didn't want a break. He just wanted her to keep going, and with his eyes closed, it felt like that moment in a dream when he might be able to drop right back into the spot where it had paused.

"Good, Ma'am. Very green."

Green was the stoplight color for doing well—green means go, go, go. And he didn't want her to stop.

"Good."

She stepped back, the spot on his back where her hand had been suddenly feeling a little cold. He didn't have very long to miss it before the flogger was coming down again.

Thudding against his skin.

A rainfall of sensation drawing him deeper.

The wooden frame creaked as he leaned more of his weight on it. His knees weren't exactly buckling, but he needed more support.

The leather rain stopped.

His dick throbbed.

A warm hand touched his sensitized skin, making it feel hot, and he groaned.

It moved across his shoulders and down his back, rubbing over all the spots that had just been flogged, sending sensation tingling through him. His cock jerked in response, bouncing off his groin as his muscles flexed.

"I think you can take a little more," Mistress Julie murmured as she caressed his back. "Do you want more, Connor?"

"Yes, please. More."

This time, when she stepped away, the thudding massage wasn't just on his shoulders and back. It was his shoulders, back, ass, and the backs of his thighs.

Fuck me.

Now, his knees did threaten to buckle, and the wooden frame creaked again. He was feeling so spacey, so good, and it was getting harder to hold himself upright. She'd made the right choice not to cuff him. He wasn't sure he wouldn't have ended up trying to let the cuffs take his whole weight.

He closed his eyes as the patter continued, sending him into a blissful haze.

JULIE

The flogger felt almost weightless in her hand as she watched Connor submit to the leather. He was nearly done, his head hanging down, his back, ass, and thighs a bright pink. He'd given himself over completely to the sensations, and she was pretty sure it was only instinct keeping him upright.

Time to stop, regrettably. At some point, maybe they'd get to do a public scene where she'd have help getting him down if she needed it.

Putting the flogger back in place, she was pretty sure he didn't even notice things had paused until she put her hand on his back. He sucked in a breath, shuddering and lifting his head, straightening up as if he was coming back to himself.

Standing at his side, she rubbed one hand across his sensitized skin while the other moved over his chest, then dipped lower, following the line of hair that went down his stomach to his groin. She'd always had a thing for happy trails.

"Do you think you can make it to the bedroom, Connor?" she asked as the tip of his cock brushed against the back of her hand. It was velvety soft and a little wet from the precum leaking from it.

"Yes, Ma'am." He gave himself a shake, as though he was trying to shake off a spell, blinking down at her and dropping his arms. The movement forced her to step back, which wasn't the worst thing since it meant more torment for him. Something he realized as soon as she moved away, her hands no longer on him.

Julie grinned wickedly.

"Get yourself in the bedroom then. I want you in the middle of the bed, on your back, with your hand around your cock to keep you ready for me."

"That won't be a problem," he muttered, even as he started to turn.

She laughed softly, reaching out to smack his ass hard enough to leave a print on top of the already pink skin, making him jump. Just because he was funny didn't mean the backtalk would go unacknowledged.

It was nice to know that he didn't think he was going to have any trouble staying ready for her, though.

As much as she was enjoying watching his backside as he led the way into the bedroom, she was looking forward to him being on his back even more. Her personal playground for the evening. Lying on his back would mean all his weight would be on his sensitive skin, which would be pressed up against the silky sheets on the bed...

This was going to be so much fun.

"Good boy," she murmured as he got into position. His cock was completely proportional, which made her wonder if she was biting off more than she could chew... but she certainly wasn't going to go sleep tonight without trying.

He turned his head to watch her as she started to strip down. His hand was on his cock, moving, as she tugged her clothing off. Julie enjoyed the look in his eyes—an adoring man's eyes were a better mirror than a length of glass could ever be. Running her hands down her body, she enjoyed watching his gaze follow the movement, the growing hunger in his eyes showing as he clenched one hand in the sheets as if he was stopping himself from reaching for her.

Under his gaze, her puckered nipples tightened even more, her body humming with arousal. He was a big man buffet, all laid out for her to enjoy... and she certainly planned to.

"Keep your hands to yourself unless I tell you to touch me," she ordered as she crawled onto the bed. Her breasts hung beneath her, his gaze dropping to them for a moment before returning to hers.

"Yes, Ma'am," he agreed, then groaned as she knelt beside him, placing both of her hands on the middle of his thighs. The wiry hair beneath her palms was softer than his chest hair, but not by much. Julie grinned as she pressed her thumbs into the sensitive spot on his inner thighs, then began to move her hands up his legs.

His fingers gripped the sheet and his dick, his hips moving upward, cock bouncing against his lower stomach as her hands slid across his skin. The large but tender sack hanging below them was her first stop. Watching his face, Julie straddled his thighs as she gently cupped his balls... then tugged.

"Fuck!" His hips surged upward again, though they couldn't do quite as much with her on his thighs... but he was so big that she ended up moving a little more than intended, sliding toward his dick.

It was like riding an earthquake—he was so big, and she was so much smaller, yet it didn't matter.

He was letting her do whatever she wanted to him.

The rush of power of having such a big, strong man at her command was heady.

Size had never mattered to her before, but she couldn't deny the difference between them gave the experience a little something extra.

"Do you like a bit of pain?" Julie asked, her tone almost sympathetic. Almost. She tugged on his balls again, a little harder this time, and his cock bounced. Wrapping her hand around the base of the thick, hot shaft, she elicited another groan from him. "You certainly seem to."

"I think I just like you touching me."

"Mmm, so it doesn't matter what I do, you'll like it?" She twisted his balls slightly, allowing her to get a finger twisted around underneath them so she could drag her nail across his sensitive perineum. He whimpered. Oh, she liked making Connor whimper. Maybe a little too much. Her core tightened.

"Unfortunately for me, yes." The expression on his face was almost sheepish, offset by the burning need in his eyes.

Fuck, she wanted to ride him... but she was also enjoying torturing him too much. The sadist's dilemma.

11

───────

His balls ached, his cock ached—for two totally different reasons —and Mistress Julie was scraping the sensitive spot just under his balls and making his sphincter tighten in fear. Not because he didn't want her finger in his ass; it was just an instinct. That and if she scraped her nail over the sensitive skin around his anus, it was probably going to hurt even more than the strokes over his perineum.

Before tonight, Connor wouldn't have said he enjoyed pain that much. During the classes, he'd liked the flogger and the crop, while he'd tolerated the belt, the paddle, the whips, and the cane. None of the latter had been a turn-on. He hadn't had much use for sensation play.

Now, he was wondering if his disinterest had been because of his lack of interest in the person causing the sensations... and conversely, his current interest was because it was Mistress Julie touching him. Tugging on him. Squeezing his balls.

He groaned again, thrusting his hips up through the tight grip of her fingers, yet also trying to keep from moving too much because he didn't want to accidentally tip her off his thighs. The curve of her bottom rested on his legs, her knees pressed against the outside of his thighs, and if he moved too much, he might trap her hand between his legs or even send her tumbling.

Since he wanted a reward and not a punishment, he was determined to do neither.

Fuck, he wished he was tied up. Gripping the sheets to keep himself still was getting harder and harder.

As if she heard his thought, Mistress Julie released his balls—and sadly, his cock as well.

"Arms above your head, Connor." She smiled as he let out a sigh of relief. Being cuffed to the bed would be so much easier than trying not to touch her on his own.

Of course, he hadn't considered exactly how torturous the process would be.

Mistress Julie didn't move off him or to the side. Instead, she moved over him—breasts hanging down in front of his face, pussy hovering over his body—but she'd told him not to touch her until directed.

No, she told me to keep my hands to myself unless she told me to touch her.

It was a semantics argument, but as her pert, dark pink nipple dangled in front of his lips, he wondered if it might be worth arguing. His tongue flicked out, wetting his lips... then she shifted, dangling the other nipple in front of him. Leather closed around both of his wrists now, holding him in place, giving her full access to his body.

His cock felt like it was going to break off, it was so fucking hard.

Pressing his lips together, he breathed through his nose and closed his eyes. Maybe if he couldn't see her breasts hovering right above him, he'd forget they were there... forget her nipple was right...

Something brushed against his lips, and he jerked his head back, eyes flying open.

Mistress Julie looked down at him with amusement, running her hands from the cuffs down his arms to his neck, then up to cup his face. Her fingers stroked the scruff on his cheeks, the sensation rippling through him. Even though she was no longer holding his dick and balls, he could still feel the strain, the tightness around them for some reason.

"You are... a *very* good boy," she whispered before pressing her lips against his.

It was a sweet, hot kiss that deepened quickly, and suddenly, Connor really wished that his hands *were* free. His arms jerked, pulling at the restraints, wanting to wrap them around her, wanting to touch her. She tightened her thighs around his chest, her hair brushing against the inside of one of his arms as she kissed him.

His lower body was moving again, pushing up, his cock seeking her... but she was too far away. He groaned against her lips, and her tongue slid into his mouth, dancing with his. The wood of the bed creaked, his muscles flexing, and his desire to touch her grew with every second.

When she lifted her lips from his, he was panting from the strain, from the need coursing through him.

For a long moment, she studied his expression, her dark gaze fathomless, then she smiled again. Let go of his face. Put her hands against his chest and used that to leverage herself back and up, so that her pussy hovered above his cock.

"When was the last time you had sexual contact, Connor?" she asked.

"It's been months, Ma'am," he admitted. Though he'd scened, they'd all been platonic. He'd done an awful lot of cuddling, but his dick had become less and less interested post-scene as he hadn't been getting what he truly wanted—needed. He knew why she was asking, though. "I was tested last month."

Reaching down, she grasped his cock.

"For me, too, and I was tested this month. I'm on birth control." She pumped her hand, and he shuddered, the wooden frame creaking again as he pulled at the cuffs. "We can still use a condom." Raising one eyebrow at him, she waited for his answer, giving his dick a little squeeze.

"I'm good without if you are, Ma'am." Connor completely trusted her. If she wasn't worried about getting pregnant, then he wasn't worried about her getting pregnant.

And, hell, if she did anyway, they'd make it work. He'd make sure of it.

A slow smile spread across her face.

"Then I very much think I'd like to feel you inside me." Mistress Julie pressed the tip of his dick against her pussy, moving the head back and forth to slicken it with her arousal. The hot, wet touch of her body made him whimper, his hips trying to thrust up, but her grip was too strong, all of her weight pressing down on him to keep him in place.

Fuck.

Being at her mercy was the best and worst thing that had ever happened to him.

The worst only because he couldn't do anything he wanted to do. The best because not being able to do anything allowed him to completely relax and enjoy himself. It didn't matter what he wanted to do—or, at least, it mattered to her, but *he* didn't have to think about it. She was going to take care of it... take care of him. The weight of responsibility for her pleasure had been completely taken off him— she was going to make sure he pleased her.

Not that he was able to think about that for more than a few seconds. Mistress Julie started sinking down on his cock, and all the thoughts flew out of his head. He groaned, thrusting up into the soft, wet heat of her pussy, pushing deeper. It was like she weighed nothing on top of him, her body lowering to meet his, his upward movement going unchecked as she took him within her.

"Oh God..."

"I think you mean 'goddess'," she corrected in a murmur, her hands pressing against his chest as she rose up and then sank down again.

Connor could only moan in response as the hot, slick pleasure rolled over him, taking away his thoughts and his words.

Woman on top had always been his favorite position, even before he'd realized it was partly because he liked the woman in charge of her own pleasure. This was different from any other experience, though.

With vanilla women, they might enjoy being on top, but they still expected him to be in control often enough—using his hands, moving them, thrusting beneath them. Submissives even more so, constantly checking to make sure he was enjoying himself and that they were doing what he wanted.

Mistress Julie just did exactly as she pleased, taking what she wanted—and what she wanted was the whole of his cock. She sank down onto him, gasping a little when the head bumped against her cervix before she'd quite reached his groin.

"Damn, you're big," she said, flexing her fingers on his chest, the tips ruffling through his chest hair. His cock ached as she clenched around him. "It's a good thing I like that feeling."

He didn't have a chance to ask what feeling before she was rising and falling over him again, coming down hard enough to make herself shudder when he filled her up again.

Oh. That feeling.

Yeah. He fucking liked that, too.

---

*J*ULIE

Connor was too big.

At least his dick was in this position. There were other positions that wouldn't cause him to completely bottom out every time they joined together, but Julie didn't care. She liked the feeling of him coming to the end of her, the sensation of his cock bumping against her cervix again and again. It hurt, but it felt good, too, like she was as full as she could possibly get.

She knew that it wasn't a sensation every woman enjoyed, but she always had... she'd just never experienced it with a real cock before. While she'd been with other men who were well-endowed, Connor was the most endowed.

"Fuck!" He jerked against the restraints again as she sank onto him, making her wonder exactly what he would be doing with his hands if she hadn't cuffed them to the bed.

Hearing the wood creak every time he pulled on them made her clench around him. All that power, all that strength, all tightly leashed just for her. Flexing her thighs, she moved up and down, riding him at the pace and rhythm she wanted to, using him for her own pleasure and enjoying the way he writhed beneath her in response. His panting groans were coming faster as she moved, his body rippling underneath her.

It was a little like riding a stallion or a bronco. She didn't always have full control... he was able to lift her up when he lifted his hips.

Wild and exhilarating. That's what riding Connor was.

She kept her hands on his chest, her breasts bouncing as she moved, breathing heavily from the exertion as their mutual pleasure grew. Digging her nails into his flesh, she curved her lower legs around, her ankles pressing down on his thighs to help her keep her balance. The effect was that he wasn't able to thrust upward quite as easily, giving her fuller control over their movements.

"Mistress... please..."

"I like the way you beg," she murmured, scratching her nails down his chest. Her own orgasm was hovering just on the edge of her senses, but she was holding it back the same way she was making him hold his. "Beg me again, Connor."

"Fuck..." He groaned. "Mistress, please, I need to cum..."

Her body shuddered, pussy clenching around the thick shaft filling it, and she slammed herself down on him again. The head of his cock mashed against her cervix, taking her breath away at the fullness of the sensation, the impact of his dick against her insides.

"Come for me, Connor." She moved her hands to his nipples, pinching them hard and making him yelp. "Come for me."

She moved again, up and back down as she spoke, and he let out a hoarse cry, his hips thrusting upward to meet her stroke. Liquid heat billowed inside her, his cock throbbing and pulsing against her clenching muscles as she let her own pleasure run free. Wave after wave of intense ecstasy washed through her, accompanied by the hot spurts of his cum flooding her.

It was a damn good thing she was on birth control because he was so deep inside her, he was practically cumming in her womb.

"Fuck..." Julie sighed with repletion and slumped over atop him, panting, her head coming to rest on his chest. She could hear his heart pounding, her head lifting with his breath, as they both quivered in the aftermath.

His chest was a little damp, but so was her cheek.

Talk about a hot session.

"That was..." His hoarse voice trailed off, as though he couldn't find the words.

Julie tensed, then made herself relax. Just because he didn't know what to say didn't mean he was thinking anything bad. She lifted her head, propping her elbows on his chest so she could rest her head on her hands and look at him.

His hazel eyes were slightly glazed, darker than they normally looked—though it might just be the lighting. Lips parted, he was still panting slightly for breath. It probably didn't help that she was lying on top of him, but she didn't feel like moving yet. And he hadn't complained.

He met her gaze.

"That was amazing."

Relief rushed through her, and her lips curved in a slow smile.

"I'm so glad to hear that," she said sincerely. It had been amazing for her, too. Just like their first date had been. Amazing enough that part of her was already wondering what she was getting herself into, but she pushed those thoughts to the side.

She didn't know where they were going; that was the point. If she was falling a little faster than she was comfortable with... well, those were her emotions to deal with. Especially when it came to her emotions and the baggage she came with.

"Let's get cleaned up." Stretching forward, she brushed her lips over his in another kiss, making him sigh. But a good sigh. The sigh of a content man, a happy submissive.

The grin didn't leave his face even when she left him there, still cuffed to the bed, to go clean up in the bathroom and get a cloth to wipe him down with. When he did get his arms free, he carefully wrapped them around her, snuggling her against him. She'd never been in quite this position before, on her back with a man literally wrapped around her while he rested his head on her chest, her legs draped over his.

He was on his side, one arm beneath him, the other curled over her body. Her feet dangled a few inches above the bed, thanks to how thick his thighs were. His groin was snugged up against her ass, but he was completely soft at the moment.

Julie played with his hair with her free hand, fighting back a yawn.

"Connor..." She trailed off as she was met with a light snore. He'd fallen asleep.

She could wake him. Probably should wake him. Spending the night together was intimate in a way she wasn't sure they were ready for. They'd said they'd date, not jump right into a relationship.

But...

She didn't want to wake him up. Didn't want to disengage from the way he was wrapped around her. Didn't want the night to end.

So, she didn't.

Even as she fell asleep, though, the thought lingered in her mind...

I hope I don't regret this.

12

Julie

"Hey, Mom, I'm here." Here and trying not to be grumpy about it. Julie took a deep breath as she closed her parents' front door behind her. The cats had a tendency to try to escape out the door if it was left open.

Having to say a rushed goodbye to Connor before leaving Marquis had not been on her agenda this morning. She'd wanted to spend more time with him. Have breakfast with him. See where his head was after last night.

Instead, her mom had called, and she'd had to hurry away because her mom needed her help *right now*. No, she couldn't explain over the phone. Just 'get over here, Julie. I'm your parent, and I need you.'

Thankfully, Connor had been very understanding, although disappointed. He'd walked her to her car, and she'd gotten a very nice goodbye kiss before getting into it.

"Mom?" She raised her voice a little louder, walking down the hall. "Where are you?"

"We're back here," her father called from the sunroom.

Suppressing another sigh, Julie headed back. What did her mom need help with that her dad couldn't take care of? When her mom had demanded she come over, she'd assumed her dad was out of the house for some reason.

Walking into the sunroom, she came to a dead stop. Her dad was kneeling on the floor, assembling what looked like a new television and wall mount, while her mom was standing beside him, holding the instructions in one hand. One hand because the other one was in a sling.

"Mom!" Julie rushed forward, her gaze scanning over her mother. Other than the sling, she looked like she always did. Her hair was dyed black, so not a single strand of grey showed, but the wrinkles on her face gave away some of her age. She still looked years younger than the sixty-five she'd turned on her last birthday, which was how it was with most of Julie's family. Her mom liked to joke that Asians didn't age until all of the sudden, they did, usually overnight. With her long hair up in a bun, she was wearing neatly pressed beige pants and an orange silky blouse, even though it was a Saturday. No casual clothes for her mom. "What happened to your arm?"

"Nothing." Her mom huffed. "At least nothing I know of. My shoulder has been sore for a while, so I'm trying not to move it around and make it worse."

"How long is 'a while'?" Julie demanded to know.

"Oh, I don't know. I don't keep track." Her mother waved the hand holding the instructions at her. "That's not why I called you over, though. Your dad needs help lifting the TV. I can't do it."

But she'd probably tried.

Gritting her teeth, Julie closed her eyes for a brief moment, sending up a prayer for patience. When she opened her eyes, her dad was looking up at her with a slightly guilty expression. Probably because he hadn't been able to stop her mom from trying.

"Right. Got it." Julie kept her sigh inside. Her parents were who they were, and they weren't going to change. All she could do was try to set reasonable boundaries with them, and convincing her mom not to overdo certain things wasn't within her power.

Plus, if she didn't help, her mom was likely to try again and injure herself.

Or, worse, call Julie's ex to come over and help.

Crouching, Julie helped her dad pick up the television. The good news was it was going where a picture of Julie and John's wedding had formerly hung. Part of her was happy to see it gone, but she was trying not to get too hopeful because there was always the chance her mom was just moving it to a more prominent position somewhere else in the house.

"Oh, careful... yes... right there..." Even though she couldn't be part of the actual lifting, her mom was determined to be involved. "Good! Ow." Her mom had tried to clap her hands together, apparently forgetting that her shoulder was sore.

Pressing her lips together in amusement—because it was better to be amused than annoyed when she could direct her emotions—Julie held the TV in place while her dad got it secured to the mount.

"I think that's good. Come look at it."

Julie and her dad dutifully moved over to stand beside her mom to take a look at their work. It looked good to Julie, but she wasn't going to be the one watching it.

"So, why a television in here?" she asked, hoping her mom would also tell her where the huge, framed wedding picture it was replacing was being moved to without having to ask directly.

"This way, we can watch TV and the bird feeders at the same time," her mom replied. "And your dad can keep an eye on the squirrels."

Ah. Her dad had a long-standing feud with the neighborhood squirrels. He liked birds. He didn't mind squirrels, as long as they weren't 'stealing' food from the birds.

"I got a new birdfeeder, too," her dad said, stepping around to where Julie could see him and pointing out the window into the backyard. "This way, I'll be able to watch and see how well it works."

She looked out the window at the birdfeeder in question. It was in the middle of the yard on a post, what looked like a giant dish attached about four feet up from the ground.

"I take it that's an anti-squirrel birdfeeder?" she asked dryly.

"Exactly." Her father beamed at her, and she shook her head even as she smiled back. He looked so proud of himself. Only a few inches taller than her and her mother, he had embraced aging and let his hair start to go grey. He was also losing some of it on top of his head, but there was still enough that it couldn't be truly called a comb-over. When he grinned, the wrinkles around the corners of his eyes were far more pronounced.

Damn. Her parents were getting older.

The resentment she'd felt about being pulled away from Connor vanished. She was glad she could come over and be the dutiful daughter. As much as they drove her crazy sometimes, she did love her parents and didn't want them struggling with anything she could help with.

"Does it work so far?"

"I think so." He turned to look out the window, tilting his head as he studied it. "I haven't seen any squirrels make it to the feeder, but I want to watch just to be sure."

"That's why the television is in here," her mom said, not exactly interrupting but interjecting fast enough that no one else would have been able to get a word in edgewise. "I can watch my shows, and your father can watch the birds. And squirrels."

Shorthand for, her father had been watching the birdfeeder, anyway, and her mom didn't like being alone on the other side of the house to watch her shows. Which was pretty cute. The cats would enjoy it, too, since they liked to be around her parents but also liked to watch the birds.

Before she could get too caught up in how cute her parents could be, the doorbell rang. Julie was turning to go to get it when she heard the door open, and she froze. While she could just walk into the house without compunction, there was only one other person who had ever done that. Even her parents' siblings waited for the door to be answered.

"Sun?" John's voice called out her mother's name, pronounced more like 'soon.' Her freaking ex was here. "Daniel?"

Julie whirled back around to face her parents. Her father at least had the grace to look guilty before averting his gaze back to the backyard, but her mother's face had lit up.

"We're back in the sunroom!" she called, then she caught sight of the glare Julie was giving her. "What? I wasn't sure if you would be able to come help, so I called John just in case."

And, of course, her ex came running. Her parents conveniently forgot how unreliable he'd been when she was actually married to him. It was only since their divorce that he'd suddenly been far more available to make time for her family. They ate it up, as if the past had never happened.

Then again, John had always been more about appearances than substance.

"Julie, I didn't know you were going to be here," her ex-husband said from behind her.

Julie's back went ramrod straight, and she tugged on her emotions, pulling them within before turning to face him, leaving absolutely nothing showing on her face.

Tilting her head back, she looked her ex square in his handsome, smug face. She suspected he was his hospital's Dr. Dreamy, no matter which building he was working in. Tall, striking features, dark hair, and grey eyes that could change from a tempest to a clear sky blue depending on what he was wearing. Today, they were more grey than blue, thanks to the green polo shirt he had on.

"I was just stopping by to help out. I only had a minute, though, so I'll be going now."

"No, you should stay!" Her mother interjected, stepping to Julie's side and putting her free hand on her arm—which, of course, drew attention to her sling. "Stay and let us feed you as a thank you. You too, John, even though we turned out not to need you. You can stay for lunch, can't you?"

"Of course," he said, flashing her mom a smile as Julie's chest tightened. Yeah, of course, he could. Somehow, her mom had managed to get him on his one day off during the month. *More likely, Mom knows his schedule and planned this for today. Dammit.*

Suckered in again.

So much for being the dutiful daughter. It was a total trap, and she'd walked right into it. What she would never understand was why John didn't put a stop to it.

No, she knew why. She got out from under his emotional control. While she'd been in charge in the bedroom, he'd felt the need to run everything outside of it, and when she'd left him, that had all fallen apart. Sometimes, she also thought he was afraid she would go around telling everyone that he liked to be submissive in bed and that he really liked being pegged... It had taken her a long time to recognize how much shame he had about that.

The fact she would never, ever reveal their private business had apparently not occurred to him, which made her wonder what he might be telling people about her. Not that she cared what he said to his friends. She had her own friends now. But she did sometimes wonder what he told her parents.

Probably all sorts of dirty laundry she'd rather not have aired. People weren't usually paranoid about people talking about them unless they were the kind of person who did that.

Both John and her mother looked expectantly at her. Out of the corner of her eye, she could see that her dad had gone to the window. Possibly avoiding the conversation, possibly there was just a bird out there that he wanted to watch. Or a squirrel.

"I can't." She kept her voice clipped and short as she stepped around John, eluding the hand he reached out for her, as if he was going to try to get hold of her arm to stop her. Asshole. "Bye."

"Julie!"

"Julie—"

She walked away at a fast clip. Sure, they could catch her, but at this point, they should know to let her go. This was a boundary that she had laid down again and again... and again...

"Julie!"

Crap, her mom was still following her right out the front door. Normally, she was safe once she made it outside because her mom didn't approve of putting on a 'show' for the neighbors. Hmm. Maybe her mom and John had more in common than Julie thought when it came to appearances. No wonder they got along so well.

"Julie Kim, you stop walking right now!"

Raised voice out in the front yard? Her mom really was serious.

Spinning on her heel, Julie crossed her arms over her chest. Her mom might be serious, but she was, too. She couldn't stop her parents from talking to her ex. She couldn't stop them from inviting him over. But she could damn well remove herself from the situation when they did.

"What, Mom?" She snapped the words out, the Domme voice popping up unexpectedly, and felt both satisfied and guilty when her mom pulled up short, eyes widening in surprise.

"I... I really didn't know if you'd be available, so I called you both. I left him a voicemail. I didn't *know* he was going to show up." Her mom's tone wheedled, but Julie wasn't having any of it.

"You also didn't call him back to let him know he was unneeded. And once he was here, you invited him to lunch."

Her mom huffed.

"Well, it would be rude to have him show up and send him away immediately. You can't expect me to be rude, Julie."

Expect? No. Want? Yes.

"He was our son for years, Julie. It wasn't our choice for that to change."

Ah, yes, here it came. The guilt trip. She'd deprived them of their perfect surgeon son. Never mind that she'd become incredibly unhappy married to him. Never mind that she'd been the only one putting any work into the relationship for years because she'd known how disappointed her parents would be when it ended. Nope, what mattered was that she'd chosen herself and her own happiness, and somehow, that wasn't what her parents wanted for her.

"You haven't found anyone since him. Maybe you two should—"

"I'm seeing someone." She said it before she could really think through whether she *should* say it. But seeing the look on her mom's face was nearly as satisfying as her reaction to Julie's Domme voice.

Her eyes bulged even more, and her mouth dropped open in pure shock.

"You are?" Her mom's voice was high and squeaky.

"I am," she said firmly. "So you'll understand why I certainly can't stay here and have lunch with my ex-husband."

Turning on her heel, she hurried to her car before her mom could recover from the shock of the announcement. Maybe her mom would stop trying to reconnect her and John now... or maybe she'd just made things worse.

13

<hr>

Connor

Julie: *Dinner this Friday at six?*

Connor: *Yes, Ma'am.*

Julie: *Marquis is booked up.*

Connor: *Just dinner is fine, too. We can always go somewhere afterward.*

Julie: *Stronghold?*

Connor stared at the text message as though it was about to jump out of his phone and bite him.

He wasn't sure he was ready for that. Even though his friends had been accepting. Even though his friends' girlfriends had been accepting.

After Friday night at Marquis, he hadn't gone to Stronghold over the weekend. If someone asked him why not, he wasn't sure he'd be able to explain.

Maybe partly because he liked Marquis better. The privacy. The room to sleep in afterward. Falling asleep holding Mistress Julie had resulted in the best sleep of his life. Other than waking up with one of his arms also asleep. But it hadn't mattered because he'd been so damn happy.

Even that she'd had to rush off to help her parents didn't bother him. He'd been able to hear the phone call—her mom talked kind of loudly—so he knew she wasn't blowing him off.

None of that bothered him. The idea of scening publicly at Stronghold—just the idea of walking in and having to face everyone he'd been lying to—he wasn't sure he was ready for that yet. He knew that eventually he would have to, but eventually didn't mean 'now.'

His phone dinged again.

Julie: *We don't have to scene there; we can just hang out at the bar. Or we can go somewhere else if you're more comfortable.*

Dammit. Now, he'd disappointed her. Was he really going to put off being at Stronghold just because of his own insecurities? Especially when it was clear that was where she wanted to be?

She'd already done Marquis twice for him. Now, he needed to give.

Connor: *Hanging out at Stronghold would be fun.*

There. He hadn't said he wanted to scene there. Just hang out. That was hopefully clear enough.

He stared at his phone for a long moment. That was probably clear enough, right? He didn't need to outright say he didn't want to scene. Besides, they were supposed to be dating and getting to know each other, not just scening and having sex. People dated without scening.

They didn't usually go to a sex club for that date, though.

Maybe he should say something.

"Whatcha doing?"

Connor jumped, spinning around guiltily and tucking the phone behind his back as his thumb hit the button on the side to turn off the screen. He looked down at Sandra, who was standing just behind him, hands on her hips, one eyebrow raised. As usual, her hair was pulled back in a ponytail, so none of her suspicious expression was hidden.

"Nothing."

It was the wrong thing to say. Sandra's eyes immediately widened, sparking with interest.

"Oooh, you were texting her, weren't you?"

"I'm on my break," he replied, rather than answering the question, stepping to the side to move around her. Not that Sandra let him. She stepped with him, hands still on her hips, keeping herself between him and the door.

"Obviously." She narrowed her gaze. "You're in the breakroom. The question is, why were you in the breakroom, nowhere near the table, and instead over by the wall, hunched over your phone."

Because he'd been texting with Mistress Julie and doing it completely out in the open had felt wrong. Not just because he was at work, either.

"I just had to check something on my phone, and I happened to be standing there." It was sort of true. He hadn't intended to look quite so conspicuous, but after throwing out the trash from his snack, he'd felt his phone go off, and he'd stopped moving to check it... then turned toward the wall when he'd seen who it was.

"Hey, Connor... can I ask you a favor?" A pretty blonde poked her head in the door, smiling her brightest smile. Inwardly, Connor groaned. Whenever Beth wanted a favor, it was usually a pain in the ass.

"He can't do it," Sandra said without turning around, and Beth's face fell, turning sad and pleading.

"Well, I don't know what it is yet. What do you need, Beth?" he asked, moving around Sandra again. This time, with a witness there, she didn't block his way. Which meant he owed Beth since she was saving him from the Sandra Interrogation.

"I have Mrs. Malley this week every day at five. Would you mind taking her instead, so I don't have to rush to pick up Robert?" Robert being her son, who needed to be picked up by six fifteen every day. With most clients, a five o'clock appointment wouldn't be a problem for that, but Mrs. Malley could be... difficult.

"Sure, no problem."

Behind him, Sandra made another aggrieved noise as Beth brightened.

"Thank you, Connor! I'll go tell Aubrey to make the change!" She scurried away, as if afraid he was going to change his mind. Or maybe that Sandra would intervene.

"You're too nice. You know that, right?" Sandra asked, following him out the door into the main room, around the equipment that was scattered throughout. She kept her voice low, though, since there were a few clients being run through their stretches on the other side of the room.

He shrugged.

"I don't mind." Yeah, he'd need to stay an hour later than he normally did, but that was fine. It wasn't like he had anyone to rush home to. Beth's husband apparently wasn't around much, or very helpful, so he could help make her life a little easier.

"You should have at least had her trade one of her morning clients with you."

"But then she would have to rush here after dropping Daniel off," he replied reasonably. He knew because there'd been times in the past when he'd taken an early morning client off her hands. "I like helping. It makes me feel good. And you do want me to feel good, right?"

Sandra was silent for a moment before she grumbled, "I hate it when you do that."

He grinned, still heading toward the front. He'd just felt his phone vibrate in his pocket, which meant Julie had probably texted him back, and he wanted to see what it said. Sandra couldn't follow him into the bathroom.

"Where are you going?"

"Bathroom."

She made another disgusted noise but peeled off. Connor didn't fool himself into thinking that was the end of it. She'd be back to bother him about his dating life and probably about being too nice again. He didn't mind. It was nice that she cared.

As he passed by the front desk, he waved to Aubrey and Beth, both of whom waved back. Aubrey gave him a look that made Connor think he agreed with Sandra about being too nice, but it really wasn't a problem.

He did need to let Julie know he'd have to move their date to seven, though.

JULIE

Escorting her most recent patient out of her office, Julie smiled and waved before closing the door behind him and letting out a deep sigh. Not because of him, just because she was tired. It had been a long day, and she needed to call her mom back. She'd seen the call come through while she was making the next appointment for Tristan.

She hadn't talked to her parents since Saturday—five days ago—so she knew she wouldn't be able to put it off.

Granted, her mom hadn't reached out since then, either, probably waiting for Julie to cool off. Sometimes, Julie wondered if her mom thought Julie would forget everything if she let a few days pass, even though it had definitely never worked that way before. Just thinking about making the call had her feeling uncomfortable, but it was necessary.

If she didn't call back today, it would be even worse the next time they talked.

Sitting down at her desk, Julie closed her eyes and leaned back. Counting to four as she breathed in, she held the breath for another four beats, then slowly let it out as she counted to four again. As she did, she focused on trying to imagine the numbers in her head, clearing the rest of her mind as she calmed her nerves.

Once.

Twice.

Three times.

Four.

Good. Now, she didn't feel quite so jittery.

Box breathing didn't always help, but often it did. Taking a walk and doing it usually helped even more, but she only had fifteen minutes until her next client. It was probably a good time to call her mom back... after she wrote a few notes about her discussion with Tristan.

By the time she was done, there were only ten minutes until her next appointment, which was perfect. She had a good reason to keep the call short. If she waited until after this appointment, she'd have all evening to talk. It was better to do it now.

Listening to the phone ring, she wasn't sure whether she was hoping her mom would pick up so she could get the call over with or hoping her mom wouldn't pick up so she could just leave a message and feel like she'd done her duty. It ended up being a moot point after two rings.

"Hello?" It didn't matter that her mom had caller ID on her phone. She always answered as if she wasn't sure who would be on the other line.

"Hello, Mom." She did her best to keep her voice neutral and not to sound like she was bracing for her mom's response. "I saw you called and wanted to call you back. I only have a few minutes before my next appointment, though."

Her mom made hmphing noise but didn't protest.

"Your father and I want to meet your new... boyfriend." She said the word like it was dirty. "Bring him to the family cookout next weekend."

"What?" Julie froze. That was the last thing she'd expected to come out of her mother's mouth. An admonishment for the way she'd left, sure. A series of questions about Connor, absolutely at some point. But an invitation for him to come meet the family?

"This... man... he is important to you, yes? So he should come meet everyone. Unless, of course, he is not important to you." *Or does not exist.* There was more than a little challenge in her mother's words.

Either Connor was made up, or he wasn't actually important enough to invite to a family event. The problem was, Julie did think he was important... at least, he could be important. So much potential was there for something amazing between them. But her family could be a *lot*.

Especially the whole family. All at once.

With her parents there watching his every move and mentally comparing him to John.

Talk about pressure.

"His name is Connor. I can ask him, but it's kind of short notice. He might already have plans." If he was smart, he'd already have 'plans.' Julie rubbed her forehead, leaning forward to rest her elbows on the desk. Just like her mom to know how to give her a headache in two minutes flat.

Her mom sniffed.

"John always made time for family."

"That is a complete rewrite of history," Julie said flatly. "Should I be worried about memory loss, Mom? Do I need to talk to your doctor?"

"Do not be disrespectful, Julie. No matter how old you are, I am still your mother," her mom scolded, neatly avoiding answering the question. Uh-huh. "If not this one, then the next one. Your aunties want to meet him, too."

"You told the aunts?" She didn't know why she was asking. Of course, her mom had told her sisters, Julie's aunts. Her entire family was terrifyingly codependent. Some small part of her had hoped her mom wouldn't tell the aunts, though, if only because it might break the illusion that she and John would one day get back together.

If her mom had told the aunts, that meant she was serious about meeting Connor as soon as possible, and she was gathering allies. Crap.

That also meant all of her cousins were going to know, too. If she didn't bring Connor, she'd be getting the full-court press.

"Of course, I told them." Her mom sniffed again. "This is the first man you've dated since John. At least, the first that you've felt was important enough to tell me about."

There was that word again. Julie's chest clenched.

Connor was important. Which was why she didn't want him chased off.

"I'll ask him if he can make it." And make sure he didn't feel too pressured, even though part of her wanted to panic at the idea of being surrounded by her nosy family, all asking questions about her new boyfriend. Especially her cousins. They were so nosy, they were probably already trying to find out who he was and look him up.

Maybe she shouldn't have told her mother his name. Just a first name was all her cousin Sandra needed most of the time. She was the reason Julie had so much of her social media on lockdown. That girl should be working for the FBI.

"Good. I won't take up any more of your time. We look forward to meeting this... Connor." Her mom really was good at making someone's name sound like a mortal insult.

Julie made a face as she hung up the phone, very aware that her mom had also acted like meeting him was a foregone conclusion. She still hadn't even told Connor that she'd told her parents about him. They hadn't discussed when that would happen. Or maybe it didn't need to be a discussion? Maybe he'd already told his parents about her.

Though, from what he'd said about his family, he probably hadn't flung the information at them like a slap after they'd sprung an ex on him. And she was pretty sure he hadn't been married before. She'd told him her parents were still friendly with her ex, but she hadn't really gone into detail.

Hopefully, their date on Friday didn't go off the rails. He'd already hesitated about going to Stronghold with her, which she tried not to be hurt by. It might not have even been hesitation. Maybe he'd just had to talk to someone. They had been texting while he was at work. Maybe the gap in response time hadn't been about that at all. There'd been another gap after that, an even longer one.

Though, he had made it pretty clear he didn't want to scene at Stronghold.

Not yet, she told herself sternly.

It wasn't anything personal to her. It was about him.

Yeah. Time to do some more box breathing before her next appointment. But at least the call with her mom was over. Now, she just had to face all the repercussions.

14

CONNOR

"A family cookout?" Connor stared at Julie, trying to get a feeling for where her head was at. He hadn't realized they were quite there yet. Not that he objected to meeting her family on principle. It just seemed... fast. They hadn't even spent time with each other's friends yet. At least not together as a couple.

He was still nervous about doing that after dinner tonight.

Family seemed like the kind of thing that happened after a few months. Well, even more for his family since his parents lived hours away.

Julie sighed, tapping her fingers on the table as she fidgeted in her seat. He realized she was nervous, too. He didn't think he'd ever seen her fidget like this before. Normally, she was cool, calm, and collected.

"You don't have to say yes," she said quickly. "I... well, remember how I had to rush out on Saturday to get to my parents? I went over to help them out, but my mom had called my ex-husband to come help, too." She huffed in remembered frustration. "He showed up, and I immediately left because that's the boundary I set with my parents about him remaining in their lives, and my mom chased me out the door and reminded me that I haven't been seeing anyone since him. Which she apparently takes as a sign that we could still possibly end up back together."

"Uh-huh." Connor reached out and put his hand over hers, rubbing his thumb along her pulse to hopefully help calm her. He didn't feel jealous. She'd mentioned her ex, and right now, it was clear that she felt nothing but annoyance at her parents for still having the man in their lives. Connor couldn't imagine how he'd feel if his parents were still constantly in touch with any of his old girl-friends. He was pretty sure his mom was Facebook friends with his last serious girlfriend, but they weren't hanging out or anything.

"So, I immediately told her that I *was* seeing someone." Julie squeezed his hand, her expression turning sheepish. "Which... that's not how I planned on telling her. It just came out because I was so frustrated. And I'm sorry. You deserved a better way to be introduced to them."

"That's okay," he said immediately. It really was. Now he under-stood why she wanted him to come to the cookout. She needed him as a shield against her parents' expectations and also to prove that he was real.

"She called on Wednesday to invite you." Julie winced. "That's when I found out she'd basically told the whole family. My cousins have been texting me almost nonstop since, trying to find out more about you."

Connor snorted. "That's funny. I have nosy coworkers doing the same thing about you. At least our friends don't have to do that since they already know both of us."

"Small blessings." She gave him a crooked smile. "Anyway... I know it's short notice, and honestly, if you just don't want to come, that's fine, too."

"Do you want me there?" That was his only concern since it seemed like she was trying to talk him out of it.

She hesitated but squeezed his hand at the same time, which was confusing. A little bit of mixed messages.

"I do want you to meet my family, eventually. But I don't want to put a whole lot of pressure on us before we're ready. We just started seeing each other. But…" Her voice trailed off.

"But having me there would be helpful when it comes to your family." It didn't take a genius to finish the sentence, and he could tell she was struggling with the desire to have him there but also the desire not to push him into something he wasn't comfortable with.

He could go meet her family. Was it earlier than he'd ever met a girlfriend's family before? Sure. But hell, he was getting older. Things moved faster, right? Plus, she needed him.

Julie sighed.

"I don't want you to feel like you have to—"

"I don't," he said, reassuring her. She was watching him intently, clearly trying to read his expression. He smiled at her, hoping she'd seen the sincerity in his gaze, hear it in his voice. It was no hardship, and he wanted to help. "I'm happy to meet your family."

"Right." She sighed. "I don't want you to think that I don't want you to meet them. I just also don't want you to feel forced to."

"I don't. I'll meet them to help, and also because I want to. If we keep seeing each other, it'll happen eventually, anyway. Why not sooner rather than later? If it makes you feel better, you can join me on one of my video calls with my parents sometime." That was the right thing to say. He could see her relax. Not all the way, but he'd take what he could get.

"That would be nice." The smile that now curved her lips looked much more genuine than the previous one.

Their server appeared at their table again, effectively halting the conversation.

"Can I get you anything else?" she asked hopefully as she picked up their plates. "Would you like to see our dessert menu?" Julie and Connor glanced at each other.

"I think I'm good," Julie said slowly when he didn't speak right away.

"Me, too." He could always go for dessert, but he didn't *need* it. However, answering in the negative made his nerves rachet up a bit more. That meant they'd be heading to Stronghold next.

On the other hand, getting it over with would probably be better than prolonging the wait. He wasn't going to get *less* nervous.

"Just the check, then." Julie was the one directing the server, but Connor was already reaching for his wallet. He hoped she didn't think she was paying.

He wasn't sure what the rules were when it came to being a submissive and paying for dinner, but he was still a gentleman, and they were on a date. Was it odd to feel a bit of relief when she let him pay without a fight?

⁂

*J*ULIE

The tension inside of Connor was twisting tighter and tighter as they walked toward the door to Stronghold. Julie pressed her lips together. Maybe she was asking too much of him. Maybe this was too fast. And on the same night that she'd asked him to meet her family, too.

Which might be a mistake if they couldn't even go out with their friends together.

On the other hand, her family wouldn't know their dynamic, which she was pretty sure was his problem with going into Stronghold.

She put her hand on his shoulder to stop him from moving forward, even though it was a bit of a stretch for her despite the heels she was wearing. As soon as he stopped, she shifted around to stand in front of him, her hand on his chest, head tilted back to look up into his face. The lights in the parking lot created odd shadows, making it harder to read his expression.

"We don't have to go in."

Taking a deep breath, he let it out, lifting his head to look past her at the front door of the building. Unlike Marquis, Stronghold was in the warehouse district, and that's exactly what it looked like from the outside. There wasn't much to see other than the front door and the long, featureless exterior walls. The club didn't have a sign because they didn't want to advertise what they were.

If you knew, you knew.

"I think I need to," he said after a moment, his shoulders hunching slightly. "If I chicken out now, it's going to be so much harder next time."

Julie nodded slowly.

Letting her hand drop, she moved back to his side, sliding her fingers through his. It was a little odd to feel like such a big man might need her protection when she was practically a third his size, but she felt protective. Connor was a giant teddy bear. Everyone had thought so, even when they'd thought he was a Dom.

Now, he was *her* teddy bear, and she wasn't going to let anyone hurt him.

Not that she thought anyone would. In her opinion, he was worked up over a completely imaginary situation. But if anyone did give him a hard time about not knowing that he was a submissive when he'd first started his kink journey, she was going to cut them the fuck down to size. Then she'd send Patrick after them. If there was anything left worth sending him after. Which there might not be when she was done with them.

Connor looked down at her, giving her a lopsided smile that looked a bit more like a grimace.

"It's not you, it's me," he quipped, making her laugh. Strangely, her laughter seemed to ease some of his tension. He took a deep breath as he straightened back up, squaring his shoulders. "Okay. I'm ready."

"Okay." She squeezed his hand and started moving again. He moved with her, tension slowly seeping back into his frame as they got closer to the door. By the time they reached it, he was nearly rigid, but he still reached out with his free hand to grab the door and open it for her.

As he did, Julie made a calculated risk assessment.

Dropping his hand, she pulled it back and gave him a hefty

whack on the ass, hard enough to make her palm sting. He jumped, letting out a sharp cry of surprise, before staring down at her.

"Breathe," she ordered. He had taken a breath in so he could make that noise, but now she wanted him to keep breathing.

A small but real smile played on his lips as he stared down at her. "Yes, Mistress."

Yup. It had settled him. That little spark of pain, the little shock, and the reminder of who was in charge. He didn't need to worry about what was going to happen when they got inside because she had it handled.

"Good boy. Let's go. And keep breathing."

They got their first greeting when they walked through the door. Traci and Shonda were behind the front desk, and the moment Julie and Connor walked in, they both squealed and clapped their hands excitedly.

"Connor! Connor!" They both came around the desk, arms open, skidding to a stop in front of them as though they weren't sure they could touch him. Laughing, Julie let go of his hand, giving them a nod, and they immediately surrounded him with their arms. She didn't know what was better—their enthusiastic greeting or the sheer confusion on his face.

She could tell he was trying to figure out if they were just happy to see him or if they were greeting him this way because they'd heard about him being a sub. It was easy for her to see it was the latter. They were welcoming him into the group.

"Um... hi?" He was hugging them back but sent a slightly helpless look at Julie.

"Told you there was nothing to be worried about." She smirked at him. Both Traci and Shonda looked at her, then back at him, frowns on their faces.

"You were worried?"

"About what?"

"I..." Connor hesitated.

"Ladies, we need to get inside," Julie said firmly, cutting off his answer. That was his business *if* he wanted to share. She probably shouldn't have said that in front of them, but she had wanted to point out that he was being warmly welcomed. He could share his worries later if he wanted.

Both of them instantly understood, leaning in to give Connor another hug. She wasn't surprised when they picked up on what Connor might be worried about, even without being given an answer.

"We're so happy for you, Connor," Shonda said warmly.

"Happy you're one of us!" Traci grinned up at him.

"Um... thanks?" He was still baffled, but he was smiling.

Gratitude welled in Julie. There was still the rest of the club to face, but she was pretty sure it was going to be easier for him to walk through the door now.

Though as they turned to face the stoic Master Jared standing outside the door between the lobby and the club, she felt Connor stiffen again.

"Mistress Julie," Jared said with a nod of acknowledgment as they approached. His dark gaze shifted. "Connor." His lips twitched. "Have a good night."

There was something in his voice that made her wonder...

The only way to find out for sure was to walk through the door.

15

____

Connor

Stronghold looked like it always did inside, even though he felt different. The huge main room didn't look much like a warehouse other than the size. A long wooden bar ran along one side of the room on the right, accompanied by high-top tables and chairs. To the left, before reaching the various doors for the main office and the locker rooms, was a small sitting section known as 'the Lounge.'

The Lounge was where the unpartnered submissives hung out, or sometimes, they had a partner, but they were hanging out with their friends there. The bar was where the Doms hung out before and after a scene unless they were spending time with a sub. Couples—or polyam groups—usually took over the bar tables between the two spaces.

When he and Julie walked in, his gaze went to the tables because that's where his friends were usually located. It only took him a moment to find Law, Asad, and Q—but it did take a moment because he was so used to looking for their partners with them. He didn't see Morgan's distinctive red or Sam's honey blonde. Iris was shorter, and her darker hair didn't stand out quite as much, but he was so used to seeing her by Law's side, he didn't see Law right away.

In fact, there were almost no submissives on that side of the room at all.

That was weird.

"One of us!"

Connor blinked and turned his head to the Lounge. It was full of the missing submissives, with Iris, Sam, and Morgan standing at the front of them, beaming at him. Beside them were more submissives he knew, some he'd scened with, some he hadn't. Freddy was there along with an entire contingent of male submissives, including Luke—Mistress Olivia's fiancé, who rarely came into Stronghold these days.

"One of us! One of us!"

He stood there, not knowing what to do as the entire crowd surged forward en masse. Despite the loud chanting, he could still hear Mistress Julie's peal of laughter as she let go of his hand, letting the submissives surround him. The guys hung back a bit, but the others all wrapped him up in a hug, still chanting.

"One of us! One of us!"

Something was lodged in his throat. His eyes burned.

Fuck.

He was going to fucking cry.

Everything hurt, and he didn't know why.

It shouldn't hurt.

But he just hadn't expected...

He hadn't thought...

Now, he was surrounded by chanting submissives, all of them so damn happy for him, even though he'd been lying to them—lying to himself—and they accepted him completely. Fully.

Enthusiastically.

The sob lodged in his throat welled up, and he bowed his head, closing his eyes.

"Aw!" It was a big group 'aw' that echoed through the room.

"Okay, everyone, get back. Connor needs a minute. Thank you for the warm welcome." Mistress Julie's voice cut through the din, followed a moment later by the woman herself as she took her place at his side again. No longer hampered by hugging everyone, Connor was able to lift his hands to his face, covering it while he tried to compose himself.

He didn't know why he was so choked up.

Memories pushed at him. The fearful looks he'd gotten in high school just walking down the hallways. The way he'd always been chosen first for dodgeball, and the other team had always been afraid. The weight of expectations that had hampered him from the moment of his first growth spurt in ninth grade when he'd shot up above the rest of his classmates, towering above even his teachers.

Always trying to make himself smaller. Always trying to make himself less intimidating. Always trying to make himself *acceptable*.

Here he was in Stronghold, showered with acceptance, and all he'd had to do was show up as fully himself.

"Sit," Mistress Julie ordered, and his knees buckled. Thankfully, someone had actually placed one of the high-top chairs behind him, so he didn't have far to go. He heaved in a breath as she rubbed slow circles on his back, trying to get himself under control.

Crying in public had not been on his agenda today.

"Sorry, Connor, are you okay?" That was Iris, her voice a little tremulous, as if she was afraid she'd done something wrong. He couldn't bring himself to look up yet, but he nodded, moving one of his hands away from his face so he could give her a thumbs-up, which made her giggle.

"I don't think he was expecting that kind of welcome," Mistress Julie said, her voice low and soothing against his rattling nerves.

"Aw, but... of course we wanted to welcome him. He's done so much for... all of us." That was Emery, a non-binary submissive who he'd done aftercare for several times. Connor nearly choked again. He hadn't done anything he wasn't supposed to as a Dom.

Of course, he'd wanted to take care of them. That's what Doms did. And subs took care of their Doms. Everyone was supposed to take care of everyone.

But not everyone does, whispered a little voice in his head.

And he knew that was true, too.

He still didn't think he'd done anything out of the ordinary, though. At least his fears about being rejected by everyone were assuaged. There had been no mistaking the genuine welcome, the sincerity in their happiness that he was now one of them. It wasn't something he could explain away. It wasn't something he could deny. And he didn't know what to do with it.

So, it all came leaking out his fucking eyeballs.

He was so damn happy.

"We just wanted him to know we're happy he figured out what he wants," Iris said earnestly. She sounded so worried that she'd done something wrong, Connor couldn't take it anymore. He lifted his head, opening his arms as he did so, and Iris rushed in for a hug.

Behind her, Law was standing there—his hand in the air from where it had been on her shoulder. He grinned at Connor, and his own eyes looked suspiciously watery, so at least Connor wasn't the only one. Beside him, Emery looked worried, and Connor waved at them, too, so they could come in for a hug.

Which started a hug stampede.

"Hey! Ack!" Mistress Julie protested as she was inadvertently caught up in the middle of the hug, too. She started laughing. "Okay, subbies, back up again!"

"Cuddle puddle!" Angel, one of the submissives, sang out the words as she threw herself into the mix, drowning out Mistress Julie's order. Squeals met her announcement, and everyone squeezed in tight, making Mistress Julie groan again. She was laughing too hard to say anything, though.

"Okay, everyone, back up. Let them breathe," Law barked out the order, managing to make himself heard over all the squeals. This time, everyone actually dispersed, giving them some real space. Connor took in a deep breath.

"Are you okay?" Mistress Julie asked, softly enough that probably only he, Iris, and Morgan could hear it since they were still right beside him.

"Great." He choked on the word, trying to get it out. He really was. He was just a little emotional. Taking a deep breath, he wrestled his emotions back under control, surreptitiously wiping his eyes and looking up to see what was going on.

The subbies had all returned to the Lounge, though some of them had spread out to the rest of the bar, especially if they had a partner. Or partners. Off to the side, Angel was arguing with her husband, Master Adam, about something. Probably the fact that she'd ignored Mistress Julie's order and started the second big squeeze. Though Connor thought she probably hadn't heard it, he wasn't surprised Master Adam had. He also wasn't surprised when, a moment later, Master Adam flipped her over his shoulder and carried her off toward the stairs to the Dungeon.

He had to shake his head when she started tapping out a beat on his leather-covered ass like it was a bongo drum set. That subbie liked to push her limits and get into trouble. Even the answering sharp swat to her own ass didn't stop her.

Amy sent him a thumbs-up when he looked her way, followed by several other subbies who did the same. Freddy and the other male subs were hanging out off to the side, and they all grinned and waved when he looked their way. Even Luke, who Connor had never really sat down to have a conversation with.

He felt like he'd just been welcomed into a special club.

"Well, we didn't mean to make you cry," Iris said a little mournfully as Law came up beside her, slinging his arm around her shoulders. "We just wanted you to know... you know."

"I know." He was thankful she didn't actually try to explain because he might have started tearing up again. There had already been more than enough of that tonight. Connor liked to think he was evolved enough not to think there was anything wrong with showing emotion or crying, but that didn't mean he liked doing it when everyone was watching him.

"It was very appreciated," Mistress Julie said, rubbing his back. "Now... how about we go over to the bar and get a drink."

That sounded good to him.

JULIE

There was a constant revolving door of people stopping to speak to Connor while they were at the bar. Not just the submissives, but the Doms as well. Most of them just stopping to say hi, giving a show of support with their greeting before moving on. As the evening went on, Connor got more and more relaxed. It did make conversation with him difficult, so she was glad they'd gone on a date before coming here.

Several of the Dommes stopped by to talk to her, too, casting curious glances at Connor. She didn't blame them for their curiosity, but she couldn't help but bristle a little. Apparently, she was feeling a little territorial, even though she had no reason to think he was interested in anyone but her.

Still, it was their first time publicly at the club. Once people got used to seeing them together, got used to him as a submissive, all the interest would die down. Hopefully, her possessiveness would as well.

"So, Julie, tell me about yourself." Asad sent a winning smile her way, which made her snort. He was a charmer, all right. At least, he certainly thought so. Next to him, Morgan elbowed him in the side. The look he shot her way was full of heat. "Behave, Red."

She wrinkled her nose at him.

Damn, they were cute together.

"What do you want to know?" Julie asked, amused, when Asad finally turned back to her. Beside her, Q and Sam were involved in a conversation with Connor and a male submissive named Steve, who had come over to say hi. On her other side, Law was now watching her and Asad's exchange. Iris was, too, though she was openly grinning while Law was harder to read.

Julie still wasn't entirely sure how he felt about her and Connor hooking up. It was one thing to accept Connor as a submissive, another to accept two of his closest friends dating. Though if things did end up going south between her and Connor, she was going to do her level best to make sure it didn't affect any of the friendships.

"Oh, you know... any crazy exes in the past we need to watch out for... if you were ever the crazy ex... if you have a police record… all that kind of stuff." He winked at her, but his tone was semi-serious. It was always hard to tell with Asad. Julie's lips quirked.

"Not as far as I know." The answer to all three questions. John wasn't crazy. Her family might be. But Asad hadn't asked about them. "How about you? Because I'm pretty sure I remember something about getting arrested after stealing a goat."

"It was supposed to be a high school senior prank! Who calls the cops on the high school senior prank?" He shook his head. "Besides, that's been expunged." Beside him, Morgan's mouth had dropped open.

"I didn't know you got arrested for stealing a goat! Why would you steal a goat?"

"Because it was our rival high school's mascot." Asad shrugged, though he looked a little sheepish. "They stole our mascot's uniform, so we stole their mascot. It was only a small escalation." He looked over at Julie. "How did you even know about that?"

"I have my ways," she replied airily, making a mental note to ask Olivia for more dirt on Asad. If he was going to give her a hard time, even jokingly, she was going to dish it right back.

With his kind of personality, he'd probably just respect her more for it.

"Hey, Connor… can I ask a favor?" The question, asked by a deep, masculine voice, grabbed Julie's attention.

"Sure, what's up?" Connor replied to Master Will.

"Do you mind taking my Dungeon Monitor shift tomorrow night? Sorry about the late notice. Gina's mom needs some help tomorrow, and while they *could* do it with the baby there, it—"

"But I'm a sub," Connor interrupted, sounding a little shocked. Will stared at him.

"You're still you, man."

Connor opened his mouth. Closed it. Julie gave him a nudge. If he wanted to take the shift, he should. It might go a long way to showing him that nothing had really changed. There was a part of her that was a little sad, though. They hadn't discussed getting together tomorrow, but now that it wasn't going to be a possibility, she wished they had.

Still. At least she'd know where he was. She could always come by. Dungeon Monitor duties didn't take all night.

"Um, yeah. I can cover for you."

"Thanks, appreciate it." Will clapped Connor on the shoulder and walked away.

It wasn't until he was moving away from the table that Julie frowned. Sure, Will could have asked Connor because he realized Connor was struggling with being publicly a submissive and wanted to show him that things hadn't changed, but she wasn't sure Will and Connor knew each other that well. Would Will have realized that was going to be a problem?

She looked around at the other Doms at the table.

"What's wrong?" Law asked, frowning back at her.

"Just trying to figure out why Will only asked Connor to cover for him, instead of asking if any of you were available." Any one of them could have served as Dungeon Monitor tomorrow, including her.

"Oh, everyone always asks Connor because he never says no," Asad replied easily. Julie blinked, turning to look at Connor, who shrugged.

"I don't mind helping out."

Hm. She was going to have to poke at that further. There wasn't anything wrong with helping out, but she also didn't want anyone taking advantage of her submissive's giving nature. At least she knew this was a long-running thing and not *because* people knew he was submissive and, therefore, thought he'd say yes.

Having Will ask did seem to make Connor happy, though, so she'd leave it alone.

For now.

16

—————

CONNOR

Dungeon Monitor duty wasn't any different as a sub, other than getting much more enthusiastic greetings from the other submissives. He felt as if he'd been on one side of the wall, and now he was on the other. Or maybe as though the wall had been knocked down completely. It wasn't as if any of the dominants were treating him any differently.

It made him feel as if he was going a little crazy. No one was reacting the way he'd thought they would. He was the only one who thought it was a big deal that he'd lied to people. Even if it hadn't been an intentional lie. Even if it hadn't really affected anyone but himself.

And yes, when he thought about how he'd feel if someone he knew discovered they were submissive when they thought they were a dominant or vice versa, and it wouldn't matter to him, somehow it felt like it should matter to everyone else. Maybe he needed therapy.

Maybe having a psychologist for a girlfriend would count?

If Julie was his girlfriend. They hadn't exactly discussed titles yet, but she did want him to meet her family, so...

Though that was extenuating circumstances.

Traveling around the club, pausing to observe scenes as he went, Connor's brain was whirling with thoughts. One of the nice things about being a monitor at Stronghold was that people knew the rules and mostly followed them. At most, he needed to keep an eye on some of the newbies, make sure they were paying attention to how tight restraints were, and keep an eye on submissives who didn't want to say their safeword... that kind of thing. There were very few instances of actual emergencies or abusers here—Patrick ran a tight ship—and while some assholes managed to sneak in every now and then, they didn't last long.

Which meant it gave him plenty of time to think. Observe. Especially when it came to watching the male submissives scening. He and Mistress Julie were still exploring what his limits were, and he honestly didn't know. Some things he thought he might not like, but then he'd think about her, and he'd figure that he could maybe put up with it if it made her happy. Thinking about crawling on the floor didn't do much for him, and he could definitely go without having someone kick his balls... but he wasn't sure he'd want to tell her no if she wanted to try something.

Shit.

He might be one of the submissives who didn't want to say their safeword and disappoint their dominant.

Connor blew out a breath as he moved away from watching Frank getting his balls spanked—with a full-blown erection throughout. Not for him. *But could I say no if Mistress Julie wanted it?* He wasn't sure.

The sound of a sob—not an impassioned sob, not a pleasure-pain sob, but actually full-on tearful crying—had him turning with a frown. A busty blonde wearing nothing but her underwear was sobbing, strapped to one of the St. Andrew's crosses, and a tall, dark-haired man was by her side, hurriedly trying to get her out of the leather cuffs holding her to the wooden X. Red streaks marred her pale skin across her thighs, buttocks, and upper back—the kind of raised welts that came from a whipping. The cuffs were quick release, but Zach was fumbling in his haste.

"What happened," Connor demanded to know as soon as he stepped up next to Zach, both of them crouching down to get to her ankles.

"It's not his fault, Connor," Amy said, though she was still crying harder than he'd ever seen her cry before. As soon as she was free, Connor straightened up and held out his arms for her to fall into. She did, burying his face against his Dungeon Monitor vest.

Beside them, Zach frowned and looked like he wanted to say something, but instead, he clenched his jaw, keeping his mouth shut. There were bags under the other man's eyes and a bit of a five o'clock shadow on his jawline, which wasn't like Zach, but he'd been a lot less put together ever since he and his boyfriend had broken up. Connor had heard they were working on getting back together or that things were on the mend or something, but Kincaid was nowhere to be seen right now.

"She..." Zach sighed, scrubbing his hand through his dark hair, making it stand up on end. Somehow, he didn't notice. Which was also very unlike Zach. Though now Connor wasn't sure if the other man's state was caused by his ex or by Amy's slowly quieting sobs.

"I asked him to make me cry," Amy said, sniffling. Her voice was a little muffled since her face was still buried against him, but he could make out what she said. Zach looked at him guiltily.

Ah. Well. Amy was a masochist. Zach was a sadist. The two of them had been scening off and on fairly regularly over the past year... or was it two years? Damn, time flew. Amy had a vanilla fiancé who didn't mind her doing platonic scenes at the club, and Zach had been scening with her pretty regularly. The fact that they were both partnered up had made it seem like a good fit for platonic scenes, though sometimes, Connor thought maybe there was more to it than either of them was willing to admit.

Still, they always kept it within bounds, never scening in any of the private rooms. Which was why he knew he'd never seen Amy cry like this before.

"Let's go over to the aftercare corner," he said, scooping her up in his arms, leaving Zach to clean up his equipment and follow after them. Feeling her soft curves trembling against him, he had to sit on the protective feelings that were threatening to run rampant. Amy was one of the sweetest, kindest, most giving people he'd ever met, and he hated to see her upset.

Considering how often she and Zach had scened together, Zach should know her limits. She shouldn't have been crying like *that*, even if she'd asked him to make her cry. That was way more than tears over physical pain. He didn't think Zach would have done anything to deliberately hurt her, but he also knew it was his duty to make sure. He wouldn't be leaving Amy's side until he was completely convinced she was alright and that he could leave her in Zach's care.

"He really didn't do anything I didn't ask him to," Amy said, sniffling, as though she could read Connor's mind.

"I know." He did believe that. But one thing he'd learned about being a Dom was that sometimes what the submissive wanted and what the submissive needed were two different things. And some submissives were too willing to go past what was actually good for them. He sat down on the couch, cradling her on his lap and reaching over with one hand to grab a blanket from the top of the stack. Zach was already on his way over, so Connor figured he could take care of the water and snack. "Why did you want to cry?"

She sniffled again, her voice turning watery. "It's so dumb."

"I bet it's not."

"It is, though." Sorrow threaded through her voice. "I saw this stupid challenge online... you're supposed to ask your partner to peel an orange for you. And then see how they react. Jeremy didn't want to do it for me, and I started to get upset, but when I explained it to him... I mean, he's right. I was trying to trap him into a certain kind of reaction without telling him my expectations, and that wasn't fair to him. It was a trick. It was really shitty of me, yet even though I know I messed up, I'm still upset he didn't peel the orange for me, which makes me feel even worse."

"Why didn't he just peel the orange?" Connor's brain was having trouble getting past that one simple fact. If Julie asked him to peel an orange for her, he would, and he didn't think it had anything to do with being submissive. Hell, if Amy asked him to peel an orange for her, he would.

"Because I can do it myself. Which I can. But you know, it's just… it's stupid. It's a stupid test that's supposed to tell you if your partner cares enough about you to do something for you that you can easily do yourself, but he's right. It's a trick and a trap, and he didn't know what I was trying to do. I was being dishonest. I was setting him up to fail." The words poured out of her, leaving her breathing hard. Zach had caught up to them by then, a bottle of water in one hand and a chocolate bar in the other.

"You did not," Zach said grimly as he opened the bottle and handed it to her, making it clear that he'd had a conversation with Amy before the scene about why she was asking for a hard one. "You made a perfectly reasonable request, and he was a jerk, then he made you feel bad because he knew he looked bad."

Amy sniffled, keeping her gaze averted from both Connor and Zach.

"I was testing him, though. We're getting married. I shouldn't be testing him. It's childish."

"Maybe he shouldn't be failing the tests," Zach muttered. Taking the bottle from her, he held out the chocolate, which she took—still not looking at him.

Privately, Connor agreed, but he wasn't sure it was his place to say anything.

"Anyway, I was feeling… well, bad, so I texted Zach to see if he could be here tonight because I needed some release." Amy spoke loudly, as if she could drown out Zach's words, even though they were already out there. "I'm grateful he was available." *Even if he does need to keep his opinions to himself.*

The words hung unspoken in the air.

"I'm glad I could be here for you." *Since your dipshit fiancé wouldn't be.*

Maybe Connor was just imagining things or projecting. Maybe they weren't really thinking those things. But even if they weren't, he was starting to feel uncomfortably like he'd stepped into a couple's fight, even though Zach and Amy weren't a real couple.

He cleared his throat.

"Right, well… you're okay?" he asked Amy.

"Other than being embarrassed that you felt like you had to step in, yes." She lifted her gaze to his, giving him a sheepish smile. Connor smiled back at her reassuringly, rubbing his hand over her blanket-covered back. It didn't hurt that the blanket was very soft, so rubbing her back meant he got to rub the soft blanket, too.

"Any time," he told her seriously. "We're both just here to make sure you're okay."

Her smile shifted, just the slightest bit, going from sheepish to something else. Something a little sad, despite the curve of her lips.

"I'm fine. I learned my lesson about testing Jeremy. He doesn't respond well to it. But he loves me. He proposed. We're getting married. That's the only test he should need to pass." As she spoke, her tone picked up strength, and even though she wasn't looking at Zach, it felt as if that's where her words were really directed. Once again, Connor felt as though he'd stepped into the middle of someone else's fight.

Zach didn't respond, just pressed his lips together like he *really* wanted to say something, but was holding back. Unsure of what to do —whether leaving the two of them alone would really be a good idea —Connor glanced around as a distraction while he tried to think.

It only took a moment for his gaze to be arrested as Mistress Julie was watching him from near the row of spanking benches. She smiled at him when their gazes met, and he felt his heart jump in his chest. She was dressed for an evening at Stronghold in a black PVC corset, black PVC skirt, and boots that laced up to her thighs. Her hair was pulled back in a high ponytail that swished to the side when she tilted her head at him and winked.

"Hey, Connor, I'm good," Amy said gently, patting his chest where his heart had just done its little bounce. "If you want to go see Mistress Julie." She grinned at him, a much more sincere smile again now. She was happy for him.

"I still have…" He turned his head, looking for the clock. "Five more minutes of being Dungeon Monitor."

Damn. Mistress Julie had overheard Will asking him to cover. Had she appeared because she knew his shift would be almost over?

I hope so.

Connor had never considered himself a particularly jealous person, but he didn't like the idea that she'd come here for anyone but him. Of course, she came here for you, dumbass. You're together. Or dating. But she's not dating anyone else.

"Then go monitor the Dungeon for five more minutes. I'll be okay." Amy grinned cheekily at him. "Zach's got me."

Zach huffed. His expression was like granite when Connor looked at him, but he nodded confirmation.

Truthfully, his duty to Amy was done. He'd checked in on the situation, she was okay, and she was perfectly comfortable being left to Zach's care. Even if they were going to argue about what kind of treatment she should be getting from her fiancé. As much as Connor wanted to tell her she deserved better than how Jeremy was acting, she'd probably take it better coming from someone who was closer to her.

Probably. Though she and Zach seemed like they were butting heads over it.

Sighing because there wasn't anything he could do about it, Connor lifted her up and passed her over to Zach. The other man cradled her in his arms much the same way Connor had been before turning and sitting down on the other side of the couch.

As he got up, Connor grabbed the bottle of water and the chocolate and brought it over, placing it on the side table next to the couch arm.

"Thank you, Connor," Zach said, giving him a nod.

"Thank you, Connor," Amy echoed. Despite the bickering, she was now snuggled up against Zach's chest, looking perfectly comfortable. More than comfortable, she looked like she had fully relaxed now that she was on his lap, which she hadn't done while she was on Connor's.

Probably just because they were closer than her and Connor. After all the scening together. And Connor was probably just reading into things that Zach seemed as if he was holding her in a possessive manner.

"Have a good rest of the night," he said, making himself turn around and walk away. They didn't need his help. They hadn't asked for his help. He'd done what he was supposed to do. Just because something felt unfinished didn't mean he needed to finish it.

If Mistress Julie hadn't been waiting for him, it would have been much more difficult, but thankfully, she was. As he walked toward her, a smile lit up her face that nearly made him forget about the not-couple behind him.

"Hello, handsome," she purred as he stepped up in front of her, tilting her head back. Her hands came up to rest against his chest, one of them immediately sliding up to reach for the back of his neck, pulling his head down to meet her lips. Connor went eagerly, his hands fluttering for a moment by his sides before he moved them to her hips.

She hadn't told him to, but then, they hadn't discussed protocol.

And she didn't seem to mind as she gave him a very thorough kiss in greeting.

That or he was going to be punished for putting his hands on her without permission.

Her tongue slid against his, making his cock stand at immediate attention. A sharp scream cut through the air, reminding him of where they were and what he was supposed to be doing. Immediately, he jerked his head up, turning in the direction of the cry.

17

———

Julie

Watching Connor cuddle Amy had been interesting.

It hadn't been good. But it hadn't been necessarily bad, either. Just... interesting. She'd enjoyed watching how caring he was, and at the same time, she'd definitely felt a little jealous. It was an interesting dichotomy.

If she was Kincaid, she'd be jealous of the way Zach was holding Amy. She happened to know that Kincaid was out of town this weekend. Did he know Zach was here? Probably, she answered her own question. It would be extremely foolish to be here out in the open if Kincaid didn't know.

The gossip train ran Stronghold. And Marquis.

Especially with Connor needing to intercede at the end of the scene—everyone was going to be talking about that for a bit.

She wondered if Kincaid had seen Zach and Amy together recently.

Though, with Amy getting married...

Not my circus, not my monkeys.

Besides, Connor was almost to her. She tilted her head back, smiling up at him, reaching up to his chest. The leather Dungeon

Monitor vest was cool under her palms, and she slid one hand up to his neck, encouraging him to bend down for a kiss.

When his hands came to rest on her waist, she shifted closer to him, feeling the growing bulge in the front of his pants as it rubbed against her stomach. She'd deliberately arrived when his shift was almost over, so she wouldn't have to wait long. Since she was surprising him, she wasn't sure if he'd be interested in a scene, but either way, they'd get some time together.

Even if he wasn't interested in a scene, she wanted to spend more time with him. If showing up at Stronghold because he'd taken on an extra DM shift was how she had to do it, so be it.

The kiss deepened, lingered—and abruptly cut off when a shrill scream echoed through the Dungeon. Connor jerked upward, fully at attention, and Julie was already going up on her tiptoes, trying to see where the noise had come from. The woman screamed again, a word this time, but Julie couldn't make out what it was.

"Who is it?"

"I don't know... I can't..." Connor's head was turning, his gaze scanning over all the equipment, looking for whose scene it was coming from. If he couldn't see them, she sure as hell wasn't going to be able to, no matter how much taller she tried to make herself.

Several more shrieks from different voices, then a moment of silence followed by chatter that had an oddly relieved sound to it.

"What the hell is going on?" Julie snapped, not liking that she was completely out of the loop. Especially since whatever it was had interrupted a very nice kiss. There was a stir among the crowd between them and whoever had been screaming, and suddenly, Master Michael came shouldering his way through, holding out his hands out in front of him, one atop the other, like there was something between them. Like Connor, he was dressed in leather pants and a Dungeon Monitor vest, indicating that he was currently on duty this evening. His eye-length brown hair swished as he walked, and he shook his head to move it back out of his eyes—since his hands were full.

Julie automatically stepped back as he moved, getting out of his way.

"What happened?" Connor asked as Master Michael approached.

Julie wondered if it would be too obvious to hide behind Connor. Master Michael was in the classic 'I'm holding something gross in my hands' position, and it was likely the something gross had too many legs and was moving.

"Spider," Master Michael said, his lips starting to twist up before he managed to stop the smile. "A really big one. Angel just about took out Adam when she saw it, and for some reason, it kept running right for her. I've never seen her jump like that."

Managing to suppress a shudder, Julie took a deep breath. It wasn't that she was afraid of spiders or bugs. She just didn't *like* them. And she really preferred not to have to touch them. She also didn't want anyone thinking she was afraid or that she couldn't handle a spider. Especially when someone else was holding it.

"I'm gonna take this guy outside where he'll be safe... and so will Angel." Chuckling to himself, Micheal moved past them, heading for the stairs. Julie sighed with relief once he was past them.

Turning around, Connor looked down at her, amusement clear on his face.

"Don't like spiders?" he asked.

"Does anyone?"

"They've never bothered me much, but no, I guess I can't say I like them, either. My dad does, though. He likes watching them spin their webs. When I was a kid, he had a wolf spider that we kept as a pet. He named it Drake."

Julie didn't know what to do with that. While she knew people sometimes kept spiders as pets, she'd never known anyone who had one. Spiders were meant to be removed from the house immediately, along with any other bugs that made their way inside. But it sounded like Connor had fond memories of it.

"Did you play with Drake a lot?"

"Not really. Dad was worried about me being gentle enough with him." Connor shrugged. "I was kind of a clumsy kid. But sometimes

I'd get to hold him if I kept very still, and he'd run up my arm and sit on my shoulder."

She suppressed a shudder.

No, thank you.

The way Connor was looking at her made her think that he realized he was making her uncomfortable. She narrowed her eyes at him.

"It's been five minutes." She was done talking about bugs. And spiders. "Do you want to scene?"

The smile that bloomed across his face was much more to her liking since it had nothing to do with being amused by her dislike of things with more than four legs.

"Yes, please, Mistress."

Good. Because she was in the mood to torment him a bit now.

<u>CONNOR</u>

By a stroke of luck, the Locker Room was available, though only for a short time before the next reservation. Connor relaxed as soon as they found out. He still wasn't ready to scene down in the main room of the Dungeon where anyone could see them. And if asked, he wouldn't have been able to explain why.

Thankfully, Mistress Julie didn't ask. She just looked at him with her fathomless, dark eyes and slowly nodded in agreement when he'd requested to see if any of the private rooms were available. If one hadn't been, maybe he would have been able to work himself up to it... but more likely, he would have suggested going out to the walled-in gardens behind Stronghold. Fewer people.

Less of an audience.

The submissives had accepted him. None of the Doms seemed angry at him. No one was treating him any differently. Yet he still wasn't comfortable scening in front of them, not if he didn't have to. Though once he'd said yes to Mistress Julie, he would have done so rather than disappoint her... but he was relieved it wasn't necessary.

She closed the door behind them. There was a window that looked into the hallway, and the shades could be drawn, which she went and did. Connor knew that meant whoever was monitoring the cameras tonight would be paying extra attention to the audio from this room, just in case he safeworded. Safety came first. Having one watcher didn't bother him, especially since he couldn't *see* them watching.

The Locker Room was exactly what it sounded like, with the walls mostly made up of lockers—other than where the window was—and there were two long benches down the center of the room. It could accommodate a couple or quite a few people if someone had a football team and cheerleader fantasy they wanted to fulfill. As rooms went, it wasn't the most comfortable, but this particular room was all about the fantasy—and there was plenty of function to go along with it.

For instance, the lockers were full of implements and toys that could be used. They served as both aesthetic and storage. Mistress Julie went over and opened one.

"Hmmm... we don't have long," she said out loud while Connor stood by the benches, hands at his side, watching her with slowly growing nervous anticipation. She turned her head to look at him. "I'd like to plug you, Connor."

It wasn't a request; it was a statement. His cock immediately hardened even further, his cheeks clenching automatically. She seemed to be waiting for some kind of answer or maybe just making sure he wasn't going to say his safeword.

He sure as hell wasn't.

Ever since he'd realized what pegging was, he'd had multiple fantasies about Mistress Julie doing it to him. But he hadn't had anything in his ass since the introduction class, so it was probably best to start with a plug.

"Yes, Ma'am."

Standing still, he felt like he was quivering in place as she smiled at him, then turned back to the locker she was looking through. He happened to know it was full of a lot of different kinds of plugs, all for sale if someone hadn't brought one from home. If they used one, it would be added to her account. He made a mental note to pay her back for it later.

"Strip down." She wasn't looking at him, but it didn't matter. Connor immediately started to strip. Heck, at least it gave him something to do while he waited. By the time his clothes were off, so was the packaging on the plug she'd chosen for him.

Shit.

The black length of silicone she was holding didn't look *that* big, but it wasn't little, either. His muscles clenched again, trying to protect his ass. In her other hand, she held a small pack of lube.

"Bend over, feet apart, hands on the bench."

Holy shit. She had the bossy teacher voice down pat. Then again, she was a teacher for the introduction classes, but this was the first time in a while that he'd had the opportunity to hear it. Besides, during the class, it had always been directed at all the students at large—now it was just for him.

Completely naked, dick bobbing in front of him, he felt her eyes moving up and down his body as he got into position. It felt awkward, maybe even a little embarrassing, but when she ran her hand down his back and spoke, he completely relaxed.

"Good boy. You please me very much."

Fuck, he wanted to please her.

Her hand ran down the small of his back, then over his ass. With his feet spread apart, even when his cheeks automatically clenched, they couldn't entirely close. Bent forward, feet apart, the little hole where the plug was going to go was entirely vulnerable.

"Hold still, Connor. We're going to take this slowly... but I am on a bit of a time crunch." That last part was said a bit reprovingly, probably because it was his fault. He was the one who had wanted a private room, which was why she couldn't take her time.

"Sorry, Ma'am." He really was sorry. Next time, he wouldn't ask. Not if it bothered her enough to make a remark about it, even though she'd agreed.

He heard her let out a long, slow breath as her hand caressed him, sliding down to cup his balls and give them a little tug. Just enough to feel really damn good. Connor groaned as she cradled them in her hand, panting for breath at the pleasant sensation of her fingers rolling them.

"No, I'm sorry, Connor. That wasn't fair." She tugged his balls again, like an apology. It hurt just enough to make the pleasure feel even greater. "We'll make the most of it, and next time, I'll make sure I have a room reserved for us."

"You don't— Ah!" Her hand squeezed a bit harder as the tip of the plastic nosed against his anus. It had already been lubricated, and he could feel the small hole being pushed open as she added pressure.

"Breathe, Connor. I promise I'm not going to hurt you... much." There was a certain amount of devious, sadistic glee in her voice, which made him shudder even as his anticipation shot even higher. He groaned as she pulled the plug back just a bit, then pushed it deeper, his sphincter aching as it was stretched.

It hurt.

It felt good.

He felt more vulnerable than he ever had in his life, with his balls in her hand and a plug slowly pushing into his ass, yet he wouldn't have traded this moment for anything.

18

CONNOR

The plug moved back and forth as Mistress Julie worked it in deeper, stretching him wider with every stroke. The slick feeling of it gliding in, the discomfort of it stretching the small hole, made him gasp and groan—especially when the tip rubbed over his prostate. His fingers tightened around where he was holding the bench, and he leaned forward. It wasn't that he was purposefully trying to get away from it, exactly—it was an instinctive reaction.

As soon as he started to move away from the plug, she grabbed his balls again.

"Hold still, Connor." Her voice was soft, only a little louder than a murmur, but he froze—and not just because of where she was gripping. "You're almost there. Take the plug for me."

He groaned as her fingers tugged on his balls, pulling him back so that instead of her pushing the plug forward, *he* was moving himself back onto it.

Fuck.

With his sack in her grip, his dick bounced against his body, leaving behind wet spots as precum leaked from the tip. The tug on his balls pulled him back, the plug pushing forward, rubbing over that sensitive spot deep inside again and making him gasp. The sensations were almost too intense to be pleasurable, yet he didn't want them to stop.

The discomfort, the burn, grew as the plug went deeper, and he cried out as he felt himself stretch to the point of pain—then it was over. The plug was inside him. His body had snapped shut around the neck between the bulb and the base.

Panting, his head hung down between his arms, his balls still throbbing in Mistress Julie's grip.

Holy hell.

That had been a *lot* more intense than in class. Not just because the plug was bigger, either.

"Good boy," Mistress Julie murmured, and he felt the plug move inside him as she twisted it back and forth, igniting all the little nerve endings around his sphincter. The slickness of the lube made it easy to spin, and when his muscles clamped down instinctively, all it did was amplify the sensations.

"Fuck!" The word came out in a hoarse bark, the muscles along his back rippling as his body tried to curl inward, tried to adjust to the new stimulation. She laughed low in her throat, then gave the plug a little tug, starting to stretch him around the bulb again before releasing it.

"Very good. Now, I want you sitting down on the bench for me, one foot on either side of it." Releasing his sack, she patted his ass.

Right.

Sitting right on the plug.

Great.

His dick throbbed as he straightened up and turned around to look down at her. The wicked gleam in her eye as she watched him just turned him on even more. His dick bobbed as he stepped back, one leg on either side of the bench, and he took a deep breath. Every movement jostled the plug inside him, bumping it against his prostate, making his cock jerk in reaction.

Lowering himself onto the bench under Mistress Julie's watchful gaze made his face heat, but at the same time, he didn't feel embarrassed exactly—incredibly vulnerable for sure, but not embarrassed. Still, his face was turning red, which might partly be from exertion.

Sitting on the plug meant he was definitely not going to be able to forget it was there. With his legs spread, the bench between them, most of his weight was right on the toy. It wasn't big enough to hurt, but it sure as hell made its presence known.

"Fuck." He let out all the air in his chest as he settled his weight onto the bench, his ass clenching around the plug, the wood cool against the underside of his sack. Mistress Julie smiled at him, pleased, and he felt something flutter inside his chest. Damn, but he liked making her smile.

"I do like a man who listens," she quipped, winking at him.

Connor grinned back at her, eager to please.

"Yes, Ma'am."

"Now. Hands behind your back. Fold them up to hold on to your elbows." As she gave him instructions, she moved around behind him. He could hear her pulling something else out of one of the lockers while he did as she said, then felt the leather wrapping around his forearms, locking them together and holding them in place.

It was a good thing he was flexible. Holding the position wasn't the easiest, but the leather strap around them helped. Not too tight, but it gave him some support, so he wasn't straining to stay in place. He was able to relax his arms just a bit, allowing the leather to do some of the work.

Mistress Julie's hand slipped up his back, her nails trailing across his shoulders as she circled back around him, making him shudder at the rivulets of sensation. By the time she came back around to face him—with him sitting on the bench, they were nearly of a height, with her just a little taller than him in her heels—he could feel himself begging for more with his eyes.

Having his hands behind his back meant he wouldn't be able to touch her, which, of course, made his desire to touch her so much bigger.

Her nails trailed down over his chest, scraping over a sensitive nipple, and he hissed out a breath between his teeth. It stung, making the little bud throb, yet his dick throbbed in response because right now, it was struggling to tell the difference between pleasure and pain.

"I think some jewelry next," Mistress Julie announced, smiling down at him. He groaned when she opened her other hand, and he could see that she was holding clamps connected by a thin metal chain.

Yeah, he remembered those things from class. They fucking hurt.

But he'd take the pain for her if that was what she wanted. Hell, he was already taking pain in the ass. The plug hadn't hurt at first, but it was growing more uncomfortable the longer he sat on it, and he found himself squirming in place a bit to try to secure a more comfortable position.

"Is there a problem?" she asked, raising her eyebrow at his groan.

"No, Ma'am. Just remembering how much those hurt."

"They do." Mistress Julie leaned forward, her lips hovering over his as her free hand moved down to grip his dick. This time, his groan was of pure pleasure as she wrapped her fingers around his shaft and pumped, moving her hand along the thick length. "And you're going to take it for me, aren't you, good boy?"

"Yes, Ma'am," he said immediately, desperately, and was rewarded with another pump of her hand along his cock.

She released him, and he had to hold back a whimper. Fuck, his cock was aching from the teasing. But if he was a good boy, he'd get a reward. And he liked being good for her. He liked knowing she was pleased with him. That he was doing a good job.

He liked being the one putting a smile on her face, even if that smile was a little sadistic.

Whatever she wanted.

He hissed but didn't protest when she put the first clamp on the tiny bud of his nipple, flattening it. Such a small part of his body, but it throbbed like a mother fucker as it was crushed between the rubber tips of the clamp. A moment later, the other one matched it, leaving him panting for breath as he adjusted to the sensation.

Not that he had time to fully adjust before Mistress Julie was straddling his lap, pulling her tight skirt up to her hips.

She wasn't wearing anything underneath it.

And she wasn't going to get undressed, apparently.

Nope, she was going to ride him—in her boots, skirt hiked up around her waist, corset still on, so that her heaving breasts were right in front of him yet not accessible—all while he was buck ass naked, hands bound behind his back, plug up his ass, and clamps hanging off his nipples. It was the hottest thing that had ever happened to him.

The wet heat of her pussy as it touched the head of his cock agreed with the assessment. Mistress Julie moaned as she began to slowly impale herself on his dick. Her hands came up to cradle the back of his head, and she tipped her head forward to take his lips in a kiss as his cock slid into her. The combination of wet heat gliding over his cock, her tongue in his mouth, his nipples and ass throbbing from the toys...

Fuck, he didn't know how long he was going to be able to last.

As if she'd heard his thought, she lifted her lips from his, one hand gripping the back of his hair, so she could twist his head enough to get her mouth next to his ear.

"Don't you dare cum until I do."

The hot, heavy whisper made his jaw clench, and he shuddered as he pushed back the wave of pleasure. He groaned, trying to think about anything—cold showers, Amy and Zach's issues, Law's bald head—to keep himself from cumming as Mistress Julie started to glide up and down on his cock, using him for her own personal sex toy.

JULIE

She'd never considered herself a size queen, but Connor made her feel like one. The size of his cock as she worked herself up and down the long length, and the size of the man himself as she moved atop him. It was intoxicating having him under her control, submitting to her, letting her take the power.

If he'd flexed hard enough, he could have easily popped the snap on the leather strap around his arms.

If he stood, she'd be dumped onto the floor.

If he'd wanted her to stop at any point, all he had to do was say the word.

But he didn't do any of those things. And he wasn't going to. Because he wanted to please her.

To pleasure her.

To take whatever she was willing to give him.

Fuck.

Her pussy tightened around him, making him groan again. She could see the desperation in his eyes—the need to cum, and the struggle to obey her command. That was so damn hot, her pussy clenched around him again.

There was also something incredibly arousing about being mostly clothed while he was entirely naked. It was a show of power that aroused her as much as everything else. And the boots helped give her the height she needed to be able to ride him the way she wanted.

If only she had more time...

Maybe next time.

Julie dismissed the thoughts. There was no point dwelling on what might have been. Connor had wanted privacy, and she had chosen to give it to him without pushing the point. They were still new. The time to show him off, to show *them* off, would come eventually.

"Fuck... Mistress... please..."

He did beg so nicely, accompanied by a heartfelt groan as he struggled against cumming before her.

"Not yet," she murmured, dragging her teeth down his earlobe and making him cry out as she rose up again, slamming herself down. "I'm getting close, but not yet."

He whimpered as she sucked his earlobe between her lips, a

small sound that sent delicious tingles up and down her body. Julie started moving harder, faster. Connor's cock felt like a steel bar as he struggled to hold back his orgasm, hardening to the point where it felt bigger than ever, her pussy clenching and spasming as she impaled herself again and again.

Ecstasy swirled inside her, twisting and rising as her body began to shake.

"Now, Connor." She managed to gasp out the words as she tipped over the edge into the waves of her climax.

He surged up beneath her for the first time, as much as he could, and she clung to him as he lifted them both up just a bit. His hoarse cry was a counterpoint to her moans as she ground herself down on him, rubbing her clit against his body, shuddering as she felt him explode inside her.

Their mutual pleasure went on and on, and she clung to him like he was a buoy in the sea of her ecstasy until they were both utterly spent.

19

CONNOR

Watching Kevin do his leg lifts, Connor nodded. The man was moving much better than in the past; Connor could tell he'd been doing his exercises in between appointments. He had a good handle on things.

Which was why Connor's mind kept wandering.

Back to the late evening with Mistress Julie. Just thinking about it made his ass clench all over again.

He looked forward to their date tonight. She was going to come over for dinner after work. He was cooking. Well, he was smoking a brisket and making a salad. He'd buy bread from the store on the way home and pop it in the oven to crisp up a little. Hoping she liked it all. Wondering what might happen after.

It was her first time coming to his place, after all.

Then, this Sunday, he'd go meet her parents. Not just her parents—her family. She'd warned him she had a big one, though so far, she'd talked about them in bulk. The aunts. The uncles. The cousins.

He'd always wondered what it would be like to be surrounded by a big family. The only time he'd got even a taste of that was during the occasional family reunions, where all the far-flung second and third cousins showed up. From the sound of it, Julie had more first cousins than he had second and third cousins combined.

"What's up?" Sanda popped up at his elbow, phone in her hands, her gaze focused on the screen. Connor looked down at her with bemusement.

"You aren't still looking for my... date, are you?" he asked. He wasn't sure if he could call Julie his girlfriend yet. Even if he could, he wasn't sure if he wanted to in front of Sandra. That would likely just push her to greater heights of internet stalking. So far, she hadn't found Julie, and he was happy to keep it that way a little longer. Maybe after he'd met her family, he'd feel secure enough to let Sandra do some online sleuthing.

"Are you still dating?"

"Yes."

"Then yes. Though, that's not what I'm doing right now. I've been given a second assignment." She scowled down at her phone. "My mom wants me to find out some stuff about my cousin."

"You should do that instead. That sounds much more important." Funny that he was thinking about cousins, and here Sandra was, investigating hers.

"Oh, don't worry. I can do both." She looked up at him and winked. "I'm gonna find her. Just because you haven't connected with her on social media doesn't mean I won't. It just means it'll take me longer."

"Uh-huh." Thankfully, Sandra had no clue what he did on the weekends. He'd never talked about Stronghold or the second floor of Marquis at work. It hadn't seemed appropriate. He just said he'd gotten together with friends and let people assume it was at someone's house or a bar.

The lack of personal information he had online and that he'd given out at work was definitely working in his favor.

He probably could have told Sandra more about Julie now, but honestly, he was kind of curious about what she'd manage to come up with if he didn't. He'd give her until Monday after he met Julie's family, then he'd tell her and Aubrey all about Julie. Minus a few pertinent details.

She sighed.

"My cousin is almost as bad as you about online details. What is it with you people and not putting your life online?" She shook her head and started walking away again before he could ask any questions about her 'assignment.' "Good thing I love a challenge."

Chuckling under his breath, Connor went over as Kevin finished his rep set.

"Good job, man. I can really see the improvement."

"Mostly thanks to you being a total task driver." Kevin grinned, rubbing his leg a little as he stretched it out post-exercise. "I can really feel it. I'm moving a lot better."

"You are. Let's go over to the table." He gestured for Kevin to lead the way. The man was walking almost completely normally, even after the exercises, which was great. That's what made it easy to tell he'd been keeping up with working his leg at home, which was why his recovery was going so smoothly.

Now, it was time for the massage to loosen things up a little, then Kevin would be on his way home. Pretty soon, he wouldn't need to come in at all. It kind of sucked that success in his field meant not seeing the person again, especially if they became friendly, but Connor knew that was also the sign of a job well done. At least with the kind of injury Kevin had. Granted, there were chronic conditions that meant he got to see the same person over and over again, but he wouldn't wish anything painful on someone just so he could keep seeing them regularly.

"You're a lifesaver," Kevin said, sighing as Connor dug his fingers into the man's leg, loosening up some of the muscles that had tightened during the exercises.

Connor grinned. He really did love his job most days.

---

*J*ULIE

It was days like this that Julie hated her job. At least she had her date tonight with Connor to make up for it.

Cassidy was a submissive who had been in an abusive relationship with a dominant. She'd been lucky—they'd come to Stronghold, and Don had gotten kicked out after ignoring her safeword. The problem was her ex wasn't done with her, and there was nothing she or Julie or anyone could do about it. Not legally, at least.

He'd started stalking Cassidy, at first with notes left on her car or in her mailbox, and now with calls coming from duped phone numbers. Not that he said anything. He just breathed heavily into the phone and made growling noises, which might have been comical under other circumstances, but knowing who it was made Cassidy fall to pieces every time.

Even with the restraining order, there wasn't shit they could do about it since they couldn't prove it was him. The police were no help. Basically, until he did something violent, they were useless—and from many of the instances Julie had seen, even after there was violence, the police were often far from helpful.

There was only so much she could do to help Cassidy's state of mind when her biggest problem was currently external, not internal.

"I just want to stop being afraid all the time." Cassidy huddled on the couch, arms wrapped around herself, hugging herself. Her long dark hair fell forward, covering most of her face, as though she was trying to hide behind it.

"I know. And you deserve that." Julie kept her voice soothing, even though she felt like screaming in rage at her own helplessness. It wasn't fair that Cassidy was having to spend her life in fear while that asshole Don strutted around with impunity.

The fact he'd gotten more fixated on Cassidy rather than moving on didn't bode well. Neither did the slow escalations from notes to phone calls and the decreased time between contact. That he was going to keep escalating, that he was eventually going to hurt Cassidy again, Julie had no doubt.

But there was nothing she could *do*.

"Patrick thinks I should relocate." Cassidy lifted her head, meeting Julie's gaze. Her face was incredibly pale. "His cousin works for a security firm in Pittsburgh."

"The one that Kincaid is working with now?" Julie asked automatically. She knew the Dom had recently moved from the police force to a private security firm that wanted to open a DC office.

Cassidy nodded.

"They have a good reputation. Do you want to move?"

"No... yes... I don't know." Cassidy dropped her head down again and shuddered. She took in a deep breath and let it out.

Julie waited patiently, proud of the progress Cassidy had made. She was working her way through her breathing exercises, through her emotions, rather than allowing them to control her.

"Part of me wants to run away. Part of me is mad that I feel that way. But I also... what's worse, running away or dying? It feels like he wins either way, but at least one way I'm still alive."

Dammit. And Julie couldn't even reassure her that staying wouldn't mean her death. There was every chance it would. She couldn't diagnose Don since he wasn't her patient, but his obsessive fixation wasn't going to just suddenly go away.

"So, you'd be staying with Patrick's cousin?" It was a bold move. Send her hours away to live with someone who had the skills to protect her if asshole figured out where she was and followed her.

Not that there weren't people here who would be willing and ready to protect her, but none of them belonged to a security firm. Well, except Kincaid, but he was helping set up the new office, so he could hardly be on call 24/7. Plus, he was distracted by whatever was going on with him and Zach. Throwing a submissive in danger into the mix was hardly going to be good for any of them, including Cassidy. She needed to be around stability, even if asshole Don wasn't a factor.

Cassidy nodded.

"Drew and his wife, Naomi. They're the ones who rescued Morgan." Hope crept into her voice, giving it a little lift. The fact that they'd already rescued another abusive submissive seemed to make her feel better.

Julie hadn't been around then, but she'd heard some of what had brought Morgan to Stronghold.

"It sounds like you want to say yes."

"I..." Cassidy blew out her breath, lifting her head and staring out the window of Julie's office. "I think I do, but I hate the idea of leaving. I hate the idea of being chased away. I hate feeling this weak. And..." Her voice trailed off.

"And?" Julie prodded gently after a moment of silence.

Cassidy gulped and closed her eyes. Wet tears dotted her lashes.

"I don't want people here to think I'm ungrateful."

"Oh, honey." It might not be professional, but Julie didn't care. Sometimes, when it came to her clients from the club, the lines blurred a little. Especially with someone like Cassidy. Julie reached out and put her hand on Cassidy's, prompting the other woman to open her eyes again. "No one is going to think you're ungrateful. They're just going to be happy you're taking care of yourself. That you're safe."

Hitch in her breath, Cassidy nodded.

"No one will think you're weak, either. They'll think you're smart, going to a place where you're more likely to be safe. That's not an option for everyone."

Nodding, Cassidy reached up to wipe away some of her tears before they could slide down her cheeks.

"I know. I'm lucky in that way. Patrick said Drew and Naomi would help me get a job, too. Something where it won't be easy to track me down. They even... well." She coughed. "Let's just say they said they could even get me a new name if I wanted."

"It sounds perfect."

"Sort of." Cassidy's face crumbled. "But my friends are here. I've made friends here. I like living here." And friends were all Cassidy had. Her parents had been killed in a car accident when she was in her early twenties. She had no siblings. While she had two aunts, an uncle, and several cousins, they were spread out across the country, and she'd never had much contact with any of them, even when her parents were alive. She hadn't had a close family, which was why she valued her friends so much.

All of which were things they'd talked about in previous sessions, so Julie knew how hard it would be for Cassidy to leave.

"You won't be far enough away to prohibit visits. And there are definitely ways to keep in touch, even without social media. You can talk with your friends every day if you want."

"That's true. It won't be the same, but..." Cassidy perked up a little. "And I know there's a club in Pittsburgh."

"The Outlands." Julie smiled at her. "It's a very nice club, especially since the renovation. Kind of a cross between Marquis and Stronghold."

"I heard Master Mitch's dad owns it."

"He does." Master Gavin. Incredibly hot and with a very slight Scottish accent that made the submissives swoon. Julie had met him. Even felt a little swoony herself, though she had no desire to do the submissive thing, and he was utterly devoted to his formerly ex-wife, now wife again. "He runs a tight ship, just like Master Patrick."

And sometimes assholes slipped through, but they all did their best. That was all they could do.

Cassidy nodded but didn't say anything. Giving her hand a little squeeze before letting go, Julie sat back.

"You don't have to decide anything right now," she reminded her. "There is still time to think about it." Probably. She hoped. But it was a big move—literally—and she didn't want Cassidy to do something she regretted later because she felt time pressured to make a choice.

There was always the chance that Don could get hit by a bus tomorrow, though they probably wouldn't be that lucky.

"Right." Cassidy nodded and took another deep breath. "If I... if I did move, could I keep seeing you?"

"Of course!" Julie was touched as she suddenly realized that part of Cassidy's hesitation was not wanting to leave Julie. Of course, it wasn't quite the same as not wanting to leave friends behind, but it still warmed her to know she was part of Cassidy's decision-making process. "We can do video appointments. I also won't feel hurt if you decide you want to meet with someone in person. I can make you a list of recommendations if you decide that's the case."

"Okay, thank you. I'd want to stick with you for now. If I moved."

Julie could hear the change in Cassidy's voice just from having talked it through with her. She didn't sound as uncertain. And the addition of "if I moved" was more of an afterthought than a caution. If Julie was a betting woman, she'd be putting all of her money on Cassidy taking the leap. She just hoped it was far enough of a leap to get the woman away from that asshole Don.

The fact she was probably going to be doing video appointments with Cassidy from now on—because she'd been forced to change her life thanks to a shitty man—made her want to scream. She hid it behind a smile for Cassidy, though. Now that Cassidy was actually looking hopeful about the future, she didn't want to ruin that for her.

She was in a seriously bad mood, though. Maybe she should cancel her date with Connor.

20

———————

JULIE

Canceling might have been the better idea. Julie had hoped that the drive to Connor's would help even out her emotions, and it had a little... but she was still pissed. At the world. At society. At men. Even knowing Connor was nothing like that asshole Don didn't totally help because then she just felt guilty about subjecting him to her bad mood. He didn't deserve that. He sure as hell hadn't earned it.

But here she was. As much as she'd wanted to go home and just rage privately, she hadn't wanted to cancel the date.

Especially after he'd texted her a picture of the brisket he was smoking. He'd smoked a whole brisket for her. That was expensive. And time-consuming. She would have felt so bad about canceling, knowing all the time, money, and effort he'd put into dinner with her.

I'm mad at the world, and everything I can't do to right its wrongs didn't seem like a good enough reason to hurt his feelings.

At the same time, she could feel how on edge she was. Connor deserved a better date. A better version of her. One that was focused on him and properly appreciative of everything he'd done for her. Not one that was distracted by how shitty the world was and how unfair it was that Dickhole Don got to run around harassing and intimidating Cassidy with impunity.

Closing her eyes, she took several deep breaths. In through her nose. Out through her mouth. In through her nose. Out through her mouth. While she did so, she pictured balling up all her negative energy, all her anger, all her frustration and sending it straight into orbit into the sun to explode in fiery demolition.

Too bad she couldn't do the same thing to Dickhole.

Stop it. You're ruining the exercise.

Yeah, well, sometimes the exercises didn't help as much as she wanted them to, but it had helped a little. She felt a bit looser, a tad freer. The important thing that she needed to remember was Cassidy was safe, and she would be even safer in Pittsburgh, surrounded by an elite security team. She might even be able to find happiness. She was incredibly lucky to have such an option.

Giving herself a little shake, Julie lifted her chin and started up the walkway toward the house, taking in the details for the first time. It was a cute blue house with white shutters, one story, with a well-maintained lawn. The front of the house was lined with bushes, the kind that didn't need much care other than the occasional trim but added to the overall picturesque quality of the house. There were two trees on either side of the house—and a little in front of it—creating a natural kind of frame. The leaves on the branches had started to turn, adding a pop of yellow and rusty orange to the scenery.

The front door, which matched the white shutters, opened before she reached it, and there was Connor, filling the doorframe behind the storm door. He raised his eyebrows at her as he pushed the storm door open and stepped to the side for her to enter.

Just seeing him made her feel a little better. So maybe she could hold it together to give him a nice date night after all. She still thought he deserved better than her current mood, but she'd do her best.

"Hi," she said, smiling up at him and pausing in the doorway to go up on her tiptoes and collect a kiss. He bent his head down, a small brush of the lips as she passed, which left her wanting a little more.

"Hey. Everything okay?" he asked, closing the door behind her while she looked around the space.

The door opened into a great room, basically, since the whole area had an open floor plan, making the most of the square footage. It was a cozy space. To her right was a living area with a small sectional, an entertainment center and television, and two bookcases, although only one had actual books on it.

On the left was the dining area with a table with four chairs, though it could probably fit six more if a chair was placed on either end. Just past that was the kitchen, which was set up a little like a galley kitchen, but one side of the wall was open, with the counter creating an overhang. Bar stools were tucked underneath, providing another area for sitting and eating if someone didn't want to use the table. It also doubled as prep space and a serving area.

"Yeah... just a long day."

"I was starting to wonder if you were going to come in."

She turned to look at him again. There was a bit of hesitation in his expression. Damn. He must have been watching her standing out there, debating on whether or not a date was actually a good idea.

"I just needed a few moments to gather myself," she replied with an apologetic smile. "Nothing to do with you. It was just a really *long* day. I can't really talk about it, though, because it had to do with a client."

"Gotcha." Sympathy replaced hesitation in his expression. "Can I get you something to drink? I've got water, wine, or beer. Or something stronger if you want."

"Water to start and wine with dinner sounds great." She'd forgotten to eat a snack today, so she'd save the alcohol until she had something in her stomach in hopes that it wouldn't hit her so hard.

"Great." He headed to the kitchen, and she breathed in, happily sighing at the scent of well-roasted meat.

"That smells incredible." Following him toward the kitchen, she veered off to the left to pull out one of the stools and sit on the other side of the counter to watch him. There was a large bowl on the counter full of salad and what she assumed was the brisket resting under a cloth on a wooden cutting board.

"Good. Hopefully, it tastes incredible, too." He gave her a little wink before opening one of the cabinet doors to pull out a water glass, pivoting to the fridge's water dispenser to fill it up. "Ice?"

"No, thank you." Yes, she knew it was weird, but ice made water too cold, then her teeth ached.

If Connor thought it was odd, it didn't show. He just filled up the cup and passed it across the counter to her.

"The bread is almost ready, then we'll be able to eat." He grinned at her, seemingly very pleased with himself.

Julie couldn't help but smile back. Yes, just being around Connor made her feel better. He was a nice reminder that there were good men out there. Men who were nothing like Dickhole Don. Men who didn't tolerate men like Dickhole.

Which was why Dickhole had gotten himself kicked out of the club. Too bad there hadn't been anything more they could do.

"How was your day?" she asked, lifting her glass to take a sip, which ended up turning into a gulp. She was thirstier than she'd realized.

"Pretty good. A couple of my coworkers are intent on trying to figure out who I'm dating." His eyes sparkled with mischief while he opened the oven door.

Damn, that smelled good, too. Maybe part of her problem was that she was hangry.

"I figure I'll give them a little more time to spin their wheels before I tell them your name."

Julie laughed.

"Isn't it amazing how people can get so caught up in what's going on in someone else's life?" she asked, shaking her head. "At least that's not something I need to worry about at work."

She had her own practice and no coworkers, and her clients definitely weren't asking about her dating life. Not even the ones who were members of Stronghold and Marquis. They might ask her about it outside of their appointments but not during. Her whole day was about other people, with no one poking in her business, which was normally how she liked it.

"It was more fun when it wasn't aimed at me," he admitted with a chuckle. "I think the bread's ready."

"Mm, that smells amazing." She loved the smell of fresh baked bread. And meat. Her stomach rumbled, making Connor raise his eyebrows at her again. Blushing, she put her hand on her stomach. "I might have missed eating my afternoon snack today."

"Well, then, let's get you fed." He winked at her, pulling the bread out of the oven.

It looked as good as it smelled, and Julie sighed happily.

CONNOR

Julie had been wound up tight when she'd first arrived at his house—Connor had been able to see it in the set of her shoulders, the tightness of her jaw, and the stiff way she'd moved.

Food had made a difference. While she hadn't been able to talk about whatever was bothering her, he managed to make her smile as he told her about the conversation he'd had with Asad earlier that day. Asad had called him to ask for strap-on recommendations.

"I told him he should probably ask you." Connor chuckled, shaking his head.

"Is he actually going to go through with it?"

"Maybe. He hates being left out of things. Or being told he can't do something. I think the bigger question is whether or not Morgan would do it."

Though, if Asad wanted it badly enough… Connor had to shake his head again.

"You have to admire a man who's secure in himself." The small smile danced on her lips.

As much as Connor wanted to be the one making her smile, he would take what he could get. Especially when her smile dipped a moment later, as if an unwelcome thought had suddenly occurred to her.

Whatever was bothering her, he'd be willing to bet it was something to do with a man.

Reaching across the table, he slid his hand around hers, grabbing her attention, and she looked up at him. The little smile returned to her lips as she focused on him, which was definitely gratifying.

"You're still out of sorts." He didn't ask it as a question; it was a statement. He didn't want her to try to deflect with her answer.

Julie sighed, turning her hand so she could hold his, her fingers moving over his wrist.

"I am. It's not your fault, though. Dinner was wonderful. You've been wonderful." The smile she bestowed upon him now was a little crooked. Her free hand toyed with the stem of her wineglass. Yes, she'd relaxed, but not enough as far as he was concerned.

"Take it out on me."

"What?" She blinked owlishly at him, clearly taken aback by the sudden demand.

"I can see you've got something you're holding back. You can't tell me about it." He shrugged. "But you can take it out on me. I can take it. I'll probably even enjoy it."

Staring at him for a long moment, Julie lifted the wine glass to her lips, taking a long sip. Not once did she look away from him, and he knew she was considering it.

"That doesn't seem fair to you," she finally said slowly as she put the wineglass back down. "You're not the reason for my bad mood. In fact, you've improved my mood greatly."

"And I'd like to do it some more." He raised his eyebrows at her. "Besides, it's not like it's something you're secretly doing—which wouldn't be fair. I'm making a request. You've got some pent-up frustrations from your day. I'm both able and willing to let you vent on me a bit."

What that would look like, he didn't know, but he was pretty sure it would end in an orgasm, and that tended to be a pretty good mood enhancer.

Her finger tapped against the inside of his wrist while she considered his offer. He could practically see the wheels turning in her head, trying to figure out what she might do to him. Just knowing she was thinking about it made his heart start to race, his breath coming a little faster and a little more shallowly.

"Very well," she said after a long moment, a wicked gleam growing in her eyes. "I accept your offer."

21

———————

"I'll admit, this wasn't exactly what I had in mind," Connor said as she moved around him with the rope. He was seated in the same chair he'd been sitting in when he made the offer, though he was completely naked now. "I thought you were going to flog me or something."

"I thought about it," she replied, keeping her focus on what she was doing. The interweaving of the ropes could easily become confusing if she didn't keep track of where she was. She'd worked her way down from his shoulders to his midsection. His hands were already secured behind him with the Takatekote pattern, and she was now crisscrossing the ropes over his middle.

It was like doing macrame, but instead of a potted plant, she was doing it around Connor. The Nijûbishi pattern made pretty diamond patterns down his front. If he was a woman, she would have called it the beginning of a rope dress, but for him, it was more like a rope shirt.

Working on the ties relaxed her. It required her full focus, which meant her mind couldn't wander to things like Dickhole Don, and at the same time, the repeating motions helped soothe her. The fact that Connor was a huge, muscular guy, letting her tie him into place also helped soothe her.

And she did like having him completely at her mercy.

He liked it, too.

His dick was fully erect, and Julie made no effort to avoid brushing against the thick length, though she wasn't deliberately teasing him. With how she was moving around him, she didn't need to be deliberate... She was saving the deliberate teasing for once she had him totally tied down.

"How is that?" she asked, slipping her fingers under the ropes she'd just tied to check that they weren't too tight, even as she asked him. "Anything tingling?"

He smiled at her, almost dreamily. The more rope she'd gotten knotted around him, the more relaxed he'd become, and she was feeding off that, too. With every knot she'd added to the pattern, it felt like another knot released from between her shoulders.

"Just my dick."

Pressing her lips together, Julie did her best not to smile. He wasn't bratting exactly, but he also knew that wasn't the response she was looking for.

Reaching down, she gave the appendage in question a little tap on the head, hard enough to make him groan.

"Just my dick, Ma'am," he amended, startling a laugh out of her.

Dammit.

"You're being a naughty boy, Connor," she said, shaking her head and giving the tip of his cock another hard tap, making it bob in front of him. "I need to know if anything other than your dick is tingling or feeling off."

"No, Ma'am." Undeterred, he grinned cheekily at her. Julie wondered if he was getting rope drunk already.

She couldn't help but wonder how he'd react if she made him fly.

But right now, she was tying him down to a chair, not up in the air.

Reaching up, she patted his cheek, the bristles of his five o'clock shadow rubbing against her hand.

Then she got back to work, making a triangle with the rope around his groin, knotting it just underneath his balls, not quite pressing against his perineum. Connor shifted in his seat, as though he was trying to get a little more comfortable. The positions of the rope weren't going to cut off his circulation, but it was the first bit of rope that was anywhere near his genitals. He was understandably a little nervous about what she might do next.

Fortunately for him, her next stop was his feet.

Kneeling between them, she smiled when her hair brushed against his dick, and he groaned again, the chair creaking as he shuddered. This next part was quick and easy, as she tied each end of the rope around his ankles, wrapping the rope around each leg a few times before tying off the knot at the back, ensuring it wasn't too tight and that it wouldn't get tighter when he moved.

The ropes from his balls to his ankles made a V shape between his legs, a nice little spot for her to kneel while she toyed with him.

Already, she felt a million times better than she had when she'd first arrived at his house. Putting her hands on his knees, she slid them up to where the ropes framed his groin, stopping just short of them, and his dick jerked in reaction.

"What do you think?" she asked, curious to see how he was feeling in the midst of his first experience with Shibari.

"Really good, Ma'am." He smiled broadly, his eyes still hazy. Yup, he was a happy, rope-drunk submissive. "As long as you aren't going to ask me to get up."

Julie laughed. No, she wasn't going to ask him to get up. She was going to torture him instead.

"You're perfect exactly where you are," she said, getting to her feet. Suppressing a snicker, she wagged her finger at him. "Now, don't move. I have to get a few more things."

Thanks to the open floor plan, she could get what she wanted without having to let him out of her line of sight.

<u>CONNOR</u>

The first thing Mistress Julie got was a blindfold.

The sensory deprivation made him acutely aware of how the ropes felt around him. It was a natural fiber rope, a length that he'd gotten when he'd first joined the kink scene, then never used. He'd actually bought quite a few toys when he'd first joined the scene, some of which had been used, many of which hadn't. Somehow, it felt fitting that its first use was *on* him rather than him using it on someone else... like part of him had been saving it for that.

Every movement he made, every small shift of his body, moved the ropes. They were wrapped around him tightly but not painfully, and they moved with him. He was hyperaware of the sensations and the feeling of security, as though he was being held, even though Mistress Julie wasn't actually touching him at the moment.

It also made his ears strain, trying to figure out what she was doing, though he had to hold absolutely still in order to focus on that. Because the second he moved, his whole body lit up from the sensations of the rope moving against his skin, and it was incredibly distracting.

The whole time, it felt like his dick was going to break off.

She was doing something by the fridge. Or in the fridge. Or maybe the freezer. He'd heard one of the doors open. His head went to trying to figure out what he had in there that she might want.

A glass of water? Was she thirsty? Or getting more wine?

Ice? That made his balls want to shrivel, but he knew it was a possibility. *Sensation play.*

As long as she didn't plan on icing his balls, he'd probably be able to deal with it...

Footsteps came closer, and he turned his head in the direction of them, his eyes straining as if he might be able to see through the blindfold. Sadly, no. It was a really good blindfold.

At least now he knew none of the subs who had previously worn it had been lying when they said they couldn't see a thing. He'd liked using the blindfold because it had taken some of the pressure off him when he'd been the one leading the scene. Now, he liked it because it kept him guessing, but he also hated it because he liked watching Mistress Julie.

Seeing her kneeling between his legs, even though she'd just been tying him up, was going to give him fantasy fodder for weeks.

"You know what I realized, Connor?" she asked as she moved in front of him. Something brushed against the inside of his thigh, making him jerk, which moved all the ropes again.

"What, Mistress?" he asked. The strain in his voice was evident.

"I realized we skipped dessert. So, I thought I should have it now."

The slight hissing sound was the only warning he got before something cool and soft landed right on his dick.

Shit! Whipped cream!

The aerosol kind. It wasn't freezing, like ice, but it was cold enough to make him try to jerk away—which, of course, he couldn't. Both the chair and the ropes stopped him. A moment later, he was very thankful for that, as a hot tongue followed the path of the whipped cream, licking it off his dick.

Connor froze.

It wasn't a conscious decision, as though he thought she'd suddenly stop if he moved, but he felt her tongue and instinctively went stock still.

"Mmm."

Fuck. Just the sound of her pleasure made his cock throb in response, the air cool against where she'd just licked the cream from it.

The hissing noise and the chill swath that spread over the length of his cock was very welcome because now he knew what came next. Wet warmth slid over his length, lapping up the cream, making him shudder from the mixing sensations.

"Fuck..." The word came out as a guttural groan as her tongue teased the underside of his cock, all the way up to the extra sensitive tip.

"Not yet," she answered, teasing. He didn't get a chance to respond as she unleashed a whole pile of whipped cream onto the tip of his dick. He winced at the chilly sensation, then gasped as she didn't lick it off—no, she took the whole head of his cock into her mouth, sucking it off and laving her tongue over the tip for good measure.

Then she was gone again.

It was the most frustrating blowjob he'd ever received in his life and also the most thrilling.

Cool cream. The wet heat of her tongue or mouth. And then the retreat. Never giving him enough to truly work his way toward orgasm. Never doing more than what she needed to get her cream. Toying with him and the alternating chill and heat on his most sensitive parts.

She worked her way up and down the shaft, coming back to the tip several times as though she liked hearing him whimper. Connor didn't bother to hold back with the sounds he was making. Why fight it? It felt really fucking good, and he wanted her to know that.

The ache grew in his balls with every passing second, making him squirm in the seat, the ropes rubbing over his skin. She'd done a good job tying him; nothing tightened too much, but he was held securely in place too.

It was starting to drive him up the wall. The need was growing, and while he hadn't held back on the sounds he was making, he did hold back on the begging. Not because he was too proud but because he didn't want her to feel like she had to stop what she was doing if she wasn't ready. While he knew that a dominant would do what they wanted, he was trying really hard to show that he was fully submitting to her control.

That included not begging for anything specific.

Even though it was really fucking hard. As hard as his dick was. And right now, his dick felt like a steel bar. An aching steel bar.

"Fuck!" He practically bellowed the word as her mouth covered his tip again, but this time, instead of immediately moving away, her lips slid down the length, taking him deeper into the wet warmth. It took all of his willpower not to start begging her to just finish him then and there.

Julie

Pulling her head back up, Julie smiled as she lapped the last of the cream from Connor's cock. Giving head wasn't her favorite thing in the world, but she did love the way it brought a man to his knees—metaphorically, since Connor was currently tied in a position that wouldn't allow him to get on his knees.

She'd already taken the time to take off her clothes, so now she climbed up on Connor's lap. The impulse to impale herself on his cock was there, but she wanted to tease him a bit more. Since his mouth was already hanging open as he waited, it was very easy to pull his head forward so she could place her nipple between his lips.

Immediately, he realized what she was doing, and he sucked... *Hard.* Julie moaned as the sensation shot straight through her, making her insides clench. The tiny bud throbbed between his lips as his teeth scraped delicately over it, the pull of suction coming in pulses.

Closing her eyes, Julie squirmed on his lap, bringing the head of his cock around to rub against her labia, teasing both of them. When he moaned, releasing her nipple, she moved his head to the other one for the same treatment. Rocking on his lap, rubbing the tip of his cock along the wet length of her pussy, she moaned as he suckled her other nipple. The first one was still tightly budded, the air feeling cool against her wet skin, adding to her arousal as the second was engulfed in the warmth of his mouth.

The need was building up inside her, and she teased them both by sinking down a little onto his cock. He groaned again, his mouth still full of her nipple, then sucked even harder. Julie shuddered atop him, her muscles clenching around as much of his cock was inside her.

Then she let herself drop, sliding down his full length, filling herself up. With one leg on either side of him, she was riding him again, almost the same way she had in the Locker Room, but this time, he could lean against the chair, so she didn't have to worry about throwing him off balance. Her hands moved over the ropes, over his chest, and up to pull the blindfold off.

He blinked as he looked up at her, then she began to rise again, and the focused look in his eyes immediately shifted back to hazy. Capturing his lips with hers, Julie started moving.

Slowly.

Deliberately.

Taking her time, the way she hadn't been able to at Stronghold.

The way she'd wanted to.

And with him tied even more firmly in place than he had been at the club, she was able to do exactly what she wanted.

Up and down, rocking on him, leaving him tensing and shuddering as he did his best not to cum before her. She used him for her pleasure, grinding her clit against him. The movements made her nipples brush against the rope, stimulating her further as her passion grew, the pleasure swirling inside her.

Finally, she gave in to the urge to move faster, harder. Connor cried out beneath her, his hips attempting to thrust up, making the chair creak again.

"Come for me," she whispered. As her own peak neared, she impaled herself on his cock again. "Come for me, Connor."

Shuddering, throwing his head back, she felt his climax just as her own hit, her body clamping down around his cock as he released inside her. The staggering intimacy of the moment, of their mutual rapture, rocked her to her core both physically and emotionally.

It was the perfect moment.

Too perfect.

22

"There has to be something wrong with him."

"Or, and hear me out, maybe there's something wrong with you," Olivia countered.

Julie rolled her eyes even though she knew her friends couldn't see her. They were doing a three-way chat but without the video. She had pulled the starter out of the fridge this morning, so she could bake some loaves for the barbeque tomorrow. Connor was spending the day with his friends.

Was she hurt about not being invited to that? Only if the other girlfriends also weren't invited. Which she didn't know, and she hadn't asked. But if they were, and she hadn't been, then that would be a problem.

Olivia would tell me I'm looking for problems.

Which was why she hadn't said the words out loud.

"Nobody is perfect." Julie measured out the flour with her kitchen scale, moving by rote through the recipe. She'd made it once a week for the past year and barely had to think about it anymore.

"But he might be perfect for *you*," Camille chimed in.

Her positive outlook ever since she'd hooked up with Freddy had become almost nauseating. Not that Julie wanted her friend to be miserable again—before Freddy, she'd been both lonely and stuck in a terrible job—but a little cynicism now and again might be nice.

"Nobody is perfect, but that doesn't mean their imperfections are deal breakers."

"Says the Domme who actually has what is close to the perfect sub," Olivia teased. Her fiancé, Luke, had not been a submissive before he'd met Olivia, and there had definitely been some bumps on the road to happily ever after. Freddy, on the other hand, had been a club submissive for years before finally meeting and falling for Camille.

Camille snorted.

"You wouldn't think he was so perfect if you were living with him. The milk carton was empty again this morning when I went to get some for my coffee."

Both Olivia and Julie groaned in sympathy.

"Okay, so he has *one* flaw," Olivia admitted. "And it's not even *really* a flaw since you know he's leaving it there to remind himself to get more."

"Wouldn't it be a better reminder if it just wasn't there at all?" Camille hmphed. "And I know. I'm just cranky because my coffee didn't taste right this morning."

"Where is Freddy now?" Julie asked. She knew Camille wouldn't be griping if Freddy could overhear. It wasn't as if having a different system for the milk was a deal breaker, but it was one of the few hiccups the couple had hit since moving in together.

There was a moment of silence.

"At the store," Camille finally muttered begrudgingly.

Julie had to laugh, and she could hear Olivia doing the same. So, he was already in the process of fixing his so-called 'mistake.'

Camille cleared her throat, talking over her friends' laughter. "So maybe Connor's flaw will be equally benign."

Maybe. Or maybe it would slowly creep into their lives the longer they stayed together, until one day, she realized that there was a big problem that she'd never noticed because it had taken so long for it to grow big. Like a frog sitting in slowly heating water, only realizing too late that it was being cooked.

Yeah, she didn't have to say the words out loud to realize that some of her issues with John were rearing their ugly head again. Because she was introducing Connor to her family tomorrow? Because he was the first man she'd seriously dated since her divorce? Because her feelings for him were already growing faster than she was comfortable with?

Because of all the above?

Ding, ding, ding.

"You can't tell me we're not moving too fast," she said. At least she got to work some dough while she had this conversation. Stretching and folding worked her arm muscles and gave her something physical to do.

"What's too fast?" Camille asked. "Is there even such a thing as too fast?" She sounded way too much like Julie's therapist, Dr. Sime.

"Too fast is…" Julie huffed. "Too fast is getting in over your head emotionally without thinking through the ramifications. Too fast is feeling things before you really know the person. It's emotion based on nothing."

"So, you think your emotions for Connor are based on nothing?" Olivia's amusement was clear. "Not the fact that he's paid a lot of attention to your likes and dislikes and showered you with attention for a year before revealing himself? And after he did reveal himself, it turned out that what he wants from a sexual relationship is exactly what you want? And that he's just as attentive, if not more so, in person? And that you have a whole bunch in common?"

"Well, when you put it that way," Julie muttered. Yes, she and Connor liked a lot of the same things. Both of them enjoyed music, though she was a little pickier in her selections, but that just meant he was happy to listen to what she wanted to. They both liked action movies. Sure, his tastes ran more toward superheroes, while hers ran more toward *Jason Bourne*, but they'd both be happy watching each other's choices.

While she'd gotten an appreciation for independent films and documentaries while with John—since that was all he'd ever watch—she preferred things a little more lighthearted. A little less bleak. Why her ex had constantly wanted to watch depressing things, she'd never understood.

And Connor had already indicated a willingness to watch her movies with her, something John had only done a handful of times the entire time they were together. She'd stopped trying to watch with him after that because it wasn't worth the complaining and the constant critiques. She didn't care if there were plot holes big enough to drive a spaceship through. She just wanted to watch fun movies.

Considering how often she'd watched extremely depressing or even horrific movies for him, without complaining, she hadn't understood why he couldn't do the same for her.

Because he was a self-involved douchebag.

Right.

Connor wasn't.

"You're right." She sighed. "I know it's all in my head. I mean, I'm sure there will be a flaw eventually, but I do know some of my issues come from my own baggage."

"Don't worry," Camille's voice was full of false sympathy. "I'm sure some kind of flaw will reveal itself soon."

"Maybe he snores," Olivia suggested.

"He doesn't." At least, he hadn't the couple of nights they'd done sleepovers. Snoring wasn't a deal breaker for her, anyway. People couldn't help if they snored. Though, that would be the perfect example of a flaw that wouldn't cause her to run, which was probably Olivia's point.

"Maybe he doesn't return the shopping cart at the grocery store."

"Maybe he only does laundry once a month."

"Maybe he slurps his soup."

Julie started laughing as her friends threw out suggestions of things Connor might do, but she was pretty sure he didn't. Shaking her head, she moved her dough to the two Dutch ovens she had prepped for the job and put them in before going to wash her hands.

"You two are ridiculous," she admonished as she cleaned off her hands. But they'd done what they'd meant to do—cheered her up and reminded her that not all flaws meant the end of things. It was a good reminder. Connor wasn't John. Even at the beginning of her relationship with John, there had been little things she'd ignored. Little signs. They hadn't been obvious red flags, but there had been things she'd put up with that she hadn't wanted to—like the movies —because everything else had been so good. Especially the sex.

It wasn't until later that she realized the little things—like not letting her enjoy the movies she wanted to watch with him—were signs of bigger underlying problems.

There hadn't been anything like that with Connor so far.

———

Connor

A long tentacle reached up out of the water, and then another... and another... and another... it wrapped around the boat as screams filled the air, the terrified occupants bumping into each other on their way to a watery doom.

"I thought this was a megalodon movie," Asad said, frowning, looking up from his phone. "Why is there a kraken? Where did that come from? What did I miss?"

"Maybe it's a megapus?" Q suggested. "You know, like sharktopus? We haven't actually seen anything except the tentacles."

They were all gathered on Connor's couch, taking a guy's day. So far, that meant eating food and watching a double feature of megalodon movies.

"This is nothing like the books," Law muttered, then sighed. He'd been repeating that same complaint throughout most of the movie, though he seemed to be enjoying the utter ridiculousness. Apparently, the first movie followed the book more closely. Law raised his voice, even though he wasn't seated that far away from Asad. "You'd know what was going on if you were actually watching instead of staring at your phone."

"Hey, I enjoy bad shark movies—or bad megalodon movies—as

much as the next person, but I don't usually consider them movies you have to pay close attention to," Asad countered. "I just..."

"He's looking at strap-ons," Connor said after leaning over to get a peek. They were easy to identify because he'd been looking at similar things recently. Not to buy, since he was sure Mistress Julie had her own, but just to get an idea of what was out there. He frowned. "Why are you looking at strap-ons?"

"Why shouldn't he be?" Q asked. "Hold on." Grabbing the remote, he paused the movie.

"Oh, yeah, because we don't want to miss anything," Law muttered again. He seemed to be taking the epic lack of science-based plotting in this particular movie very personally. "Then the movie might not make sense." The sarcasm lacing his voice made Connor chuckle.

The movie already didn't make a lot of sense, but he was enjoying it that way.

"I didn't mean to make this a thing." Asad dropped his phone in his lap, running his fingers through his dark hair as he lifted his head to look at the screen again, where it was frozen on people creeping through the island jungle. "Start the movie again."

"No, no, which strap-ons were you looking at?" Q turned around from where he was sitting on the floor. "Maybe I can offer suggestions."

"Are you getting a strap-on for Morgan?" Connor asked in surprise. Yeah, they'd talked about the whole pegging thing, but it wasn't like he'd actually thought Asad would go through with it. Even if he didn't like being left out of things.

"No, he's not," Law said firmly. "He's just letting himself be influenced by Q."

"No, he's not," Q argued back in an uncanny echo. "He's interested in something, and you should support your friend in things that interest them, even if they don't interest you."

"I'm supporting him in not being unduly swayed just because one of his friends wants to make a club around a single sexual act." Law glared at Q from where he was sitting in the corner of the sectional, crossing his arms over his chest.

It was the battle of the balds.

Somehow, Connor managed to keep a straight face when it popped into his head, which he was grateful for. He did *not* want to have to explain that thought to his friends. Neither of them was particularly sensitive about being bald—in fact, they teased each other about it constantly—but there were some undercurrents to this conversation that he couldn't figure out, and he didn't want to get in the middle of.

"Okay, well, while you guys are figuring out whether I actually want my girlfriend to peg me, I'm going to go to the bathroom," Asad said, getting to his feet. "Might as well since the movie is paused."

Q gave him a thumbs-up while Law sighed and uncrossed his arms. As soon as Asad was in the bathroom and out of earshot, Connor looked back and forth between the other two.

"What is going on?" he asked in a low voice. "Why do you both care so much whether or not Asad buys a strap-on?"

The other two looked at each other, guilt creeping into both their expressions.

"You can't tell Asad..." Q kept his voice even lower than Connor had. "We made a bet."

"You what?" His voice rose on the second word; he couldn't help it. They were betting on whether Asad decided to be pegged? What the hell?

On the other hand, how very like them.

"Shh!" Law and Q shushed him at the same time.

"It's harmless. He'll make the decision on his own," Law said, leaning toward them so his voice wouldn't carry down the hall and through the door where Asad was.

"Except that you're both trying to push him to do what you want. And you're being weird about it." Connor shook his head, rubbing his hand over his face while he tried to decide if he should tell them to cut it out. Though, ultimately, it was harmless. Betting on friends was practically a time-honored past-time at Stronghold, though usually it was about relationships and when people would get together, not on whether they'd take it in the ass. "What does the winner get?"

"If I win, Law has to let Iris peg him if she wants to," Q said with a grin, making Connor choke. Holy fuck.

"And if I win, Q has to wear the couple's costume that Sam wants for this year." Law didn't grin, but there was smug satisfaction in his voice.

"What's the costume?" Those two things seemed a little uneven to Connor, but Law appeared to be very happy with his choice. Q slumped as soon as Connor asked.

"She wants to be Han Solo and Princess Leia in the bikini... but she saw a picture online, and she wants to be Han Solo, and she wants Q to be Princess Leia." Law smirked. "Though in the pic she saw, there's no bra, but it's got everything else."

"She should be the one in the bikini." Q's gaze unfocused, the corners of his lips twisting up. "She'd look amazing."

Connor was pretty sure there wasn't a straight guy alive who hadn't had some fantasy of his girlfriend dressed in the Leia bikini, so he couldn't blame Q for wanting to see Sam in it. On the other hand, he also thought the genderbent version sounded pretty great.

"So, the timeline is Asad has to get pegged—or not—by Halloween?"

"Pretty much." Q cleared his throat as the door to the bathroom opened, raising his voice a little. "So, you should invite Julie to come with us to Renn Fair next weekend."

"I'll ask her tomorrow after the thing with her family." Asking her to come with him and his friends to the Renaissance Festival wasn't quite the same as being introduced to the family, but it was still kind of a big thing. He also wasn't sure how she'd take it. While they'd talked about how he was kind of a nerd—as if the action figure collection on his bookshelf hadn't been a clue—he wasn't sure if she knew how far that would go. Somehow, he didn't peg her for a Renn Fair person, but he could be wrong.

First, though, he needed to get through tomorrow.

"Okay, let's start the movie again. I need to find out what this giant octopus is doing in a megalodon movie," Asad said, walking toward them and gesturing at the television.

They all settled back onto the couch, and Q hit the play button.

Connor sat back and wondered if he should say something to Asad or just see it play out.

He was probably going to go ahead and see what happened.

23

<u>CONNOR</u>

The noise coming from the backyard as they approached the gate in the fence was what made him realize that maybe he'd gotten in over his head.

"How many people did you say are going to be here today?" he asked Julie, not bothering to lower his voice because he doubted anyone on the other side of the fence would be able to hear them, anyway. The fence was solidly built with vertical slats that made it impossible to see through unless you were right up next to it, and tall enough that even he wouldn't be able to see over it until they were closer.

The little path of stones leading from the driveway around to the back suddenly seemed far too short.

As soon as they'd pulled up to the house, he'd been surprised by the number of cars parked in the driveway and along the street, but the house next door also had balloons on their mailbox. He'd figured at least some, if not most, of the cars were there for whoever was having a party. Now, he was wondering if he had been wildly incorrect.

"I didn't," she replied a little grimly. "I just said my family. I don't know how many of them will actually be there, but probably most of us."

The path was almost at its end, and Connor could see over the fence now. Not that he could see much because the gate was on the side of the house rather than right at the back, so he only had a partial view of the backyard. Enough to know it was full of people. Almost all of whom had black or grey hair, though he did spot a blond man and a woman with auburn hair.

"It'll be fine," Julie said, though from her tone, he wasn't sure if she was talking to him or to herself. It really could go either way. "We don't have to stay the whole time."

"No, I want to." He was determined to impress her family. Even though she hadn't said it, and she'd tried to downplay it, he could tell this was a big deal to her. She wanted this to go well. "Don't cut the visit short on my account. I'll be fine."

Glancing up at him, she smiled, though it looked a little forced.

"We'll see," was all she said before reaching out to open the gate.

No one turned as it swung open, and they were able to approach the crowd in the backyard without drawing too many eyes to them—at least, until they reached the edge of people, and several of them caught a glimpse of Connor. He towered above everyone in the yard, which was normal, making him impossible to miss. He did his best not to hunch his shoulders as a slow ripple of quiet spread through Julie's family, those who were facing him looking with either wide eyes, dropped jaws, or both, only for whoever they were talking with to turn around and see what they were looking at. Which meant more wide eyes and dropped jaws.

"Hey, everyone," Julie said loudly, her voice carrying. "This is my boyfriend—"

Before she could say his name, she was cut off by a scream.

"Aaaaah!" Out of the crowd, Sandra—Sandra from his work, his work wife Sandra—suddenly jumped in front of both of them, pointing at Connor. Then her finger swung to point at Julie as she let out a second cry. "Aaaaah!"

Now it was Connor's turn for the jaw drop as he stared at his coworker.

"Sandra?"

Her finger swung back around to him.

"Aaaaaah!"

Julie stepped forward, batting Sandra's pointing finger away.

"Would you stop that?!"

Instead, Sandra swung around to glare at an older woman, pointing at her. She blinked in surprise.

"You said Jules' boyfriend's *last* name was Connor!" It was a clear accusation of misinformation.

"I thought it was!" The older woman turned to look at another couple, a man and a woman who looked an awful lot like Julie with just a few more wrinkles and grey hair. Her arm was in a sling. "You said his last name was Connor."

"Of course I did. What kind of first name is Connor?" The woman with her arm in a sling frowned at him. Julie slapped her forehead with her own palm.

"Oh my God, Mom. You set the aunties and cousins on him, and you couldn't even get the name right?" Julie groaned, shaking her head before lifting it. "And it's a pretty common first name."

Ah, shit. Those were Julie's parents. So much for a good first impression. But Sandra was Julie's cousin, apparently, so maybe she could put in a good word for him. If she wanted to. Right now, she had her hands on her hips and was glaring at him.

He looked down at her.

"Um. Hi?"

"You're dating my cousin, and you didn't tell me?!" She was five feet of total outrage, demanding his focus, which meant he couldn't pay attention to what Julie and her mom were arguing about. Not that he wanted to be part of an argument about his name. That seemed like something he could let her handle for him.

"In my defense, I didn't know until just this moment that she's your cousin. I told you I was dating a Julie." If he'd given her a last name, she wouldn't have even needed to look it up on the internet.

And she might have told her mom, who would have told Julie's parents before Julie had the chance to. So, he wasn't exactly sad at how things had worked out. "You didn't think to mention you had a cousin named Julie?"

Sandra threw her hands up in the air in obvious frustration.

"We call her Jules! And Julie is a super common name! And… well, Jules never dates anyone, so why would I think she was dating you? Argh!" She stomped her foot in frustration as her husband, Terry, who Connor had met a couple of times, came up behind her. Tall with dark blond hair, he must have been inside or tucked away in a corner when Connor first came into the backyard. If he'd seen Terry, he would have realized Sandra was around somewhere.

"Hey, man, welcome to the family," Terry said cheerfully, a mischievous glint in his eye as he reached out a hand for Connor to take. They clasped hands for just a moment while Sandra elbowed her husband in the side.

"Hey, now, don't scare him off. Jules finally brought someone around. We need to keep him." She brightened. "Plus, if they do get married, we'll be related!"

"Now, who's going to scare him off?" Terry laughed, and Sandra scowled at him.

She didn't get a chance to respond, though, before Julie turned back to them, her parents beside her. The tension in her body was clear; she held herself stiffly. To Sandra's credit, she immediately moved away, saying something to Terry that had him nodding as they went.

"Connor, these are my parents, Sun and Daniel." Her smile was a little strained, but she moved back to his side so she could face her parents while holding his hand. "Mom, Dad, this is Connor."

"Hello, it's so nice to meet you," Connor said, putting his hand out. He wasn't sure who to put his hand to first, so he kind of put it toward their general direction. Julie's father took it first. He was only a little taller than Julie, so he had to tilt his head back a fair amount to look up at Connor.

"Nice to meet you, Connor," Daniel said, taking Connor's hand in a firm grip. Connor shook it before they released, and he offered his hand to Julie's mom. At his side, Julie had a death grip on his other hand.

Her mom really did look an awful lot like Julie, and he'd seen this exact look on Julie's face before. Blank, not giving away anything... which meant that she was displeased but refusing to show it.

Great.

"Nice to meet you," she said in a short, clipped voice. It didn't sound like she actually thought it was nice, so he was glad that Julie had prepared him for her parents' lack of welcome. At least he knew it wasn't personal. They'd gotten to know and love her ex-husband, welcomed him to the family, and were still struggling with letting go.

Hopefully, they'd give him enough of a chance that he could get them warmed up to him.

"Okay, well, I'm going to take Connor around and introduce him to everyone... and also go grab us a drink."

"Drinks are in the kitchen," her mom said.

"I know," Julie muttered, tugging on Connor's hand to lead him away.

He went with her, smiling at her parents as best he could, not sure of what else to do. There were an awful lot of people to meet, but he'd really wanted to make a better impression on her parents. That was hard to do if he wasn't going to be given the opportunity to talk to them. On the other hand, he also needed to be here for Julie and what she wanted. So, he let her lead him away.

Rather than introducing him to anyone, she took him straight into the back of the house, quickly closing the door behind them.

"My parents have two cats," she explained as she did so. "They like to try to escape. But you probably won't see them unless they're streaking past you out the door. They really don't like people other than my parents."

"Gotcha." He'd known cats like that. His grandmother's cat had rarely let anyone near her. Connor had eventually gotten her to come sit with him, but whether he'd be allowed to pet her was always up in the air. Sometimes, yes; sometimes, he got his hand scratched for his efforts.

It seemed as though almost everyone was in the backyard. The house was quiet and empty. The door had opened right into the kitchen, and she headed over to the coolers that lined the wall next to the fridge.

"What do you want?" she asked. "There's water, beer, wine, sodas..."

"A soda would be good," he said. At his size, he could definitely handle his alcohol, but he wasn't sure how her parents would feel about him drinking the moment he showed up. He'd rather be firing on all cylinders, anyway. "Thank you."

"No problem." As she bent over to open one of the coolers, movement out of the corner of his eye caught his attention. He turned to look into the room that was connected to the kitchen. It looked like a living room with a couch and a coffee table. He didn't have a full view, so he couldn't see what else was in the room, but what surprised him —after Julie's previous statement—was that the movement had been a cat. Not just any cat, either. It was the kind of cat he'd only ever seen in pictures—totally hairless.

Awed, he was drawn toward it. He'd never known anyone who had a hairless cat. It was pale with huge blue eyes that watched him unblinkingly as he slowly moved closer. Despite Julie's claims of unfriendliness, it didn't go running or even look like it was unhappy to see him coming into its space.

Sitting on the glass coffee table, it held completely still.

"Connor?" Julie asked from behind him.

"Shh, I'm almost to him," he whispered, not wanting the cat to run. He really wanted to touch it, just to see what it felt like.

"Oh, that's Avery," she said, a little closer to him now. Obviously close enough that she could see the cat. "He's the slightly friendlier one, though I'm surprised he's out right now. Normally, when the backyard is full, they don't leave the second floor."

"Hi, Avery," Connor crooned. He was close enough now to stoop down a little and rub his finger over the cat's head. Rather than running, Avery leaned into the touch, purring. His skin was soft, softer than Connor expected, and warm. Different from fur, definitely, but the reaction from Avery was the same.

"Well, shit." Julie sounded very surprised. "He likes you."

Turning his hand, Connor kept an eye on the cat as he moved his hand down Avery's head to scratch his neck. The cat kept purring, stretching out his neck and turning his head to let Connor scratch under his chin.

"Wow. He *really* likes you."

Fairly certain that the cat wasn't going to suddenly attack him, Connor kept giving him scritches while he looked down at the glass table the cat was sitting on. There were several odd circular marks on it, far too small to be from a glass or cup and definitely not something that looked like it was supposed to be on the surface.

"What is that?" he asked, reaching down with his other hand to rub one of them and see if it came off.

"Don't touch that!" Julie's sudden command made him jerk back from both the coffee table and the cat.

Avery yowled indignantly as Connor pulled away. Tipping his nose in the air, the cat stood up with a faint popping sound.

What the...

It wasn't until Avery hopped down from the table, leaving behind a little circular spot on the glass—just like the one Connor had been about to rub—right where he'd been sitting that Connor started to understand. He stared at the little circle.

"They have no hair, so they get kind of... suctioned to the glass when they sit on it. I keep telling my parents to get a different kind of table, but mom likes the glass one, so she usually just cleans it twice a day..." Julie's voice trailed off, caught somewhere between exasperation and amusement.

"Thank you so much for not letting me touch it," Connor said, straightening up. He hadn't thought about that aspect of a hairless cat. Butt marks on the furniture... good grief.

Granted, he knew cats put their butts on everything—that was a running joke of most cat owners he knew—but they didn't usually leave behind such clear evidence. Most people got to be 'out of sight, out of mind' about it.

"You're welcome," Julie grinned at him as she handed him a soda. She'd gotten herself a glass of wine. "Okay, everyone should have had enough time to talk about us and get used to the idea that I really did show up with a new boyfriend, so we can go back out there, and hopefully, it will be a little less awkward."

Ah, so that was why she'd gotten them inside the house right away. That made sense and made him feel a little better about being introduced to her parents, then immediately dragged away. It was just to let her family take a minute. If he was really lucky, Sandra had taken that time to talk him up.

"I can't believe I didn't realize you worked with Sandra," she said, as though his own thoughts of Sandra had summoned hers. "But I have so many cousins, I never remember the names of the places where they work."

"And there are a lot of physical therapy places around here," he said reassuringly. "I doubt you would have expected us to be at the same one."

"Honestly, I'm not sure I even remembered that she's a physical therapist," Julie confessed as they walked through the kitchen. "I..."

Her voice trailed off as they faced the large back window and sliding glass door. The entire yard was visible through it, and it only took Connor a moment to realize there was a newcomer to the party. Mostly because he stood out, as he was tall, white, and standing in the middle of a small circle of people, throwing his head back in jovial laughter.

"Fuck." Julie cursed.

"What?" Connor felt a sneaking suspicion in his stomach, as if something really bad was about to happen. Surely her parents wouldn't have...

"That's my ex."

Apparently, her parents had.

24

JULIE

Her parents had invited John.

Again.

She wanted to scream into the void.

Actually, she wanted to scream at her parents, but truthfully, that was about as useful as screaming into the void, and at least the void didn't scream back.

"We should go." Dammit.

"What? No. Don't let him chase you off." Connor gave her hand a squeeze. "This is *your* parents' house. This is *your* family. And we came here today so I could meet them and help get them off your back. If we leave now, he not only wins, but we don't get to show your family how much better off you are without him."

Emotions were tumbling through her, making her stomach churn like a washing machine. The problem was none of them were coming out clean. None of them were coming out clear. The waters were full of mud, and as much as she wanted to leave and hold the boundary that she'd set down with her parents, Connor had a point.

This was *her* family. This was *her* parents' house. Why should she have to be the one to leave?

Because the second my parents get an inch, they'll take a mile.

Dammit. She didn't know what to do. She needed a minute to think.

She needed John to disappear.

It wasn't like she wanted him to get hit by a bus or anything (probably), but a transfer to a hospital on the other side of the country would be nice.

"Come on, we've got this." Connor smiled at her and stepped forward, and since her hand was still in his, she found herself being pulled along with him. And because she wasn't sure she should leave, she found herself going... even though she wasn't sure that was what she wanted to do.

The blow of having her parents invite John, knowing she was bringing Connor to meet the family today, had rocked her off her axis. And Connor wasn't giving her time to regain her equilibrium. They were outside and back in the middle of her family before she realized she really did not want to be there.

"Hello. I'm so sorry about the mix-up with your name," Aunt Ji-woo said, coming up to Connor with an apologetic look on her face. Julie was pretty sure she even meant it. Sandra's mom was a lot more relaxed than her own mother. Who was currently over-talking and laughing with her ex-husband, showing him a lot more welcome than she had Connor.

Dammit.

They should have left.

But she couldn't pull away from the conversation without being rude, and if she could get Aunt Ji-woo on her side, she didn't want to ruin that by being rude to her.

"No problem." Connor smiled his most charming smile at her aunt, who automatically smiled back at him. He was *on* in a way she hadn't really seen before. "I'm grateful, actually, since it let us tell everyone on our own terms. And I missed out at least on several days of being hassled by Sandra at work about the fact that I'm dating her cousin."

"That is quite a coincidence," Aunt Ji-woo said, smiling at him.

"I'm sure Sandra will make up for it now. She's talked about you before, but I had forgotten your name because she calls you 'work hubby' all the time."

Okay, well, now was definitely not the time to get jealous. Julie realized that she'd heard Sandra mention her 'work hubby' before, too. There was no harm in it. Sandra and Terry were utterly devoted to each other, and she knew it. Sandra had never talked about her work hubby in anything but friendly terms.

It was probably only bothering her a little because she was already out of sorts, knowing John was less than ten feet away, talking to her parents. No, less than less than ten feet away because, for some reason, her mom was bringing him over.

Are you fucking kidding me?

If it wasn't for Connor standing there holding his ground, she would have walked out. And she wasn't sure she would have come back again. Ever. There had to be an end to this. Even though she knew it was likely her parents wouldn't have invited John today if she hadn't been bringing Connor, the fact they were willing to do so at all made her want to scream. It had been one thing having to hear updates about his life and a whole other thing to have her mom invite him over when she knew Julie was going to be there, but this was too far.

They should have left, and she was starting to get pretty peeved that Connor had taken that decision away from her.

The only joy she got out of this moment was the slightly stunned expression on John's face as he realized exactly how tall Connor was. Not just tall but muscular. John had always prided himself on his physique, but Connor was taller, his shoulders were wider, and his body was packed with twice as much bulky muscle as John's.

Not the kind of thing that mattered to Julie, but it suddenly struck her that it was very much the kind of thing that would matter to John. His insecurities ran wide and deep.

"There you are," her mother said, as if Julie had been gone for a lot longer than the five minutes they had been inside. "This is John. John, this is Connor."

"I'm Julie's ex-husband," John said, seemingly recovered from his shock. He gave his widest, most charming smile as he held out his hand for Connor to shake. "I hope that's not too awkward. When you become part of the family, it can be hard to leave that."

"Not awkward at all," Connor said, sounding completely sincere, despite the fact that this was incredibly awkward. "It's nice to meet you. I've heard about you, of course. Julie said you're a surgeon?" She couldn't believe that the first thing her mom had done was to introduce her current boyfriend to her ex-husband.

No, wait, scratch that. She totally believed it.

Which was why they should have left.

It was all she could do to stand there seething instead of exploding all over everyone. She was just so damn mad at all of them.

Her mom for inviting John.

John for showing up.

The rest of her family for acting like this was somehow normal.

Connor for deciding they were coming outside.

Herself for feeling like she had to stay here just because Connor wanted to.

At least her dad had had the good sense to make himself scarce once John appeared. Unlike her mom, who had decided to force the issue. Why couldn't she just turn around and walk away right now? Yes, Connor was holding onto her hand, but he would let go if she pulled away.

But then her whole family would see her walk out, abandoning her boyfriend there.

It would be clear they weren't working as a unit.

Her mom would see the crack between them and work even harder to push at them.

Which, if she and Connor broke up over this, she did not want it to be because of her parents. It would be because she'd decided that was the best thing to do. And she wasn't sure yet that she wanted to break up with him over this... but was that because she truly didn't or because she didn't want her mom to win?

She couldn't think. Not with everyone standing right there around her.

"Ah, yes," John cleared his throat, looking increasingly uncomfortable, which was the only joy she was getting out of the situation. Connor's obvious confidence in the face of meeting her ex had clearly thrown him. He'd probably expected Connor to react the way he would—with anger or insult. "Head of surgery, actually. I was just telling Sun that we might need to talk about her shoulder." He pushed his smile back onto his lips. "It's the least I can do for family."

"Hopefully, surgery won't be necessary, but I appreciate the concern," her mom said, beaming at John as though he'd just offered her the moon. Because, of course, she did. "I don't even know what's wrong with it. I didn't hit it or do anything; it just started hurting one day, and it keeps getting worse, no matter how much I rest it."

"You didn't injure it when that started?" Connor asked, frowning.

"No, nothing. I noticed it was sore one morning, so I started resting it, but it doesn't seem to have helped. I can't move it as much as I want to, but I don't know what else to do."

"Which is why we need to take a look and discuss surgical options," John said pompously. At least, it sounded pompous to Julie, but her mom didn't seem to notice, so maybe she was a little biased. Or maybe her mom was.

"Do you mind if I take a look at your range of motion?" Connor asked, leaning forward slightly, seeming to ignore John's remark.

Her mom blinked in surprise.

"Oh, well..."

Connor smiled at her easily, totally focused on her, though his grip on Julie's hand remained firm.

"We get a lot of shoulder injuries and other issues at the clinic. Did you have Sandra look at it?" he asked.

"No." Her mom was frowning, but not as if she was upset. "What do you need me to do?"

"Can you hold this?" Connor asked Julie, holding out his cup. Dropping his hand, she took it, allowing him to step forward. It was a good opportunity to run. She could leave John and Connor there competing to see who could impress her mom the most, but at the same time, she felt stuck in place. She didn't really want her mom to have to have surgery, and she was strangely fascinated by this other side of Connor.

It struck her that this was his work side. When he'd gone "on" for her family, that was probably the Connor his clients got to see. He was still "on" right now, handling her mom in a completely professional, firm, caring manner that seemed to have thrown John completely off.

Then again, John wasn't used to being ignored or questioned. And he could hardly try to physically intimidate Connor the way he might someone else. Did she get more joy than she should out of that? Yes, yes, she did, no matter how irritated she was at Connor.

Connor helped her mom out of the sling, murmuring soft instructions as he worked through her range of motion. It wasn't much, and Julie could see how much it distressed and worried her mom that she couldn't move the way she should be able to. It distressed Julie, too. Was this why her mom had been calling John lately? Because she was worried about her shoulder?

No, don't do that. Don't justify it. That way lies madness. If she was worried, she could make an appointment to see a doctor. One who isn't my ex-husband. And she was constantly giving me updates about him and pushing my boundaries long before her shoulder was an issue.

Julie took a deep breath.

"I think it's frozen shoulder," Connor said. "You shouldn't need surgery. Frozen shoulder even goes away on its own sometimes, but physical therapy can help you get back to normal faster."

Scoffing, John stepped forward, puffing up his chest. "You're hardly an expert on whether or not someone needs surgery."

"No, but I am an expert on when someone needs physical therapy," Connor said cheerfully, stepping back to take his place beside Julie again. He looked at her mom. "You should get a second opinion if you feel more comfortable with that, but I'm pretty confident that it's frozen shoulder."

"What is that?" Julie asked. "What causes it?"

"A number of things," Sandra said, pushing her way into their little circle and pulling Terry with her. Julie's cousin beamed at Connor. "Sometimes, it just happens to women over the age of thirty-five, and we don't really know why. Basically, your shoulder starts to hurt and becomes harder to move. Of course, most of us do exactly what your mom did and rest it, which actually makes it worse because it gets more frozen." She looked at Julie's mom. "I told Mom to tell you that it sounded like frozen shoulder. Did she not tell you?"

"She did." Julie's mom had the grace to look slightly abashed. "I just wanted to get a second opinion from John."

John looked like he had bitten into something sour.

He probably wanted to say something nasty to Connor about his competence, but he could hardly do that now without casting aspersions on Sandra, too. Regardless of her mom wanting his opinion, she wouldn't take him insulting her niece well.

It was kind of fun to watch him struggle with the dilemma.

"Oh, it looks like your dad could use some help," Connor said, giving her hand a squeeze. "I'll be right back."

Julie started. She didn't even know where her dad had gotten off to, but now that she looked in the direction Connor was headed, she could see her dad trying to get out the back door with a huge tray of meat in his hands. Normally, her mom would have been helping him with the door, but she'd been too busy talking to John.

Connor had both noticed and immediately gone to help.

It didn't sweep away her annoyance with him entirely, but it didn't hurt, either.

"Hmph. Well, if you want to come in for some x-rays, just let me know, Sun," John said.

"Thank you, John." But her mom wasn't looking at him. She was watching Connor as he intercepted Julie's dad, taking the whole tray of meat in one hand. Making a face, John turned away and walked over to where some of Julie's other cousins were talking. Annoyingly, they welcomed him immediately.

Sandra stepped up beside Julie. Terry was now making his way over to her dad and Connor, probably to see if he could help with anything.

"Aren't they great?" Sandra asked, sighing happily as Terry joined the other two. Now, all three of them were standing around the grill, talking about who knows what.

"Yeah," Julie echoed, wishing she felt it to her bones the way Sandra seemed to. The way she had before this afternoon. "Great."

25

CONNOR

Straining his muscles, Connor gritted his teeth as he stood up straight, forcing his arms to rise into the air to the delighted screams of the children hanging from them. He had four hanging from each arm.

They'd been adding one kid on each lift, and he wasn't sure that he could take five on each arm. He also wasn't sure they'd be able to fit, anyway.

Holding the pose for a moment, he dropped back into a squat, so their feet were back on the ground—though the shortest ones had to drop an inch or two when they let go. Applause broke out around them from the watching adults—sadly, Julie wasn't one of them. She was across the yard, talking to some of her cousins.

John was there, though, scowling at Connor. Likely because his conversation had been interrupted when the people he'd been talking to had turned to see what was going on. Connor ignored the man. He could tell a bitter ex when he saw one. John wasn't his problem, though, other than the obstacle he posed to Connor's goals.

He wanted to make this afternoon nice for Julie. John's presence had definitely thrown her and made the afternoon more of a chore than a joy. Why the man was still hovering around, Connor didn't completely understand.

The only conversation Connor had overheard him having had been bragging about a particularly difficult surgery he'd performed recently. Which was impressive, but Connor had overheard the story at least three different times now, and he wasn't even trying to listen to the man. Quite a few people seemed impressed by him, though.

He did notice that Sandra and her husband weren't part of any of the groups talking to him. Whether that was in support of Connor or just because they didn't like John, he wasn't sure.

"You're so strong!" One of the little girls, he was pretty sure her name was Mari, wrapped her arms around his leg, beaming up at him. "How did you get so strong?"

"Eating lots of veggies," he said, winking down at her.

There was a whole play area set up for the kids, but somehow, he'd become the more interesting toy. He wasn't sure how it had happened. One of the little boys had asked him how much he could lift, and it had snowballed from there.

"I need some veggies! Where are the veggies?" One of the other kids yelled and started running toward the food table. It started a bit of a stampede, which made Connor laugh. As he was watching the kids, he noticed Julie's dad at the very full trash can on the edge of the patio, pulling up the edges of the plastic bag, then struggling to actually pull the bag from the trash can.

Connor headed over, crossing the distance in a few short strides.

"Can I help?" he asked.

"If you can get it out, I'll put the new bag in. I think I accidentally vacuum-sealed this one in the can." Daniel chuckled, straightening up and stepping back.

He had, but it still only took Connor a few seconds to work it out of the trashcan.

"Thank you," Daniel said, shaking out the new bag and eying Connor.

"Of course." He hefted the full bag. "What should I do with this?"

"I've got it. I just needed help getting it out." Daniel slid the new, empty bag into the trashcan, pulling the edges over the lip to keep it in place.

"Are you sure? I don't mind."

Pausing, Daniel looked up at him. "Are you trying to impress me?"

"Well... yes," Connor replied honestly. "But not with the trash. It just seems rude to pull it out, then run."

That made Daniel laugh.

"Okay, well, you can take it around to the side of the house." He pointed to the side that didn't have the gate. "We'll deal with it after the party. If you're still around, I'll let you take it to the front then."

"No problem, we don't have any other plans for today." Hefting the trash bag up, he took it around to the side of the house. It wasn't hard to tell where it went since there was already a full bag sitting there. He set his bag down next to it.

When he turned around, John was standing on the side of the house, fists planted on his hips, between Connor and the party.

"Do you need something?" Connor asked, walking toward the other man. He wasn't worried about getting around John if he needed to, but he'd really rather this not turn physical. Julie wouldn't like that. Her parents probably wouldn't either. They seemed pretty attached to the guy, even though he was no longer their son-in-law.

"From you? No. I just want to be clear; I'm not going anywhere. Deep down, Julie knows we belong together. She only brought you to try to prove a point to her parents. She's fighting the inevitable, and that's why she's fighting so hard. She doesn't like to feel out of control... but us getting back together *is* inevitable." Clenching his jaw, John nodded firmly as he crossed his arms over his chest. The fact that he had to tilt his head back to keep his gaze level with Connor's as Connor got closer clearly irked him.

"Okay," Connor said easily, stepping around the other man as his jaw dropped with shock.

"Hey! Didn't you hear me?"

He didn't look over his shoulder to see what John's expression looked like, but he could hear the stupefied shock in the man's voice.

"Yup."

There was no point in talking to a blowhard like him. He was so wrapped up in his own self-importance, it wouldn't matter what Connor said. So, he wouldn't waste his breath. John didn't matter; Julie did. If she still had feelings for John, she wouldn't have started dating Connor. And she sure as hell wouldn't have brought him to meet her parents just to prove a point.

All John had just proven was that he didn't actually know who Julie was at her core. Didn't matter that he'd been married to her. He clearly thought she was something she wasn't.

Why he was so wrapped up in getting her back was no hardship —she was probably the best thing that had ever happened to him, then he'd lost her. Connor had sympathy but no patience for it.

Walking back out into the backyard, he found himself immediately mobbed by children, all showing him the veggies they'd gotten to eat.

"Wow! You're all going to grow so big and strong!" he said, holding his hands out in front of him. Two of the kids grabbed his hands, and he found himself being pulled along. Which was fine. He loved playing with kids and didn't mind at all being their personal playground.

---

*J*ULIE

"So... is everything... you know. Proportional?" Sandra asked in a low whisper, watching Connor getting mobbed by the kids.

"You. Are. Married."

"I'm still curious. Not to find out for myself, but like... he's a freaking mountain. Just because I'm not attracted doesn't mean I'm not curious." Sandra raised her eyebrow at her. "You've never seen a guy that you're like, 'well, I'm not into him, but I'd go for some curiosity sex?'"

The urge to facepalm was strong. That was Sandra, though. They weren't particularly close in that they didn't hang out or talk much outside of the family gatherings, but they were close in that during family gatherings, they tended to band together. Part of it was just being the same age and both girls. Part of it was that she normally enjoyed the outrageous things that came out of Sandra's mouth.

If they'd been talking about anyone but Connor, Julie would have found this conversation much more entertaining. However, since they *were* talking about Connor, she wasn't sure she wanted to think about how many women would want to have sex with him just out of curiosity.

It didn't help that she was still annoyed with him and getting more so, even though she knew the emotions weren't entirely rational.

Things would have been so different if John wasn't here. If John wasn't here, she would have enjoyed seeing her family slowly falling for Connor. She would have preened with how well he was getting along with everyone, would have been laughing at his antics with the kids, and would have felt pride at how he jumped to lend a hand.

In contrast, John was wandering around the backyard bragging about his recent promotion to each of her relatives in turn. He hadn't lifted a hand to help with anything the entire time he'd been here—hell, for the entirety of their relationship. He definitely wasn't interacting with the kids. He never had unless he had to, and most of the kids didn't want anything to do with him.

She didn't think he'd ever gotten either of her parents' cats within five feet of him the entire time they'd been together.

The fact she couldn't just enjoy how amazing Connor was being pissed her off even more.

Because they should have left.

But he'd pulled her outside because that was where he wanted to be. And now she had to question everything he was doing. Was he playing with the kids to make himself look good? Was he buttering up her parents to make a good impression? Or was he actually enjoying playing with the kids and was his first impulse to step in and help where he could?

Before today, she would have unequivocally said the latter.

Before he'd ignored what she wanted, before he hadn't given her the time to think and make her own choice, she would have been absolutely certain of his motivations.

Now, she was second guessing everything. Second guessing how well she could read him. Second guessing how well she really knew him.

As her mother walked up to her, Julie stiffened. She was still righteously pissed at her mom for inviting John. Sandra coughed, obviously unwilling to continue the previous conversation with her aunt there.

"I'm, uh, gonna get something to drink. And then maybe see if Connor wants to be saved from being buried under a pile of kids." Giving Julie a cheeky little finger wave, Sandra fled the scene. Just as well. If she was there, Julie would have felt obligated to be civil to her mom to help save face.

Because that's what good daughters did.

"Go away, Mom," she said through gritted teeth, pushing a smile onto her lips, so anyone watching them wouldn't realize how angry she was at her mother. "I don't want to talk to you."

"Well, I want to talk to you. I'm sorry."

The apology was so unexpected, it hit Julie like a blow to the stomach, knocking the breath and the retort she'd been about to sling back at her mother right out of her. She'd been about to say "no" and walk away, but instead, she stared at her mother, trying to remember the last time she'd heard her apologize.

If she'd ever apologized to Julie before.

"You are?" she managed to ask, feeling more than a little dazed. "For what?"

Her mother's lips tightened, her voice lowering just in case anyone might overhear, even though everyone was paying attention to their own conversations.

"I'm sorry for inviting John today. I..." Her voice trailed off, and she looked away. Her expression was blank, but she seemed maybe, just a little, ashamed. "Your Connor seems very nice. Your father likes him a lot."

Connor was nice. Or at least he was putting in a lot of effort to be nice. It was a different show than the kind John put on to impress people, but... was it a show? That's what she couldn't figure out, and she didn't feel as if she could trust her gut right now.

It burned her gut that she couldn't just enjoy hearing her mother say this. That Connor had to perform like he was in a circus to get her parents to approve of him. On top of the fact he shouldn't have to perform, her parents should just be happy for her and who she brought over, and she should have gotten this apology a long time ago, but only got it now because she'd brought a replacement for John, and it turned out her parents liked him...

There was not enough void, and she could not go scream into it right now, even if there was, but she felt like she was about to explode. Every single thing that happened was another shake, another jostle, and when she finally did get to release, she was going to spray everywhere and all over everything.

Which was why she smiled instead of exploding like a soda all over her mom and the rest of her family.

"Thanks, Mom." They were the only words she could get out, but thankfully, her mom didn't push her for more.

"A very nice boy." Her mom said, nodding approvingly as she turned to look at the backyard, frowning when she looked over at John. "He is a very important man, but I am starting to think he is more important in his head than anywhere else."

Great mom. Thanks for noticing.

Finally.

It had only taken bringing another man around to get there.

Julie was getting a headache.

26

———————

Connor

Something was wrong with Julie.

At first, he'd thought it was the presence of her ex, but after John finally left—called in for a consult at work, which he announced very loudly before leaving—she didn't seem any less tense. If anything, she seemed more so. But he wasn't sure what to do about it, especially as people started leaving, and he started helping her parents clean up.

He wasn't sure what the problem was.

Her family liked him, as far as he could tell. Her dad seemed like he was approving. Even her mom was thawing out toward him.

But Julie was stiff and cold toward everyone, including him. Which didn't seem very fair after he'd spent the afternoon doing his best to charm her family. He wasn't a natural extrovert, though he knew how to handle himself in social situations, and he knew he was going to be extra tired after this. He'd put on his work face for her family, on his day off, and now he was tempted to call in sick tomorrow just to get some rest.

He already knew he wouldn't do that—it wouldn't be fair to his coworkers or his patients since he wasn't actually sick—but that he felt the temptation meant something. Of course, he hadn't realized exactly how many family members she would have here today, or he might have been more prepared.

"It was very nice to meet you, Connor," her dad said, shaking his hand again as he escorted them to the door.

"Nice to meet you," her mom echoed. There was still a look in her eyes that made Connor think he was being weighed, judged, but not in a mean or malicious way. It was just that her mom hadn't fully decided whether or not she approved. That was the sense Connor got.

"It was nice to meet you. Thank you so much for having me," he said with a grin.

Julie slipped out the door past him, her gait slightly stiff.

"Bye," she said as she moved past her parents.

"Goodbye Julie," her dad called after her.

"I'll call you, Julie," her mom said right on top of him, raising her voice to make sure Julie would be able to hear her.

Connor grimaced. That had been rude. He gave them an apologetic wave and hurried after Julie, catching up to her halfway to his car.

"Hey, what was that about?" he asked, frowning down at her as he took her hand, trying to figure out what the problem was. As far as he could see, there shouldn't be a problem.

"What was what about?"

The belligerent tone of her voice meant something was really *really* off, which made him feel even more exasperated.

"The way... the way you're being right now." He wasn't sure how to describe it in a manner that wouldn't make her even more angry. Part of him was already cringing internally, not knowing how she would react to his questioning. "What's wrong? Did something happen? Did your parents say something?"

Rather than answering him, Julie took a deep breath and closed her eyes. Despite his impatience for an answer, Connor made himself hold back his questions. Whatever was going on with her, she was struggling with it, and if she needed a moment, he could give her that, even though it was hard for him to wait when he couldn't even imagine what the problem was.

Opening her eyes, she gave her head a shake. She was just as tense as she had been before she took her breath. His stomach churned, wondering what the hell was going on.

"I can't talk about this right now." Turning away from him, she put her hand on the car door handle. "Let's just go."

"Was it me? Was it something I did?" His mind shot back to the afternoon. Had he done something she didn't approve of? Had he accidentally flirted with someone? Been rude to someone? Had her parents said something to her about him? Maybe they'd only been friendly to his face.

Had John said something to her?

"Connor, I can't talk about this right now. Let's just get in the car and go, please." Despite the 'please,' her words came out clipped and angry, and it felt like the anger was directed at him.

His own frustration was starting to bubble up. He was tired after an afternoon of socializing with people he didn't know and doing his best to make a good impression on everyone, and he didn't know what he'd done to deserve this.

He'd expected praise. Gratitude. Maybe even a reward.

Not... whatever this was.

"Sorry," he said, though he was having trouble feeling like he meant it. Pulling his keys out of his pocket, he started walking around the car. "I just wanted to know if I did something. I thought the afternoon went well."

He could hear the edge in his voice. He hadn't exactly meant for it to be there, but at the same time, he wanted her to know that he was annoyed, too. A few minutes ago, he'd been really happy, thinking everything had gone well, but she wasn't acting like it had, and now, she wasn't talking to him about what was wrong either.

It hurt.

On multiple levels.

Something tickled his awareness, and he looked up, looking across the top of the car to see Julie on the other side of it. Since she was standing on the grass, just past the curb, she was tall enough that he could see her face. It was paler than usual, tight with emotion, and her eyes glittered, nostrils flaring as she took in another deep breath through them.

"You know what, I can't do this right now. I will call you later." Turning away from him, she pulled her phone out of her pocket and started typing into it.

"Julie... what... I just asked a simple question." Frustrated, Connor glanced around, trying to keep his voice down. Some of her family were still leaving, heading to the cars lined up along the street. None of them were within hearing, but they would definitely see if he left without her. Now, it was his turn to take a deep breath. "Just... get in the car, okay? We can talk about it later."

"You know what, Connor? Not everything has to be done on *your* timetable. I get a say in when I want to do things."

"Hey, we did today on your timetable." He pointed his finger at her. "You invited me here today, remember? I didn't ask to be invited or push to meet your family. I'm here because you asked me to be."

"I'm aware of that, Connor." She was looking away from him again, though, down the street like she was waiting for a ride.

Dammit. Some of her family were starting to look over at them. Thankfully, not Sandra and Terry, they'd already left, but he felt like there was probably a good chance that she'd hear about this eventually, and he was going to have to explain what happened. Even though right now, he wasn't sure what was happening. If she didn't get in the car with him, it was going to be really obvious that something was wrong, undoing all the effort he'd put in today.

He didn't want her family thinking she was scared to get in the car with him, even though they were having a fight.

He'd *never* hurt her, but he knew what it would look like if they argued. She was half his size. What would they all think if she went home separately just because they were having a disagreement?

And he didn't even know what their disagreement was about, other than the fact she wouldn't talk to him. Which he really didn't understand why.

"Just get in the car, please, Julie. Your family is starting to look at us. I think your parents are watching."

It was the wrong thing to say. Her head snapped around, gaze pinning him with a fiery glare.

"Oh, well, by all means, let's pretend everything's fine then since my *parents* are watching. I shouldn't get what I've *asked for* because my *parents are watching*. God forbid, I get a minute to think or get to make a decision about what I need, just so that you can make sure my parents *like you*." Her voice rose higher and higher with every sentence until she was shouting at him across the top of the car.

Connor stood in the street, stunned, because he didn't know what to do.

That wasn't... he hadn't...

She'd taken it the wrong way, yet she hadn't at the same time. Because everyone was staring at them now and he really wished he'd just gotten in the car and gone when she'd made the request. Why hadn't he? Why had he had to push?

"That's not what I meant. I'm sorry."

Closing her eyes, Julie pinched the bridge of her nose.

"I'm sorry too, Connor, but I really *can't do this right now*." Even though she'd stopped yelling, her voice was pitched high, like she was on the verge of losing it.

He shouldn't have pushed her. He should have seen how tense she was, how on edge she was, and he should have let her have her space, the way she'd asked him. He shouldn't have picked a fight just because he was upset that she wasn't more grateful after everything he'd done that afternoon. He'd realized something was going on, and he'd made it about how he felt instead of focusing on what she needed from him.

Some of what she'd told him about her ex, about how he was with her family, was popping up into his head now. Why it hadn't before, he didn't know. Maybe because he'd been too busy trying to make a good impression on her family.

Just like her ex.

"I'm sorry. Get in the car, and I promise I won't ask any more questions, I won't say anything. We can just get in the car and go." His voice had turned pleading, and he didn't care anymore who was listening, who was watching. It didn't matter what they thought; what mattered was what Julie wanted, and he was internally cursing himself for not prioritizing that in the first place.

What she felt should matter more to him than how her family felt about him.

For a moment, one long moment, he thought he'd convinced her.

And then a car pulled up behind him.

"Julie?"

He turned. Camille. Dammit. He'd forgotten that she and Freddy lived in this neighborhood.

Movement out of the corner of his eye, he turned his head to see Julie coming around the back of his car, heading for the passenger side door of Camille's. Pausing before she opened the door, she turned to look at him. Tears filled her big brown eyes, though none had spilled over yet.

There was more than sadness in her gaze; there was disappointment, and he felt it like a blow to his chest, making him want to crumble in on himself.

"We'll talk later, okay?" she asked.

Dumbly, he nodded his head, no longer trusting his voice, not sure of what might come out of his mouth.

Stepping forward, Julie put her hand on his chest and went up on her tiptoes. Connor bent his head down to meet her lips for a brief, unsatisfying kiss.

Then she was gone, pulled away and into Camille's car with the door closing behind her. She didn't look at him as Camille pulled away, taking his heart with her.

"Everything okay, Connor?" One of Julie's uncles called to him, concern clear in his voice.

Connor shook his head and waved at the man, getting into his car before anyone could come over to question him. No, everything wasn't okay, and he didn't know what to do about it except drive away and hope he didn't make anything worse.

———

JULIE

Staring at Camille's dashboard, Julie felt the sobs she'd been holding back clawing at her chest like they could rip through her skin and break free into the world.

It hurt.

Everything *hurt.*

Knowing she'd hurt Connor hurt.

The fact that he hadn't just given her what she'd asked for—twice!—hurt.

The way he'd spoken to her hurt.

That he'd been more concerned with how things looked to her family than how she was feeling hurt so much, she felt like her heart was breaking.

Knowing that some of this was left over from John's hurt.

Not knowing how reasonable or unreasonable she was being hurt.

She felt like a big walking open wound, and someone had just poured a saltshaker all over her. She hadn't wanted to fight with him. She'd known the way she was feeling wasn't all his fault. That's why she'd needed some *time to sort through her feelings.* She hadn't wanted to blow up at him. She'd known she needed to get herself under control before she tried to talk to him about it.

And she was so mad and hurt that he hadn't been able to give her that, even as she blamed herself for not being able to control her temper or her pride. She'd seen the way her tears affected him, yet she hadn't wanted to cry to get her way, even though if she'd started crying, he probably would have just gotten in the car and let her ride in silence.

But why should I have to cry to get what I asked for?

It wasn't the first time that question had whispered in mind, though it had been years since she'd heard it. That's why she hadn't cried. She'd sworn to herself that she wasn't going to do that again to get what she needed from a man. From her partner.

Lifting a hand to brush the hair out of her eyes, she immediately lowered it when she saw how badly she was shaking. She didn't want Camille to see.

But of course, she had.

Camille reached out and patted Julie's knee.

"It's going to be okay, honey," she murmured.

She didn't ask what was wrong. She didn't press Julie to talk, which was part of why Julie had called her over Olivia. She wasn't ready to talk yet, not sure what was going to come out of her mouth, which was *why* she'd asked Connor if they could just go. That was all she needed.

One simple request.

Which he'd ignored—the same way he'd ignored that she'd wanted to leave earlier.

Was it a sign of things to come? Was it leftover baggage from John?

Some psychologist she was—she couldn't even sort through her own mess. And she didn't trust herself to know at this point. She'd already let herself down once with John; was she going to ignore red flags a second time? Set herself up with someone who cared more about appearances than her *again*?

It hurt so much, and she didn't know what to do.

And she wasn't sure it was ever going to be okay.

Burying her face in her shaking hands, no longer able to hold back the sobs, Julie let herself drown in the bitter hurt while Camille kept rubbing her knee, murmuring soothing words that fell on deaf ears.

27

____

Ten missed calls, three voicemails, and two text messages from her mom over a four-hour period. It was a new record.

Call number eleven started ringing while Camille brewed a second pot of tea for the girls' night movie marathon. They'd already had dinner, not that Julie had had much appetite between everything she'd eaten at her parents that afternoon, then how things had been left between her and Connor.

Freddy had taken one look at Julie when she and Camille had come in the door and immediately made himself scarce, so it was just the two of them, which she appreciated.

"Are you ever going to answer that?" Camille asked as Julie's phone continued to ring.

"Wasn't planning on it," Julie answered, though she did tap the button to turn the ringing to silent. She could not deal with her mom right now. Even though putting her off was probably just going to make things worse in the long run.

She was self-aware enough to know this was a desperate attempt to regain control in one of the few ways she currently could, but at the same time, she didn't care enough to try to stop herself. Besides, if she had to listen to her mom spout off about how amazing Connor was and how dare Julie treat him like that, she was literally going to explode.

"It's not Connor calling, is it?" Camille asked, her tone totally devoid of judgment.

"No, it's my mom." Connor hadn't called. Which was good. She appreciated being given the space, even as she worried about how he was doing. But she couldn't talk to him when she was still so raw, still sorting through her feelings... there was too much of a chance she'd end up blowing up all over him. And she didn't think he deserved that.

Granted, she felt pretty righteous in some of her anger, but when she talked to him, she wanted to be able to do just that—talk. Not explode. Some of her anger was also at her parents, she realized, and he didn't deserve to take the brunt of that anger, too.

"Do you want to talk about it?" Camille asked.

Julie shook her head.

"Okay," Camille said, putting a mug down on the coffee table in front of Julie. The scent of chamomile and honey wafted through the air. "Wanna watch another movie?"

"Yes, please."

Settling down on the couch next to her, Camille picked up the remote and hit the next movie on the comfort movie list, *The Princess Bride*. A classic.

She was so thankful for Camille, who knew what Julie needed and gave it to her without pushing. She needed time and space. She needed to decompress. And then she needed to think.

It was probably why Connor's pushing had set her off so badly. John had never given her time to think. She had almost forgotten about that. Everything always had to be resolved 'immediately,' and he would push and push and push at her and demand that she talk it out *right then*. But when she did that, they only ever touched on surface stuff, not the underlying issue, because she hadn't been given a chance to figure out what was really wrong.

Then, once she did, a few days later and tried to bring it up again,

John would accuse her of bringing up 'old shit.' Of trying to start a fight about something they'd resolved. Then he'd accuse her of gaslighting him when she insisted they needed to discuss what the real problem was or even of flat-out lying because she 'hadn't brought that up when they talked about it.'

The fact she hadn't because it hadn't occurred to her until later —*after* she'd had time to think—didn't matter to him.

God, no wonder she'd blown up at Connor tonight. While she did think he shouldn't have pushed her after she'd explicitly asked him not to, after she'd requested the space, she could see that some of her reaction—specifically the desire to call Camille and get out of there as soon as possible—wasn't necessarily all about him. Which was something she wouldn't have been able to recognize in the moment when emotions were high.

She was only able to put the dots together now because she'd had time to settle, time to start turning things over in her mind and examining the interaction from every angle. Whether or not Connor would understand that better than John...

If he doesn't, he's not the right guy for me.

As much as it hurt to think about that. Despite her anger, despite how frustrated she'd been, deep down, she knew she didn't want it to end. She might not trust her judgment when it came to men anymore, but her emotions had still gotten entangled. She'd started falling for him. Harder and faster than she could have believed.

The urge to call him and go to him and cuddle up in his arms and just tell herself it was no big deal was high. But how many times had she done that with John?

What would she tell a client if they came in and told her the story of today?

She would tell them that they needed to figure out what they wanted. She would tell them that problems couldn't be brushed under the rug; they needed to be faced. She would tell them that they needed to have a conversation and see what their partner said, how they reacted, and make decisions from there.

Then she would say, 'Now let's talk through what's going on with your parents.'

Yeah, she was going to need to call her therapist this week. Connor meeting her family had brought up a lot more issues than just her past romantic relationship baggage. Even with John showing up, there was something that was still bugging her about Connor and her family, and she couldn't quite put her finger on it.

<u>CONNOR</u>

It had been a long night with no call from Julie. No text. Though he'd gotten a few from his friends, wondering how meeting her family had gone, he didn't answer. How could he? He thought it had gone really well... right up until it hadn't.

He'd called out sick from work.

His energy batteries didn't just need recharging. He was pretty sure they needed to be replaced. If things hadn't ended the way they had yesterday, he would have been able to go in. He would have made himself go in. But after a night of not sleeping on top of all the socializing... well, he just couldn't face it. Especially since Sandra would be there.

Though if he'd gone, he could have asked her some questions about Julie and her parents.

Julie had told him some things, but it felt like he had missed something, or there were things she hadn't told him. Maybe things she hadn't realized she should tell him. He was pretty sure she wouldn't have deliberately kept him in the dark about something that would upset her.

We should go.

What? No.

Her voice and his echoed in his mind, the same way they had all night last night.

Because he was pretty sure that's where everything had started to go wrong.

Because God forbid I get a minute to think or get to make a decision about what I need, just so that you can make sure my parents like you.

He'd just wanted to help. But she hadn't asked him to. She hadn't indicated she wanted him to. He'd been so sure what she really needed was to go out and face her family and show them that her new boyfriend was just as good—if not better, than her ex-husband—he'd ignored what she'd said.

She'd told him how she handled her mom, how she hung up when her mom brought her ex up. How she'd immediately left the last time her mom had sprung her ex on her in person.

Not that he had any issues close to what she had with her parents, but how would he feel if she got in the middle of how he wanted to handle an issue with them? How would he feel if she flat-out ignored what he said he wanted to do?

That was the other reason he'd been up all night. He kept trying to think of how to apologize. What to say. What to do. How to make it up to her. And he kept coming up short. He didn't know what to do or say.

The urge to text her, to call her, to at least try was strong, but after ignoring what she'd said she wanted yesterday, the least he could do was give her the space she'd requested now. No matter how much it strained him.

She'd said they would talk later.

While it was technically later, that didn't mean she was ready. She would reach out when she was. He firmly believed she was not ghosting him. He was pretty sure. It would be hard to ghost someone who was a member of the same kink club unless she decided to stop being a member and stop teaching. There was no way she would be willing to take things that far, even if she was incredibly upset with him.

He hoped she wasn't too upset with him.

Dammit.

He hoped he got a chance to apologize.

Knocking on the door made him jump to his feet before his brain had even fully registered the sound, heart pounding in his chest.

Julie?

Connor rushed to the door... only to look through the window beside it and feel his heart sink at the familiar, brown, bald head he spotted in front of it. Not Julie. Law. For a moment, he imagined the worst—Julie had sent Law to break up with him for her.

Then he shook off that thought. There was no way Julie would do that. First, she would handle her own breakups. Second, if she was going to send someone to break up with him for some odd reason, it wouldn't be Law.

New worry rushed through him. If Law wasn't here at Julie's behest, why the hell was he knocking on Connor's door in the middle of the day? What was wrong? Why hadn't anyone called him?

He yanked the door open and found himself looking down at both Law and Iris, who he hadn't realized was on Law's other side. They both stared up at him, as though they were surprised.

"What?" he asked, blinking back at them. "What's going on?"

"That's supposed to be my question to you," Law replied. "Can we come in?"

Baffled, Connor nodded, stepping back to let them pass by. Iris paused to hug him, which he sorely needed, and he hugged her back, though he kept his emotions in check. The last thing she needed was him melting down all over her just because she'd hugged him.

"So... what?" he asked again as he closed the door behind them, turning to face them.

Law crossed his arms over her chest and raised his eyebrows.

"That's what I want to know. You haven't answered any texts since last night or the call I made this morning, then when I called you at work just to check in and make sure you were okay, they said you hadn't come in. You never call out sick." Law's gaze sharpened. "So, now I'm here to find out why you're not at work and why you aren't answering your texts."

"I'm here for moral support and because Law and I were supposed to meet up for lunch," Iris chirped, smiling at him, though he could see the concern in her expression as well. She was just as worried as Law, though she showed it differently.

Oh.

Oh.

They weren't here to tell him something bad had happened to someone else. They were here because they thought something bad had happened to him. And it was lunchtime. They were supposed to be on a lunch date but had come to check on him instead.

His stomach growled, reminding him that he hadn't eaten since Julie's parents' house yesterday. No dinner, no breakfast.

"Right, um, can I get you guys something to eat?" he started moving toward the kitchen.

"Connor!" Law practically shouted his name, and Connor stopped in his tracks as his friend glared at him, flinging his hands in the air. "I don't want lunch. I want to know what's going on! What happened? What's wrong?"

Oh. Right.

"Well, we can eat lunch at the same time," Connor pointed out. It would be easier to talk if he had something else to focus on.

That's what they did. He made them sandwiches and told them about meeting Julie's family, and they listened. When they had to go, Iris gave him another hug, and Law assured him everything would be okay. Which was nice to hear, even though it wasn't as if Law could make that come true for him. But considering how cynical Law often was, knowing he thought there was a chance made Connor feel better.

It didn't occur to him until later that Law might have said that because he was going to try to *make* it true.

28

———————

The door to the Marquis office she shared with Law banged open, and there stood the man himself, glaring at her. Julie raised her eyebrow at him. She was tired. It had been a long day of dealing with other people's problems while trying to sort through her own, and she still needed to call Connor after she was done here tonight. She was kind of dreading it because she didn't know how it was going to go and just thinking about it was tying her up in knots.

"What the hell, Julie?" he asked, storming in. Iris followed behind him, a lot less dramatically, but her expression was pretty blank, which was unusual since she was normally smiling.

"What the hell, Law?" she mimicked as he glared at her from across their desks. "What got up your ass?"

"You. I mean—" He flushed, an undertone of red appearing on his cheeks before shaking his head as though he could shake the embarrassment away, and Iris snickered, moving around to the side where a comfortable seat was placed for anyone who needed to sit down in the office away from the desks. "That's not what I meant. I meant, what the hell did you do to Connor?"

Ice slid through her, making her sit up straighter and freezing her emotions. She should have realized, and she could have kicked herself for not figuring out immediately what his issue was. If she had, she never would have bantered back to him, despite how amusing his response had been, because it was none of his fucking business.

"What happened between me and Connor is between me and Connor, both in the past and anything that happens in the future."

"Is there going to be a future?" Law asked, glaring down at her.

She didn't like the advantage that his height gave her while she was sitting down, but it wasn't as if it would be that much better even when she stood up, so she did her best to ignore the intimidation factor.

"Also between me and Connor. That's an A and B conversation, so you need to see your way out of it." Was she reverting back to grade school? Yes, she was, but it was appropriate. Law was acting like a child.

"You can't dump him just because he was trying to impress your family. That's supposed to be a good thing."

Great. Now, another headache was forming at her temples. The only good thing right now was that she knew Connor wasn't responsible for Law's behavior, and she also knew that it would be wildly unreasonable for her to ask him not to talk about things between them with their friends. Though she might ask him to be a little choosier about which friends he confided in in the future.

If they had a future.

"No one asked him to help," she responded coolly, holding up her hand to stop Law before he could respond. "I have very strongly established boundaries with my parents for a reason, which is also none of your business, and rather than respecting those boundaries, Connor took it upon himself to change them for me. Which is also none of your business. But since you have partial knowledge of the situation and didn't bother to *ask* me about how I was feeling, the way a good friend would, and just jumped to conclusions and a side, I will tell you that it goes far beyond Connor trying to help."

Law made a disgruntled noise, but he was no longer glaring at her. As much as she understood his protectiveness over Connor, she was getting really tired of it. They were supposed to be friends, too, and he kept jumping to conclusions about her. It felt as though there was a serious double standard at work. She was pretty sure he hadn't done anything like this to any of his male friends—he hadn't been this bad about Morgan and Asad, even though Morgan had been in a position to possibly need actual protecting.

"I'm sorry," he said.

The immediate apology did actually go a little way toward soothing some of her hurt feelings. Not all the way, but it helped release some of the tension that was growing in her shoulders.

"I'm just struggling because he's so hurt, he didn't even go into work today, but here you are going about your day as usual, and I don't really think he did anything wrong. He might not have gone about it in the right way, but he had good intentions."

"Good intentions matter, but they aren't everything," Julie replied, feeling tired and a little judged. Yes, she'd gone about her day as usual because she was distracting herself, letting her brain work through her shit in the background while she did other things. It wasn't how everyone operated, but it was how she operated, and God, she was so tired of people misunderstanding things she did just because it wasn't the same way they would have reacted.

Iris cleared her throat.

"Excuse me, Law, but did I just hear you say that he might not have gone about it in the right way, but he had good intentions?" There was something very pointed in her tone. Law and Julie turned their heads to look at her, but her focus was entirely on Law. Something in her expression made Julie think her fellow Dom had just seriously stepped in it.

"Yes," Law said slowly, as if he sensed the trap but couldn't quite figure out what it was or where it had been laid.

Iris' eyes narrowed.

"And were you or were you not the person who told me 'impact over intent' when I reached out to *your* mom about this upcoming Thanksgiving without telling you?"

"That was different." The words came out rushed and not entirely convincing.

"Oh, really? Please enlighten me on how it was different because I'm pretty sure I got both a lecture and a spanking for engaging with *your* family without talking to you first, even though I was just trying to make things better for both of us and working on getting your mom to like me... you know, as much as she likes your ex. Sounds like a pretty similar situation, *actually*."

Law's hand came up, rubbing over his head.

"It's... I mean, I see what you're saying, but it's not the same."

"Sounds the same to me," Julie said, getting to her feet. "However, I don't think this discussion has anything to do with me and everything to do with the two of you, so I'm going to leave you to it. I have a call to make."

Perhaps talking to Connor tonight, after being confronted by Law, wasn't the best timing, but she didn't think it was fair to leave him hanging. At the very least, she could text him and set up a time and place to meet, but the main point was that she wanted to get out of there and away from Law and Iris' back and forth. It wasn't actually an argument yet but if it became one, she didn't need to be there for it.

She had her own relationship issues to work out.

Unfortunately, when she stepped out into the lobby of Marquis, Olivia and Camille were there waiting for her. Since it was a Monday and there were no classes tonight, the club was closed, which meant they were both dressed for work rather than in fetwear. Camille must have come straight from the office.

"Oh, no," she groaned, slumping. "Not you, too."

"Well, you have to admit, we're better than Law, at least," Camille commented, her lips quirking up in a smile.

"You'd better be," Julie grumbled, sighing as she made her way over to her friends. Despite their words, as soon as she reached them, they both opened their arms to hug her.

They knew she was hurting. They knew this wasn't easy for her. The fact that Law was putting everything on her shoulders was definitely a big pain point for her. Did she recognize that she'd behaved unreasonably in some places? Absolutely. But she wasn't the only one who'd been in the wrong. Connor had made mistakes, too. While she was absolutely going to own up to what she'd done wrong, she didn't get the feeling Law had seen where Connor had stepped in it, too. And the fact he and Iris had apparently had a similar situation recently, and Law *still* didn't see where Julie was coming from...

She squeezed her friends back, incredibly grateful for their support.

"So how much have you heard?" she asked as the hug broke apart, and Olivia gestured for them to go into her office. Pulling her phone out of her purse, she sent off a quick text to Connor, asking if he'd be free to talk a little later. Olivia took her own seat in the chair on the other side of the desk, and Camille settled into the one next to Julie.

"Just that the meet-the-family didn't go so well," Olivia said. "Something about Connor making too good of an impression on your family?" The dubious way she said it made Julie feel a little better since Olivia obviously didn't put any credence in the idea.

Julie had to laugh.

"It's sort of true." She sighed. "Not that I didn't want him to, but... well, we showed up, went inside to get drinks, and when we were about to head out to the backyard, I saw that John was there."

"Girl, no..." Camille gasped, putting her hand on her chest, her jaw dropping. Olivia made an aggravated noise, picking up a pen and starting to twirl it around in her hands.

"Pretty much. So you know, I said we needed to go. Because that's my boundary with my parents. I'm not going to try to keep them from maintaining their relationship with John if that's what they insist on doing, but I'm also not going to be there for it." She couldn't control what they did; she could only control what she did. "Instead, Connor decided that we should stay... something about not letting John win since it's my parents and my family, and then he took my hand and led me outside."

"And you let him?" Olivia raised her eyebrows in surprise, and Julie grimaced. Yeah, she should have dug her heels in then, but...

"Honestly, I had kind of frozen. I don't know why, but I really didn't expect my parents to invite John. I saw him and realized what had happened and... froze. I also didn't expect Connor to just decide for me what we were doing, and I wasn't really thinking. I just went with him." She sighed again, rubbing her forehead where it was creasing. For the past twenty-four hours, she'd been psychoanalyzing herself in the back of her head, trying to figure out why she'd acted the way she had, yet she felt no closer to answers.

"I'm sure him saying something about winning didn't help," Camille observed. "First, because that was definitely going to remind you of John. Second, because he was also right about that. If you keep letting John chase you off from your own family, he's definitely winning."

"But if I stay, my parents are getting what they want." Julie made a face. "And then I have to put up with John. I divorced him specifically so I wouldn't have to do that anymore."

"Fair point." Olivia was still playing with her pen, one end of it tapping lightly against her desk while she was thinking. "So, then Connor spent the afternoon showing off to your parents and focusing on them and what they wanted instead of you and what you wanted, which meant they won, and on top of that, you had to spend time around John again." Her tone had definitely turned disapproving.

"I'm sure he wasn't thinking about it like that." Which was exactly what she'd been telling herself, but it hadn't really sunk in until she was defending him to Olivia. Olivia smiled, and Julie rolled her eyes.

Yeah, she'd been set up for that one. She got it.

"Did he know about the boundaries you have with your parents?" Camille asked.

"Yeah, we've talked about how I deal with them. Granted, I didn't say, 'Hey, if my ex shows up to this, we're out of here' because I didn't think I would need to, but he knows I don't stay on the phone with them if they bring him up. He knows about me leaving as soon as John showed up the other week. That's why I told my parents about him in the first place." She sighed.

Her phone beeped, and she automatically checked it, blinking in surprise as she read the message back from Connor.

"He's downstairs." The text said he'd be happy to talk right now, but he was at the Marquis restaurant with Q and Asad.

"Who?" Olivia frowned, her pen coming to a halt.

"Connor."

"Oh." The pen started up again. "For a wild second, I thought you meant John."

That startled a laugh out of Julie, which helped undo a few of the knots that had formed in her stomach the moment she'd read Connor's message. She did want to talk to him. Should she go downstairs? Was it better to do it in a public space or wait until they were in private? She didn't want to interrupt his time with his friends.

Pressing her lips together, she texted him back, letting him know that she was upstairs and that she could come down to talk or she could call him later if he let her know when he was home.

"I do think it's a little different than with John," Camille said thoughtfully, making Julie sigh again.

"I know it's different. He was doing it for me. But like I just told Law, good intentions matter, but they aren't everything. I am grateful for the effort he put forward in impressing my family, but I'm still mad he didn't listen to me when I said we needed to leave. Especially since he knew how I've handled my parents in the past."

"Valid." Camille gave her a sympathetic look. "I just really want you guys to work out. He's made you happy."

"He has. We just... we need to talk. He needs to know it's not okay to do that again."

"And he needs to know to prioritize you and what you want over what he wants when it comes to your family," Olivia added. "Connor's first instinct is for people to like him, which isn't necessarily a bad thing, but I'd be willing to bet he realized if he left with you, your parents might not like him. Add that into the idea that they might like your ex more than him... That would be hard for him to deal with. But that doesn't mean it's more important than how you choose to deal with your family or what you want to do in regard to them."

"Exactly." Julie sighed. It was such a relief to hear her own thoughts coming out of Olivia's mouth, soothing away some of the self-doubt Law had stirred up in her.

Her phone beeped with another text message.

Connor: *If you want to come down and talk, I'd love to see you. Or I can let you know when I get home. Whichever you're more comfortable with.*

That answer helped relax even more of her tension. He was giving her the reins of control, letting her know his needs, then leaving the decision up to her. Exactly what he hadn't done at her parents'.

Maybe things would work out after all.

29

Connor

"Ah, shit." Connor stared at the text message on his phone. "Julie's upstairs." And offering to either come downstairs or to call him later, which wasn't the problem.

"So? Oh, did you not want to see her?" Asad asked, frowning at him. "I thought you did want to see her."

"He does, but remember who else went upstairs as soon as we got here?" Q asked, tilting his head significantly at Asad. It only took a moment for the light bulb to go off in Asad's head.

"Oh... *oh.*" Asad turned his head toward the back of the restaurant, where the stairs to the second floor were, as though he might be able to see through the walls and up to where Law and Iris had gone. "I thought they went up there cuz... you know." He tilted his head in the opposite direction without looking, so as not to draw attention from the booth he was indicating.

Asad and Q had known that Morgan and Sam were going out tonight with Noelle, Amy, and Marissa; they just hadn't realized the women were going to be *here* until they'd also arrived for dinner. Noelle had immediately shot a dirty look at Iris, then Iris and Law had gone upstairs, so Asad probably wasn't wrong.

"That might have been why, but..." Connor couldn't shake the feeling that Law would probably say something to Julie if he saw her. It had been all his friends could do to convince Connor to come out tonight. The main reason he'd agreed was because it would be a helpful distraction, rather than sitting around waiting for Julie to get in contact with him.

Now, he wished he'd stayed home.

But he did text her back, letting her know he would talk to her wherever and however she was comfortable. If she didn't want to come downstairs and talk to him at the Marquis bar while his friends were here, he couldn't blame her. And he fought the impulse to immediately leave and go home so she could call him.

She was here, too, which meant she might not be able to talk right away and then he'd just be sitting at home waiting, and *not* doing that was the entire reason he'd come out tonight in the first place.

"Five bucks Law couldn't keep his mouth to himself," Asad said, catching Connor's drift.

"You're on," Q replied, reaching out to shake his hand and seal the deal. "He knows not to get involved in another couple's business."

Asad snorted, releasing Q's hand.

"Yeah, but it's Connor. Law's gone all uber protective because he's worried about Connor's balls. And also the fact that he's a people pleaser." Asad glanced at Connor. "Which isn't necessarily a bad thing, but sometimes you go a little far with it and ignore what you need."

"I..." Connor cut off what he was going to say, frowning. It was hard to argue with facts. He knew he liked to make people happy. He knew that sometimes he felt like he'd been taken advantage of. Or he'd get resentful when people didn't appreciate the fact that he'd bent over backward for them.

That had been part of the problem yesterday.

He'd had that feeling of 'but look at everything I did for you.' He'd been thinking about that today. He'd been feeling resentful that Julie hadn't appreciated everything he'd done for her yesterday... but the inescapable fact that she hadn't asked him to do those things kept popping into his head.

That was something his mom had tried to help drill into him when he was younger, and mostly, he managed to remember it.

You need to ask before you try to help someone.

Connor not only hadn't asked, but he'd ignored what Julie had said she wanted—he'd been so determined to impress her family. Then he'd gotten mad at her for not being grateful, which was why he'd been so pushy at the end. But she'd already been pushed too far, and he'd been so far up his own ass about what he'd done 'for her', he hadn't been able to see it, and he hadn't backed off.

In hindsight, he could see a hundred places where he wished he'd made a different choice yesterday. All he could do today was hope she'd be willing to give him another chance to get it done right.

"I can't believe you're choosing her over me!"

The words weren't shouted, but they were loud enough to be heard over the rest of the conversation happening in the bar.

"Noelle, we're not." That was Sam. Connor recognized her voice even though he couldn't see her face from where she was sitting in the booth. She and Morgan were on one side with Noelle and Amy across from them, and Morgan and Noelle were sitting on the outside of the booth.

"You are!" Noelle's voice was bordering on hysterical. He could see her face perfectly clearly and Amy's, who was now flushed pink as she put her hand on Noelle's shoulder, trying to soothe her. "All of you are! You don't care about me, you don't care about my feelings, or you wouldn't be taking her side! Did she put you up to this? Did she tell you that you have to choose?"

"The only person who has made me feel like I have to choose is you, Noelle," Sam said sharply. Even though she wasn't as upset as Noelle, her voice carried, especially as conversation around the bar dropped, eyes and ears being drawn in by the drama. "And any friend who tries to make me choose between them and another friend is going to be sorely disappointed. Iris, on the other hand, has never asked me to choose. She never has anything to say about you, period. The only one badmouthing anyone is you."

"Oh, yes, because Iris is just perfect. I see how it is. Well, I'm not going to stay here where I'm not wanted." Noelle ran toward the door, covering her face with her hands.

Giving Sam and Morgan a resigned look, Amy scooted out of the booth and followed her.

"And there goes another people pleaser," Asad murmured, watching Amy go. He sighed, shaking his head.

Realizing he'd had his own urge to chase after Noelle and make sure she was okay—or at the very least that she got home alright, even though he didn't particularly even like her, and she'd definitely brought that upon herself—made Connor realize that his people-pleasing was maybe a little more out of control than he'd initially thought. He wasn't even sure that she was actually upset or if she was faking it, but he'd still felt the urge to go check on her... and relief that Amy was handling it.

Would he have followed her and risked Julie coming down to find him gone?

The hesitation he felt about answering was a little disconcerting. Noelle was definitely not as important to him as Julie, so it should have been an immediate and easy answer, yet he hesitated. Yeah, he needed to work on getting his priorities in order.

That was pretty bad and not a particularly comfortable realization to have about himself.

"What on earth is going on?" The familiar voice made him sit straight up, spinning around in his seat, but Julie wasn't looking at him—she was watching Amy chase Noelle out the door. Connor drank in the sight of her.

She looked as tired as he felt, with darkish circles under her eyes. Still dressed for work, she was wearing a pair of beige slacks with a white button-down shirt that had a lacy collar and black jewel buttons. Her hair was pulled back into a bun, but several long strands had come loose and were hanging down over her shoulders, giving her a slightly disheveled look.

She was fucking beautiful.

"Noelle," he said, and apparently didn't need to explain further because Julie snorted and nodded, finally turning her gaze to him. There was worry in that gaze, along with a softness that hadn't been there yesterday, and a bit of the same happiness he felt just looking at her. Her lips curved slightly into a rueful smile.

"Hey," she said.

"Hey."

"Wanna go grab a booth?"

"That sounds good." He glanced at his friends, who were conversing quietly, before looking at him and Julie.

"Ya'll can have this table if you want," Q said, picking up his beer. "Asad and I are going to go join Morgan and Sam." He gave them a little wave, turning away. Asad was already moving toward the women's table.

Connor looked at Julie. She shrugged, then pointed to a booth tucked in the corner which was currently empty. There was only one booth connected to it and that was also currently empty.

"Want to go over there?" she asked.

Relief filled him. Not that there was anything wrong with the current table, per se, but it was a lot less private than one of the booths.

Catching the eye of Marquis' bartender, who was also serving the tables since it was a slow Monday night, he indicated that they were moving. Shane gave him a nod of acknowledgment before turning to one of the patrons who was sitting at the bar to take his order.

Following Mistress Julie over to the corner booth, Connor smiled when Asad and Q saw him going, and both gave him an encouraging thumbs-up. Knowing his friends didn't think he'd fucked up beyond redemption helped a lot.

Sliding into the booth, he cleared his throat before she could say anything.

"I'd like to start off by apologizing."

Julie blinked in surprise, hesitating only a moment before slowly nodding. "Okay." Her tone was more curious than anything else, as if she wasn't sure where he was going with that.

"I'm sorry I didn't listen when John showed up, and you said we should go. I'm also sorry that after that, when we were leaving, I didn't listen to you again when you told me you couldn't talk at that moment. I didn't give you the space you very clearly stated you needed, and I pushed for what I wanted instead." As he spoke, he could see her softening, appreciation filling her gaze for the apology. "The only thing I can say in my defense is that the biggest reason I pushed to stay was because I did want your parents to like me, but I wanted them to like me for you. I wanted to make things easier for you."

A little half-smile hitched up one side of her mouth.

"To be fair, I think it will in the long run," she admitted. "But... it does hurt that their approval of me is based on who I'm dating. Which is not your fault. I need to apologize, too. My emotions were keyed up yesterday and going in every direction, and that's why I couldn't talk. I shouldn't have left like that, but I didn't want to explode all over you in the middle of the street, which is what likely would have happened."

"I should have been more sensitive," he countered. "I knew what your relationship with your parents was like. I knew the afternoon was hard for you. I was upset because... well, because I thought you should have acknowledged all the effort I put in. But you didn't ask me to do that." He rushed the words when she opened her mouth, wanting her to know that he got it. "I decided to do that on my own. And I do appreciate that even after you said we should go, and I made us stay, that you did stay."

She could have walked out then by herself, leaving him there alone with her family. He wouldn't have even been able to blame her. Though he might have been embarrassed at first, he would have also realized immediately that he'd stepped wrong.

"Well, you felt so strongly about it... and I didn't want to abandon you with them. That would have made things harder on you in the future. You know, if we have a future." Her voice lifted up at the end, so it was caught somewhere between a statement and a question.

"I hope we have a future." He shook his head. "I know I fucked up. I know we didn't communicate well. But I think we can do better in the future. I think *I* can do better in the future. Asad pointed out that I'm a people pleaser. He's not wrong. Sometimes, I choose the wrong people to try to please." Taking a deep breath, Connor decided to go all in and tell her the full truth that he'd realized just this evening. "I chose your parents and told myself I was doing it for you, and I was in some ways, but the truth is I just wanted them to like me. I didn't want them to have a reason to dislike me."

"I don't care if they like you or not."

"I know. But I cared. Too much." He shifted uncomfortably in his seat.

"I might have cared too much about having my way." She sighed. "When I said we should leave, part of that was out of anger, part of it was out of fear, part of it was out of hurt. I wasn't thinking; I was just reacting. And I wasn't thinking about how it would have affected you in the long run. It should have been a discussion, not me making a unilateral decision. I also should have found a way to let you know I was upset during the afternoon. I tend to internalize things and need time to think through things before I can talk about them."

"You deserve that time. I shouldn't have pushed you."

"I could have been kinder about telling you that I needed that time. And I could have been better about saying that we'd talk later but that I just needed to get away from my parents' house before I exploded."

"You shouldn't have had to say anything more than what you did. You were clear about what you needed, both times, and I ignored you."

"You ignored me because I wasn't being very considerate of your feelings." They stared at each other. Julie's half-smile had grown to a full one, her eyes sparkling with amusement. "Are we really going to have an argument about who did the other one dirtier, but we're defending each other instead of ourselves?"

"If we do, I'm going to win. I stepped in it first." He grinned at her. "It all could have been avoided if we'd left when you said to."

She laughed. "Yeah, but then you would have had a much more uphill battle with my parents."

"It would have been worth it."

Which was true. The statement softened her even further.

"We'll do better in the future," she said, and the tension in his chest eased.

"In the interest of good communication, I should tell you that John confronted me when I was taking the trash to the side of the house and told me that he wasn't going to give you up because you two belonged together, and eventually, you'd realize that."

Julie raised her eyebrows.

"What did you say to him?"

"I said 'okay' and walked away."

She stared at him for a long moment, and he started thinking he'd fucked up again, then she started *cackling*. One hand on her stomach, leaning back in the booth, gasping for breath laughter.

"Oh God... please tell me you got a picture of his expression!"

Grinning back at her, relieved, Connor shook his head.

"It was really good, though."

She snorted, she was laughing so hard, which made him chuckle.

"Damn, I wish I could have seen it," she said as she managed to get her laughter under control, subsiding to giggles. She shook her head, then cocked it, looking at him with an invitation in her eyes. "Ah, well. Want to get out of here?"

"Hell, yes."

30

———————

JULIE

Waiting for Connor to settle up his tab with Shane, Julie admired how Connor's ass looked in his jeans. After their conversation, she felt like she'd been able to fully relax for the first time since arriving at her parents' yesterday.

It was going to be okay.

They'd done a much better job of communicating this evening. And she definitely needed to talk to her therapist about her triggers around her parents. Someday, maybe she'd be able to handle things less emotionally, but at least in hindsight, she was able to break down why she'd reacted the way she had. A combination of feeling like no one really cared about her and her feelings, along with the many old wounds from feeling like that when she was with John.

Connor wasn't John, of course, but it made sense that her first serious relationship since her ex would reveal some major emotional baggage that needed to be dealt with. No one got out of a toxic relationship without carrying wounds that might appear unexpectedly in the next one.

Now, she and Connor understood each other better.

She could definitely see the people-pleasing thing. It was something she'd noticed before. She just hadn't realized how deep it went. From what he'd said, it sounded like he'd been doing some Monday morning quarterbacking as well, thinking through why he'd done the things he had and why he'd reacted the way he had.

A tap on her shoulder made her jump and spin around. She hadn't been paying attention to the people around her at all. Finding herself facing Law, with Iris right behind him, she let out the breath that she'd sucked in, holding back the yelp she'd almost uttered.

"Hey." Law cleared his throat, looking wildly uncomfortable. He ran his hand over his head. "I need to apologize."

Two apologies in one night. That was more than she usually got in a month. Unlike with Connor, though, this one felt like it was truly deserved and did not require an apology in return. Law had stepped way out of line.

"Okay." Julie crossed her arms over her chest. She was still smarting. Not just because Law had tried to involve himself in her and Connor's relationship, but because Law was supposed to be her friend, too... *and* they'd already had that discussion. "Go ahead."

He cleared his throat again.

"I apologize. I was a shitty friend, and I was butting my nose in where it wasn't my place to. I feel protective of Connor, but that's no reason to be a bad friend to you." He paused, then grunted, and Julie got the feeling Iris had poked him from behind. "Also, I apologize for being a massive hypocrite and coming down on you for doing the exact same thing I have done myself."

A large hand came down on her shoulder, and Julie reached up to pat it, glancing up to see Connor frowning at Law.

"I didn't ask you to talk to Julie for me," he said, obviously upset that Law had done so.

"I didn't think you had," she reassured him. "And in his defense, he was doing it for you."

Connor narrowed his eyes as he turned his gaze to her, recognizing that it was the same defense he'd used for trying to impress her parents.

"Mmm. So, that's what it feels like to be on this side of it," he said after a moment.

Law sighed. "I'm sorry, Connor. I promise the next time you need to vent or talk things out, I will be a good listening ear, and I will not attempt to intervene in anything."

All in all, it was a pretty good apology, but Julie knew it would take a while for her trust to rebuild. She probably wasn't going to be as comfortable around Law for a bit, and she doubted she would ever confide in him about anything that was going on with her and Connor. He was clearly Connor's friend first. Which was fine, she understood it, but it was also something she needed to keep in mind for her own feelings.

"Good boy," Iris said with a smirk, patting him on the shoulder.

The look Law shot her was full of warning, and Julie snickered. Iris might have won that argument, but she was skating on thin ice with that comment. But it was Iris, after all—if there was a big red button to push, she was going to slam her hand down on it.

"Ready to go?" Connor asked Julie. She threaded her fingers through his, stepping to the side so their joined hands could drop between them, and she smiled up at him.

"Let's go."

They took a moment to say goodbye to everyone as Law and Iris went to join the others in the booth. Thankfully, no one else seemed to be bothered by the fact that she and Connor had been on the outs for a day. They just seemed happy they'd worked it out.

She was, too.

Sometimes, she needed to think, but sometimes, her head got in the way of her heart, overthinking the things that she knew deep down. Fear didn't help, either. She was afraid she'd picked poorly again. She was afraid her parents would only ever see her as an extension of the man she was with. She was afraid she'd find herself trapped with someone who cared more about appearances than about her.

But Connor's motivations were totally different, and deep down, even when she'd been in the middle of questioning everything, she'd known that. She didn't expect him to do everything right all the time, but tonight, he definitely had—from letting her choose where and when to talk, to immediately apologizing and showing that he understood where she was coming from.

John would never have.

He wouldn't have even acknowledged he'd done something wrong, much less be self-aware enough—and aware enough of her—to know what he'd done wrong. Or maybe he was, but he'd certainly never admit that he was in the wrong.

With time, and probably more therapy, she'd hopefully be able to work through the triggers she had around the gaslighting and toxic bullshit he'd put her through.

Maybe it was a low bar—to not gaslight her, to apologize, to think about how to make things better in the future—but she still felt like Connor deserved a reward tonight.

Connor

Holy fuck, Julie was killing him.

Flat on his back, wrists bound to the headboard, a vibrating plug up his ass, his dick was hard as a rock, and the slow glide of her lips up and down the shaft wasn't nearly enough. He wanted, needed, more. Harder. Faster.

The vibrations in his ass were a low steady thrum that tingled through him without giving him the stimulation he really needed. Just like her mouth, it was nothing more than a tease at the moment.

Her hands pressed down on his hips. Despite their size difference, it was surprisingly hard to thrust up the way his body felt compelled to do when she was pressing all her weight down on one spot. There was nothing he could do but whimper and groan as her mouth slid tortuously slow down his cock again, tongue flicking against the sensitive underside, then back up to slide around the mushroom head.

"Fuck... please, Mistress..." The headboard creaked as his arms pulled, tugging on his wrists.

Instead of moving faster, she hit the button on the remote.

Connor cried out as his ass clenched around the toy, shuddering with the sensations that coursed through him in response. His dick jerked in her mouth, but it still wasn't enough to get him off.

Soft hands cradled his balls, then her grip tightened, squeezing and tugging hard enough to send a snap of pain whipping through the growing pleasure. It hurt so good. Connor gasped, trying to thrust up again. He wasn't consciously trying. It was a bodily response he couldn't help, even though he wanted to let Mistress Julie have her way with him in whatever manner she wanted.

Her mouth slipped off him, and for a moment, he thought she was going to impale herself on his cock... but then she turned.

The view of her slick, dark pink pussy lips filled his vision as she got her legs in place on either side of his head before lowering her pussy to his mouth. Eagerly, he latched on; all the pent-up energy from being sensually tortured finally had an outlet.

He felt her moan around his cock as his tongue slid up the center of her lips, the sweet and salty flavor of her body exploding in his mouth. Connor went after her pussy like a starving man, using his tongue and mouth to expend his sexual frustration.

He felt her move atop him, felt her shudder and redoubled his efforts. It also gave him something to focus on other than her mouth moving up and down his cock. Not that he wanted to focus on something else, but he had to if he was going to keep himself from cumming before she told him to.

Especially when the vibrations in his ass turned to pulses, making every muscle in his body tense at the sudden change in sensations.

"Fuck."

He moaned the word into her pussy, which muffled the sound, his toes curling as he struggled against the need to release. A soft hand gripped his balls, tugging on them hard enough to send a shot of pleasurable pain through him, keeping his orgasm just at bay.

Whimpering, he felt his body trying to lift up beneath her. He sucked her clit into his mouth, suckling furiously against the sensations coursing through them. Despite her thighs on either side of his head, pressing against his ears, he could still hear her moan as she started to rub her pussy against his face, riding his mouth.

Fuck, yes.

Even the air he was breathing was pussy scented, and he was drowning in the pleasure of it.

When she pulled away, lifting her pussy away from his mouth, he groaned in protest. He hadn't been done.

She moved down his body, still facing away from him, so she could impale herself on his dick. Connor liked seeing her face, but there was also something about the view from the back as she sat down on his cock, her hand still tugging on his balls, adding to the sensations.

The pulsing in his ass changed again, the vibrations starting low, then revving up higher before dropping and rising again.

"Oh, fuck..." He spasmed in reaction to the stimulation. If she didn't give him permission to cum soon, it wasn't going to matter because he wasn't going to be able to hold it back much longer.

Still facing away from him, Julie started to ride his cock, the slick heat of her pussy easily gliding up and down his length, her muscles squeezing him, tugging on his balls. Connor made a strangled noise as his hips thrust upward into her, shuddering at the effort to keep from coming. The hand on his balls made it particularly difficult as they tightened against her grip, the base of his spine tingling.

"Please... oh fuck, Mistress, please..."

"Come for me, good boy."

That was all he needed.

As the vibrator hit high—a relentless, humming high that blasted through him—he cried out, writhing underneath her. Her pussy clamped down around him as she cried out as well, shuddering atop him, grinding down on his cock while he pulsed inside her, filling her with spurt after spurt of wet heat.

It felt like all the blood rushed from his head down to his groin, leaving him floating on the bed, buzzing in an erotic haze. The vibrations stopped, and he finally went limp—and not just his dick, leaving him more relaxed than he could ever remember being.

After she undid his cuffs, after they got cleaned off, after they were in bed, Connor wrapped himself around her while she sleepily played with his chest hair, her head nestled against his shoulder.

"I know it's kind of silly because it was only a day, and it's not like we've been spending every night together, but I missed you," she murmured.

Connor's chest constricted at the admission.

"I missed you, too," he whispered back.

This. This was what he wanted. This was what was most important. He was all in. They'd need to figure out how to deal with her family, and tomorrow, he would need to face Sandra at work, but after tonight, he had faith they could do it.

Together.

31

JULIE

Life was good.

It had been a week since her and Connor's first fight and a mostly uneventful week. According to him, Sandra had given him a bunch of advice about how to 'handle' her when he'd gone back to work. Not that he would share any of the supposed advice. She called Sandra, who claimed innocence, then asked her—again—about the size of Connor's dick. Julie hung up on her.

Talking to her parents had been a little more difficult, but not much. She'd very firmly told her mom that she and Connor were still together and that it wasn't her business what they'd been arguing about. Surprisingly, her mom had been full of apologies, seeming to think the argument must have had to do with John. She'd also wanted Connor's phone number so she could apologize directly to him again. Julie had refused but had agreed to get together for dinner.

Connor said it would be okay if she did give her mom his number, but she was going to protect him from that for as long as possible. Was she also a little nervous that they'd be going around her to talk, the way John and her mom had?

Absolutely.

Which she admitted to him. He reassured her that her mom didn't need to have his number until Julie was ready for that to happen, and he would not be trying to go around her to collude with her mom. The fact that she had that worry was also something she'd brought up in therapy that week when she was recounting the events of the weekend. It had been a good appointment, kicking off a whole new round of things to work through.

Things were still a little awkward between her and Law, but they were working on that tonight.

"I'm going to build my second wonder," Law said, sliding his card into place.

When Connor had invited Julie over for game night, she'd thought they'd be playing Monopoly or something. She'd never considered herself a board game person, but she'd been willing because she knew it was something their group of friends did regularly. She wanted to be a part of his life. At the very least, she figured she should do it once, especially while things were still weird with Law, then she could bow out more often in the future.

But Seven Wonders was a lot more complicated than any game she'd played before. She liked it.

"I'm going to get some wood from Connor," Julie said, then snickered, making Law shake his head.

The number of wood jokes going around the table had gotten a bit ridiculous, but the only person who didn't seem to find it hilarious was Law. Which just made it more hilarious.

"Get it, Jules," Iris called out from where she was sitting on the couch. Only seven people could play Seven Wonders, so she'd elected to sit out the game this time since she had some emails she needed to answer.

Snickering again at Law's expression, Julie built the card she'd chosen.

It was impossible to tell who was winning, which she kind of liked. Points wouldn't be added up until the end, and there were so many things to take into consideration. The inability to know where she was in the standing actually helped her enjoyment of just playing the game.

She wasn't the *most* competitive person she knew... but who liked to lose?

"I need to get some wood from Morgan," Asad said with a lascivious leer at his girlfriend, who laughed at him.

"Oh, really?" Q asked, raising his eyebrows. "Does that mean you're going to try that in more than one way?"

"That's not what he's saying," Law said immediately, though his focus was on the cards on the table. Speaking of competitive... she was pretty sure he was looking at everyone's cards and trying to count up the current points in his head, which was a mind-boggling amount of work. "Stop pressuring him."

Julie's lips twitched. Poor Law. She was definitely rooting for Q to win the bet, though. Whether or not Iris would actually want to try pegging Law, she didn't know, but just having to offer was going to pain him. Then again, if he hadn't been open to it being a possibility, he wouldn't have made the bet.

"Don't knock it till you've tried it," she said mildly. She wasn't sure if Connor had told them that he'd told *her* about the bet. Law shot her a suspicious look, so she was pretty sure he hadn't. She smiled innocently at him.

"Ah, shit," Iris said in a disgusted voice, making all of them look over at her. There was something more than disgust in her voice, though Julie couldn't pinpoint the exact emotion. It wasn't a good one.

"What's wrong?" Law asked immediately, going from competitive board gamer to protective boyfriend in a heartbeat.

"I got a text from Noelle."

"I thought you blocked her."

"I did, but I just connected my computer and my phone, and it linked my texts, and one came through from her. Maybe the block doesn't work on the computer."

"What's it say?" Sam asked tensely, an unhappy expression on her face.

Julie didn't know what was going on with Sam's other group of friends, which included Noelle, but it seemed like it was a bit of a hot mess. Not helped by the fact that they were all bridesmaids in an upcoming wedding.

"I'm not opening it, so I can only see the preview." Iris was scowling, but she kept her voice even, as though she was trying not to show too much emotion. "Something about how she hopes I'm happy, and she's glad she knows now that she always cared more about me than I did about her."

That was some preview.

Law was already on his feet, game forgotten, holding out his hand to Iris.

"Give it to me. You aren't reading any more of those. I'll get them deleted."

Sighing, Iris handed her laptop over, leaning back against the couch and rubbing her hand over her face.

"Thank you." Dropping her hands down into her lap, she looked over at Sam and Morgan, who both looked uncomfortable. "I promise I did really care about her. I'm not trying to bully her or make people hate her or anything like that. I'm honestly glad she found new friends. I don't want her miserable or anything, I just can't be her friend anymore. I just wish she would leave me *alone*."

"She should. I'm really sorry, we keep telling her that... but she's really sensitive. Like, if we're not agreeing with everything she says, then she freaks out." Sam sighed, glancing over at Morgan. "She keeps accusing us of taking your side, and it doesn't matter how many times I've tried to explain that I'm not, it doesn't seem to matter."

"It's not your fault." Iris waved her hand. "Trust me, I know how it is. There was a reason I ended up with very few friends other than her... Shit, that sounds bad. I don't mean to talk badly about her in front of you."

"No, no, you're right." Sam sighed and looked over at Morgan, who shrugged.

"I don't think I'm going to be friends with her after Amy's

wedding is over," Morgan said baldly, which was her way. "She tries really hard to be my friend, but it doesn't feel right."

"She's good at putting on a show," Sam agreed. "Honestly, I'm not sure Amy is going to be friends with her after the wedding is over, but I think right now, she feels like she can't kick Noelle out of the bridal party. She always wants to give her another chance. At some point, though, her chances have to run out. She has to accept that someone not wanting to talk to her after a fight is not the same as being bullied. And I have never heard you badmouth her to anyone, ever. I can't say the same about her, although she always does it in a way where she says something shitty, then acts like she either didn't mean it that way or like she's super apologetic, but she's just so hurt, she couldn't help herself." Sam shook her head.

"Well, I have said some things about her, but only to people who aren't also friends with her. I would never complain about her to you guys. That wouldn't be fair."

"That's appreciated," Sam replied. "I wish she would act more like you."

Julie raised her eyebrows. It sounded like things with Noelle were seriously escalating. Then again, Sam wasn't the type to put up with the kind of hypocrisy and drama that Noelle seemed to thrive on, so maybe she shouldn't be surprised.

"There, all done," Law said, handing the laptop back to Iris.

She beamed up at him. "Thanks, honey."

"You're welcome." Leaning down, he gave her a very thorough kiss on the lips. Damn, they were cute together.

Julie was glad they'd found their way to each other. Iris needed the support. Especially after having to deal with Noelle.

The fact she'd wormed her way into the club and into making friends with people, and even getting them on her side against Iris, still made Julie want to go around smacking people upside the head. She could see so clearly how Noelle manipulated everyone around her; it was hard to understand why those being manipulated couldn't see it. Yeah, she was good at playing the victim, but why hadn't people noticed that she was somehow always the victim and that she never took real accountability for her actions?

At least Sam and Morgan had had their eyes opened. It sounded like Amy had, too, though whether she'd do anything about it was up in the air. Connor had called himself a people pleaser, but Amy's people-pleasing ways put him to shame. Julie would love to get her in for an appointment, but it wasn't like she could go recruiting like that.

A hand slid around the back of her chair, Connor's lips coming to her ear.

"You're looking a little murderous," he murmured.

Oops. Julie took a deep breath, rearranging her expression to something less... angry. People like Noelle just ticked her off.

"Sorry. Sometimes, my face has subtitles," she murmured, making him laugh.

Connor's laughter broke some of the tension as everyone turned their attention to them.

"What's so funny?" Asad asked, looking at them suspiciously.

"Nothing." Connor smiled, still chuckling as he looked down at his cards. "Come on, let's get back to playing."

"Fine, be that way."

"I will."

Good grief, it was like playing with children. But it was also fun, so she really couldn't complain too much.

Connor

Board game night was either the best or worst idea he'd ever had. Law had always been the most competitive during board game night in the past, but Julie was giving him a run for his money. On the other hand, their trash-talk banter was a lot better than the awkward tiptoeing around each other that they'd been doing at the beginning of the night. They'd settled into trying to beat each other and had forgotten about being careful with each other's feelings.

He also hadn't known that the Quacks of Quedlinburg could be so competitive. It definitely hadn't been in the past.

"Maybe we should play some cooperative games next time," he suggested as Law scowled while they put the game away. Julie was beaming because she'd won. Or maybe next time, he'd make sure that when they split into two groups to play games that Law and Julie were in different groups.

Because wow.

"Oh, that sounds fun. How does that work?" Julie had taken to board game night like a fish to water. He'd been able to tell that she hadn't been super enthusiastic about it before, then a little dubious when she'd realized she'd never even heard of the games they were playing, but she'd clearly ended up loving it.

"Basically, we all work together, and it's us against the game. *Pandemic* is a good one to play for that." He grinned when Law made a face.

Law didn't like *Pandemic* because, as he said, he liked to beat people, not a board. Julie's eyes lit up with interest, though.

"I'd like to try that one," she said with obvious enthusiasm. Connor grinned, feeling incredibly happy that she'd had such a good time tonight.

In the long run, would it have really meant anything bad if she hadn't liked board game night? Of course not. He'd still feel the same way about her that he did. But he felt as though tonight, he'd fallen a little more in love, seeing another side to her.

And he really liked how well she got along with his friends. He'd enjoyed watching her beat Law. Law cared enough about winning that it was rare for someone else to beat him, and it had been fun to watch.

Both Law and Julie's phones alerted simultaneously. Different sounds, but they'd gotten a text message at the exact same time, which was either a colossal coincidence or...

Julie glanced at Law as she pulled her phone out of her pocket and glanced at her screen. She was so much shorter than Connor when she was right next to him, and looking at her phone, he couldn't see her expression, but he could see Law's.

The scowl Law had worn when losing had been real but without any real driving emotion behind it. It had now morphed into something much more intense, with real fury blazing in his eyes as he looked up and over at Julie.

"What is it? What's going on?" Iris asked, jumping up to try to look at Law's phone. Rather than keep her away, he tilted the screen toward her so she could see, and she gasped as Julie told the rest of them.

"The upcoming introduction classes are on hold. Cassidy's ex has been seen around Marquis, and Olivia's tires were slashed today."

"Was it him?" Asad asked, getting automatically to his feet, his fists clenching at his side. The others were upon their feet as well, only a moment behind him, looking just as ready to throw down as he was. "Was it her ex?"

"They can't prove it because there are no cameras where Olivia was parked, but..." Julie's voice trailed off.

Sure, it could have been someone randomly targeting Olivia's car while Cassidy's ex was in the neighborhood. It could have been.

But what were the chances of that?

32

Julie

"I'm moving to Pennsylvania." Cassidy was pale, but her tone was resolute. With her hands folded in her lap, her hair pulled back in a severe bun, and wearing a baggy t-shirt and jeans, she looked like she'd lost all the confidence she'd fought to regain.

They'd been working their way around to this topic the whole session. Pressing her lips together in sympathy, Julie waited to see if she was going to say anything else. Cassidy looked up at her, dark eyes dull with resignation.

"I think it might be safest for you," Julie said after a long moment. Cassidy snorted, and Julie raised her eyebrows. "I take it you're thinking more about keeping others safe."

Cassidy's shoulders hunched slightly.

"If I'm not here, he'll probably leave you all alone." There was sadness in her voice and regret, but the resoluteness remained.

"He might," Julie said gently. "Or he might escalate in an attempt to find out where you've gone." She hadn't thought Cassidy could get any paler, but she did. "My point is that you need to make the choice because it's the right move for you. You don't know how he'll react. You can't make his choices for him."

Taking a deep breath, Cassidy rubbed her hand over her face, shuddering.

"I hate this. How can I make a decision without thinking about how he might react? I wouldn't be thinking about moving to Pennsylvania if it wasn't for him."

"I would hope you're moving to Pennsylvania for your own safety and your own peace of mind," Julie pointed out. "If you're moving because you think it will make everyone else safer, that's not a guarantee. Neither of us can predict how he might react because he's not behaving in a logical, rational manner."

"It's so messed up that he has to actually do something to hurt me before the cops will do anything." Cassidy's expression pinched, some emotion starting to brighten her eyes again. Julie preferred anger over resignation because at least that had some spark to it. "It's the fact that I have to rely on my friends that puts them in danger."

"Well, if they can connect him to Olivia's tires, that will be something." But the odds were slim, and it was unlikely he'd face any time for it. More like a fine. Which would make a man like him even angrier, or it would make him smug at getting off with such a light consequence.

Julie would be willing to put money on the latter. He was getting bolder, and while there was plenty of anger there, she felt like he was more getting off on the power. Which was the same reason he'd called himself a Dom. He liked feeling empowered. He liked seeing what he could get away with.

The fact that he'd had very few repercussions for his previous treatment of Cassidy had probably emboldened him. Which made a thought occur to her.

"It's very possible he'd be targeting the club and its members even if you had moved away immediately." It probably wouldn't be much comfort to Cassidy, but if she wasn't taking the total blame for Douchebag Don's actions, Julie would count that as a win. "While his main focus has been on you, the club kicked him out. He would likely see that as an insult, especially because he would have expected them to be understanding and even supportive of him. He believes he's a Dom. That rejection would sting."

"So, he might follow me, but he might not." Cassidy hefted a sigh and slumped. Then she shook her head. "I think I should still go. He might follow."

"He might," Julie agreed.

"And if he does, I'll be better protected by Patrick's cousin's team than I am down here."

"Personal security could make a big difference." And Patrick's cousin would have resources that they didn't. Especially since the club no longer had a connection to the police department through Kincaid.

"I think starting over will help me, too." Cassidy looked down at her hands. "I have so many memories around here and not necessarily good ones. I don't want to leave the people... but some of the places I can do without." She looked up again, meeting Julie's gaze. "I want to keep seeing you, over video, to start. If I start feeling like I need someone in person, I can let you know."

"I think that's perfect. I'm proud of you for making that decision."

A ghost of a smile lifted the corners of Cassidy's mouth.

"I'm proud of me, too. It's getting a little easier to figure out what I want. As much as I want something new, I think having some familiarity will be good for me. I don't want to change everything all at once, and starting with a new therapist... it would feel like starting over completely. I know part of it is not wanting to explain everything to someone new, but..." Her voice trailed off.

"That's fine, Cassidy. There's nothing wrong with that reason. You don't have to tell anyone about your past or why you're moving until you're ready to. You don't have to tell anyone at all unless you want to —well, other than Patrick's cousin and his team. Though they already know a lot of the details."

"Honestly, that makes it easier. That way, I don't have to admit to any of them how incredibly stupid I am."

"Hey," Julie said gently, leaning forward. "We've talked about this."

Cassidy huffed.

"I know. I still feel stupid. We always think, 'oh, it won't happen to me', then it does, and I can't figure out how it got there. How it was me."

"Don was very charming. Abusers often are. People tend to think of abusers as malicious, deliberately doing things to hurt their partners. They think they'll be able to spot the monster because they'll always be doing terrible things. But the truth is, most abusers don't see themselves as abusive. They justify all of their actions. Which means that most of the time, they look like everyone else. Don got into Stronghold because he was charming, he knew the right answers, and he didn't show any signs of being an abuser at the club before you safeworded and he ignored it."

"He wasn't so charming when Iris intervened."

"Because he was angry. A woman, a submissive, had interrupted him when he'd done nothing wrong. Then everyone backed her up instead of him. That shocked him. Even if he realized on some level that you were supposed to have a safeword, that kink is supposed to have consent, he didn't really believe it. He didn't walk in thinking, 'I'm going to abuse Cassidy and get away with it.' He walked in, thinking he had the right to do whatever he wanted, and you weren't supposed to protest. No one was supposed to stop him. He wasn't doing anything *wrong*."

That was the most dangerous thing about many abusers. They were very good at hiding what they were because they didn't feel guilt about what they did. Or they did feel guilt, and that guilt made them think they weren't actually abusive because they did feel bad about what they'd done. Right up until they lost their temper and did it again. They didn't consider themselves bad people.

"He could be amazing sometimes." Cassidy rubbed her forearm, the movement appearing unconscious. "Especially when we first started dating. He could be so sweet and thoughtful. It wasn't like he was always terrible to me. Most of the time, he wasn't."

"If abusers were abusive all the time, it would be easy to leave them." Julie smiled sadly at her. "It's called a cycle for a reason. That's a large part of why it can be so difficult to get out. But you did get out."

Wrapping up the appointment, Julie felt both exhausted and proud. She was just as angry as Cassidy that the submissive felt like she had to move for her own safety, but it seemed as though Cassidy had mostly gotten past the anger and moved into acceptance. Waving her off, Julie was just closing the door when her phone vibrated on her desk.

Walking over, she frowned when she saw the caller ID. Sandra never called her. They texted like proper millennials.

Her next appointment wasn't for another hour and a half because someone had canceled today. Julie picked up the phone, her stomach churning nervously as she tried to think of why Sandra might be calling.

"Hello?"

"Hey," Sandra whispered back. "Your mom is here."

"What?" Even as she said the word, Julie's brain went into overdrive, connecting the dots.

It was workday hours. Sandra was at work. Sandra worked with Connor. Which meant her mom had just shown up at the rehab center where Connor worked.

What. The. Hell.

Before she could respond, Sandra was whispering again. "She came in for her shoulder. It's definitely frozen. She requested Connor."

Julie's jaw dropped open, and she sat down heavily in her seat. What the hell was she supposed to do with that? Her mom needed help with her shoulder. Sandra probably couldn't treat her since they were family. The connection with Connor was far more nebulous.

What was she supposed to do? 'I'm sorry you're in pain, Mom, but I don't want my boyfriend to help you?'

It didn't matter that there would be a good reason for it. Her mom would harangue her about why she didn't want Connor to be the one to help her. She would ask Julie if Connor wasn't good enough. If Julie didn't think Connor was a good physical therapist. While Julie didn't care what her mom thought of Connor as a PT, she did care about not making Connor feel like she thought he wasn't good enough to help her mom.

She also knew that her reason for not wanting her mom and Connor meeting up regularly without her around had a lot more to do with her mom's past relationship with John than anything else. She also didn't want Connor to feel like she didn't trust him or as if she was painting him with the same brush as John. Taking several deep breaths, she lowered her head to her desk and very gently started banging her forehead against the wood.

What else was she supposed to do?

"I'm going to put you on speaker and get closer so we can listen in... just, don't ruin it by talking," Sandra whispered.

Immediately, Julie stopped banging her head on her desk. Just in case that sound carried over the phone.

Connor

Having Julie's mom as a client was the last thing he'd expected. She was a last-minute addition to his day. When she'd called and asked for him, Aubrey had apparently told her about a cancelation today and said he could fit her in. He hadn't realized she was his girlfriend's mom. If Connor had known she might come, he would have told Aubrey not to schedule her for him, but it was a little late now.

"Okay, I know I've already seen your range of motion recently, but let's check it again," he said, gently holding her arm as he helped her move it back and forth and up and down at various angles.

"Did Julie tell you that I wanted to apologize for inviting John to the barbeque?" she asked as he moved her arm. "She wouldn't give me your phone number so I could."

"I appreciate the apology," he said easily, backing off on her arm when she winced.

"I hope it didn't cause that fight between you and Julie." She paused. "I know she can be sensitive."

"Any disagreements Julie and I have are purely between us," he replied. "Okay, we're going to start off with a massage to help loosen your shoulder muscles up, then we're going to do some stretches. After that, I'd like to put you on the tens unit to help keep everything loose. Sound good?"

His own shoulders were bunching up because he did not like having to tell her no. He felt the urge to reassure her, to tell her that everything between him and Julie was fine, but he didn't know how much Julie would want him to divulge. He sure as hell wasn't going to guess. The best thing to do was to not tell her anything, no matter how hard that was for him.

"Yes, that sounds fine." There was a hint of exasperation in her voice. "You know, Julie—"

"Mrs. Kim," he interrupted her, keeping his voice professional but firm. His heart was pounding in his chest, knowing he needed to do this, even if it meant Julie's mother became angry at him. Even if it meant she never liked him. It felt like the wrong thing to do, contrary to who he was, but he knew it was the right decision. "I'm very happy to help you with your shoulder, but that's what we need to focus on. If you continue to bring up Julie, I'm afraid I will have to transfer you to another physical therapist. If you'd like, I can do that now."

Julie's mom looked up at him, obviously displeased, but there was begrudging respect in her eyes, too.

"I'll stay with you, thank you," she said primly.

"Glad to hear it." He smiled at her because he really did think he could help her. And he'd like to help her.

As they went over to the massage table, he caught Sandra's eye, and she gave him a thumbs-up, making him wonder how much she'd overheard. At least someone was approving. It did help with feeling like Julie would have approved of how he'd handled the situation, which eased some of the tension he was still feeling.

It shouldn't feel this difficult to say no to someone or lay down a boundary, but it did. He wondered how Julie managed to handle it for so long. No wonder she'd been so wound up when he'd broken it for her parents. He couldn't imagine how much harder it was to do with family.

That Mrs. Kim had taken it really well and they proceeded to have a good session, which she'd thanked him for at the end of it, also went a long way to helping him feel better. Even if she wasn't happy about it, she accepted it, and she wasn't mad at him.

That helped a lot when, twenty minutes after she left, Beth came up to ask him to take her last patient.

He said no. He couldn't. He had a date.

And despite Beth's disappointment, she was happy for him.

This saying 'no' thing was getting easier every time he did it.

33

____

Dinner date at Marquis, the downstairs restaurant, and Julie had something to confess. Though she wasn't quite sure how to work around to it, or if she should.

Thankfully, it didn't take Connor long to bring it up. Once they'd sat down and ordered, once the server had whisked away, he looked across the table at her very seriously. He had dressed up for the date in a maroon button-down shirt that strained across his broad shoulders and chest but fit him well enough, it didn't look like buttons were going to pop off or anything. Julie rather liked it.

"I have something to tell you," he said. It was clear he was nervous but determined. Even though she was already pretty sure she knew what he was going to say, Julie nodded.

"Okay."

"Your mom came in for an appointment with me today." His gaze was on her face, studying her reaction.

She smiled at him, reaching across the table with one hand, palm up. Connor slid his fingers into hers.

"Sandra called me when she got there and let me listen to part of your conversation."

Connor blinked.

"Dammit, I should have known she was up to something. So, it's okay?" He looked at her plaintively. "Your mom had a good session today. I'd like to keep helping her."

Because he wanted to help anyone who needed it or because he wanted to make sure Julie's mom kept liking him? And did it really matter as long as he held firm on the lines he'd drawn in the sand today?

Not really.

Her mom could use the help, and she felt reassured knowing that she was in Connor's hands. Much better than John's. If Connor couldn't help, he would say so. He wouldn't push his own agenda to salve his pride.

"It's okay with me as long as you keep handling her like you did today." It was a huge measure of trust that she was putting in him. It wasn't like Sandra was going to be able to spy every time her mom came in. "I don't want her going to you behind my back with things about me or us."

"I will definitely not talk to your mom about you at all while she's seeing me." A sudden grin lit up his face, and he squeezed her hand. "Though I hope you can make an exception for her telling me childhood stories about you."

Julie groaned, leaning back in her seat. "Oh God, which ones did she tell you?"

"I rather liked the one about how you ran through the house as a toddler yelling 'naked baby, naked baby' when your dad's boss was over for dinner."

Groaning, Julie tried to tug her hand away from his so she could bury her face in her palms, but he wasn't letting go. So, she buried her face in one palm, searing it with the heat from her cheeks.

"I can't believe she told you that story." Her mom had waited until she was engaged to John to tell him that story.

Did it mean she trusted Connor more? Or had that been an attempt to scare him off somehow? Julie wasn't sure how to parse her mother's behavior sometimes.

"I thought it was cute." He grinned at her.

Before she could make a retort, a shadow fell over their table, and they both looked up to see Olivia. She smiled at them, but it was more of a grimace than a smile.

"Hey, I'm so sorry to interrupt, but we've got an issue for this weekend. Sherry's mom fell today, and she wasn't too badly injured, but she can't be alone for at least a week, and Sherry and Mark were supposed to perform on Friday." Olivia shot Julie an apologetic look. "It's your week."

Olivia, Julie, and Law did a rotation of who was 'back-up' each weekend in case of emergency, and this just happened to be Julie's weekend. Before Connor, she would have drafted one of the submissive employees who had a night off and done a platonic scene with them. Maybe used a toy or something to add a sexual element.

But now she did have Connor.

He'd appeared slightly confused at first, but when Olivia said it was Julie's week, light dawned in his eyes. She had told him about it before.

"Can you give us a minute to talk about it?" she asked Olivia.

"Of course, just text me sometime tonight if you can." Olivia shot her another apologetic look. "Sorry again for interrupting, but since I just got the call, and I was walking through the dining room, and you were here..."

"No, I get it. This gives us an opportunity to talk about it." Julie smiled, giving Olivia a little wave as she walked away. Her smile faltered as she returned her focus to Connor.

John would never... and he would have been thoroughly insulted that she would think he would.

But Connor wasn't John.

Taking a deep breath, Julie tried to quell the nerves that were churning her stomach. Connor wasn't John. This wasn't going to be a fight just because she was going to ask him if he would perform with her at Marquis.

"Got any plans for Friday?" she asked, trying to make a joke of it.

"I don't, no," he said slowly. He was thinking.

He wasn't saying yes immediately.

He also wasn't blowing up at her for thinking it was even a possibility.

Some of her nerves settled a little. Connor wasn't John—Connor was, in fact, the opposite of John in a lot of ways. He'd described himself as a people pleaser. There was every chance Connor would say yes even though he didn't want to, just because he felt like he should or because he felt like she needed him.

"You don't have to do this," she said quickly. "I think Olivia just wanted to give us the chance if we wanted to. We could see if she and Luke could do it if you're not ready. Or Law and Iris. Or I can call around and see if someone else can be back-up—"

Connor squeezed her hand before she could ramble on, throwing out any more ideas.

"We should do it."

Her verbal vomit grinding to a halt, Julie took a deep breath.

"Are you sure? We really don't *have* to. There's time to find someone else."

"I want to." He smiled at her. "It'll be fun. I've never performed at Marquis before." He paused thoughtfully before adding on. "But... if we could wait for you to peg me until after the show is over. I don't think I want my first time for that to be in front of everyone."

Julie laughed, surprised and maybe even a little shocked, but also gratified to hear that he was open to being pegged afterward. If that was what he wanted, she was happy to reward him with it.

"Of course."

<u>C*ONNOR*</u>

"Are you sure you're okay with this?" Julie asked, frowning as she helped Connor into a leather harness with straps that wrapped around his chest and shoulders. It wasn't the same as Shibari but hugged him in a similar manner, helping him to relax. It was like being held by her, even though she wasn't touching him. The back was left mostly exposed, with one long horizontal strap across the center. There were also two vertical straps, set at an angle, coming down from around his neck. In addition to the harness, she'd already plugged him with a rather large, long plug to prepare him for later.

On his bottom half, a leather pouch contained his cock, leaving him otherwise completely naked. Strings attached to the pouch worked like a thong, so she'd be able to reach his ass.

"I'm okay with this," he said immediately, amused.

This was the fifth time she'd asked over the past twenty-four hours, as if she kept expecting him to suddenly change his mind.

"We can always grab Olivia and Luke from her office if you decide you're not."

The harness was now strapped down, and Connor turned to face her. They were in the backstage area—the green room, even though there was not a single thing in it that was green—which was a small, well-lit room furnished with a single couch, two mirrors, a shelf in front of the mirror hanging on the wall, and two chairs in front of the shelf. They had a room reserved for the evening—the Dungeon Room—though Connor doubted they would be using the front part of that room by the time they were done with the show. They'd left most of their things in there but then had come to the green room for the finishing touches.

He didn't have to look down as far as he sometimes did to meet her gaze. Tonight she was wearing thigh-high boots that laced up the sides, a short black skirt that was like a second skin over her ass, and a bright green corset that had a deep V between her breasts, pushing them together into far more substantial cleavage than she normally had.

Taking her face in his hands, Connor lowered his head, so they were nearly nose-to-nose, looking deep into her eyes.

"I promise, nothing will make me happier tonight than submitting to you for this performance... other than being pegged by you afterward. I love you, Julie." He grinned as her mouth dropped open, then snapped shut, and then opened again.

She was at a loss for words. He didn't need them said back. That wasn't why he'd said it.

Heck, he hadn't known he was going to say it until the words were coming out of his mouth.

The rush of emotion when he'd realized how determined she was to protect him, even from himself, to make sure that he wasn't going to do anything he didn't really want to do even if he wouldn't say it immediately... He'd already known he was falling, had known for a while, but this was the moment when he'd realized he'd *fallen*.

"You do?" she asked after a moment when she'd finally found her voice again.

"I do." His thumb swept along her cheek.

Reaching up for him, she wrapped her arms around his neck.

"I love you, too."

"You don't have to say it just because I did."

Mistress Julie's eyes narrowed as she glared at him.

"Are you calling me a liar, Connor?"

Well, shit.

"No, Ma'am."

"Are you saying I don't know my own feelings?"

"Definitely not saying that, Ma'am."

"So, you believe that I love you?" A smile toyed at the edges of her lips. She was enjoying herself.

Connor smiled back, happy warmth spreading through his chest.

"Yes, Mistress."

Fuck. She loved him.

And they were going truly public with their relationship. With his submission. Then he was going to give himself to her, fully. His cock, already half-hard, began to lift to full height as she went up on her tiptoes and pressed her lips against his.

The kiss had barely started when it was interrupted by a knock on the door and the sound of the door opening before they had a chance to answer.

"Hey, you two, five-minute warning," Olivia said.

"Thank you, five," Julie replied with a sigh, pulling away from

Connor. He frowned at her in confusion, and she laughed. "That's how you acknowledge that you heard the warning... by repeating the number back. Angel taught us all the backstage protocol."

Connor nodded. "Got it. Thank you, five."

Chuckling, Olivia closed the door behind her, giving them privacy again.

Julie ran her hands up his chest. "Ready?"

"Yes, Mistress."

34

JULIE

Shows at Marquis were always as much about the theatrics as they were about the sensuality. Yesterday, she and Connor had done a very brief run-through of how the scene would go, though without the actual flogging. She was going to be doing the two-handed Florentine method for the show—which was quite beautiful to watch and should be highly enjoyable for their audience—then they'd depart to go to their private room for the pegging.

Her body hummed just thinking about it.

The only thing that had thrown her off was Connor's declaration of love. Mostly because he'd said the exact words she'd been thinking at that moment and trying to find the courage to say. He'd done it first, and she'd been so thrown off by the coincidence that she had responded reactively instead of with the smooth, calm, assured response she wished she had.

Yet she had no regrets.

It had been very them.

She was still floating high off the emotions.

The lights on the stage went down, and she and Connor moved to it. They'd been waiting in the darkness, so their eyes didn't take much adjusting. The large wooden frame—like a huge doorway with braces on either side—stood in the center of the stage with two chains hanging down, cuffs attached to the end of them.

Luke and Olivia were right behind them—they were the ones who actually put Connor in the cuffs while Julie got into place behind him with her floggers. One in each hand, she hefted the weight, watching as Olivia and Luke's shadows moved away from her man.

They retreated from the stage, and the lights began to come up again, along with a throbbing base beat that pulsed through her body. With the way they were positioned, it was impossible to see into the booths. Julie had no idea who was watching them. She wasn't sure whether that would make things better or worse for Connor.

Slowly circling around him, she swung the floggers a few times for dramatic effect, not actually touching his skin with them.

Although her circling was part of the show, part of the build, she was also using it to make sure he was okay. All signs pointed to yes—his breathing was even and steady, his muscles were relaxed, and the bulge at the front of his pants said he was already hard.

Of course, that last could happen even if he was uncomfortable, but combined with the other signs she was looking for, it was pretty telling.

Breaking from what they'd rehearsed for just a moment, she stepped forward to go up on her toes and press her lips to his for a swift kiss before stepping back again. Connor grinned at her, his eyes shining. He was enjoying himself.

Julie felt the last of her tension, her nerves, relax. Now, she'd be able to enjoy herself, too.

Moving back around behind him, she swung one of the floggers, sweeping it outward in a pretty spray of multi-stranded leather before she took her place to make sure she knew the length of her reach.

The music started to swell as she lifted her hands and began to move them in the figure-eight pattern that pattered against Connor's back. She couldn't hear him groan, but she knew he did as his muscles flexed, his body arching against the sensation of leather falling against his skin. Breathing in time with the bass, Julie let herself fall into the rhythm of the flogging, her entire focus narrowing to what her hands were doing and how Connor was reacting.

His pale skin turned pinker, darker under the flogger, his shoulders rolling, back muscles flexing as he took the beating. Julie kept one eye on his hands—if he needed a break, he would open and clench his right fist twice in a row. She was watching both hands, though, just in case.

The music rose and fell, and she let the floggers drop.

This was one of the designated breaks when she was able to pace around him again. Switching her floggers to be held in one hand so she could reach up to touch his skin, Julie rubbed her palm over his warmed back and shoulders. It wasn't quite hot to the touch—yet—but it was sensitized, and she felt him shudder. The sensation of power was heady.

Moving around to his front, she kept the hand on him, so she was touching his chest by the time she was looking up at him. He was still smiling, a happy smile that demanded she smile back in return.

"Good boy," she murmured, loud enough that he'd be able to hear it despite the music. His smile widened. The pouch holding his cock had lengthened with it, showing off his very erect hard-on. Julie ran her hand down the outside of the leather to tease him before she moved on.

Walking back around behind him, she got back into position. This time she aimed the flogger lower, turning the pale cheeks of his ass a nice, bright pink, bisected by the line of black leather that was above and between those brightening cheeks. And when she was done turning it a nice bright color, it was going to be time to peg it.

Connor

Feeling almost drunk from the sensations buzzing through him, Connor grinned at Olivia and Luke as they helped him through the Dungeon Room and to the bed. Julie was following along behind him. It was nice to have the extra help, so he didn't have to try to get a hold of himself. He could just let them take care of him.

They helped him onto the bed, and Connor rolled onto his back, his leather-clad cock pointing up at the ceiling. The feel of the comforter against his sensitized shoulders and ass made him shudder, his cheeks clenching around the plug inside him. He felt dizzy and happy and incredibly aroused.

"Have fun, buddy," Luke said, giving Connor's shoulder a pat.

"Thanks." Connor had already had fun, but he was looking forward to the next part, even though his nervousness was growing. Understandably. He was going to be doing something he'd never done before.

Something that was incredibly intimate just because of what it was.

But he wanted it. With her. His Julie. His Mistress. He wanted to give her everything. Every part of him.

He wasn't sure how long he was staring up at the ceiling thinking about that—he really did feel drunk or like his head was floating in the clouds—when a noise made him turn his head. There she was. Mistress Julie. Naked now, no more corset or skirt. The only thing she was wearing was a harness holding a large, tanned cock to her hips. It jutted out in front of her.

It wasn't as big as Connor's dick, but considering where she was planning to put it, it was intimidatingly sized. Even though she'd shown it to him ahead of time, now that the moment was here, it seemed bigger. Or maybe it just looked bigger because she was wearing it. His heart started pounding faster, feeling as if it was getting ready to jump out of his chest.

Crawling up onto the bed, her eyes were alight with anticipation, her tongue flicking out to wet her lower lip.

"What's your color, Connor?" she asked as she reached for the tie on his cock pouch, pulling the string so she could tug the leather off his erection. The feel of it sliding over his shaft, the cool air in the room suddenly wafting over his skin, did nothing to quell how hard he was. In fact, it only made him harder.

"Green, Mistress."

Nervous, but green. He sure as hell didn't want her to stop.

Putting her hands on his legs, she pushed them upward, bending them at the knee and bending him at the waist so she could reach the base of the plug, then tugged gently, twisting the toy inside him rather than immediately pulling it out. Connor shuddered, reaching up to grab the headboard, so he had something to hold on to as the sensations rolled through him.

Then she tugged, and he felt himself stretch for the bulb before closing as the plug slid out, leaving him empty. Julie leaned over to put the plug in a little basin on the nightstand. She picked up a tube of lube at the same time.

With his legs still tucked up against his body, his ass was completely exposed and vulnerable.

Slicking the lube over her cock, Julie smiled wickedly at him.

"Ready?" she asked, dropping the tube beside her and shifting forward, settling herself between his feet where they were raised in the air. The head of the cock nestled against his anus, which ached emptily without the plug.

"Yes, Mistress. As ready as I'm going to be." Which was the full, truthful answer. He didn't feel entirely ready but didn't think he ever would feel entirely ready. How could he be ready for something he'd never experienced before?

He couldn't.

Mistress Julie's hands came down on his knees, pressing them back toward his chest as the cock began to push forward.

Connor groaned. The dildo was about as thick around as the bulb on the plug he'd had inside him, but the plug had been tapered. It had started out very small and grown to that size, and once it was inside him, the ring of his sphincter had been able to close around the neck between the bulb and the base.

This was entirely different.

This stretched him immediately, with no gradual taper and no end to the stretch. Connor groaned at the discomfort, the sting, and the pleasure. Mistress Julie leaned in, keeping his legs pinned to his body, her hips moving back so that the cock retreated... then thrusting in again, deeper this time. The slickness of the lube made for easier entry, but it also meant that his spasming hole couldn't slow the toy's advance the way his body was desperate to.

It was enough to make his erection subside slightly as his asshole burned. Mentally, he didn't feel any less aroused, but his bodily reaction as he adjusted to being invaded changed.

"Good boy," Mistress Julie crooned, reaching forward with one hand to rub her fingers through his chest hair. His chest moved up and down as he panted, his body adjusting to its new proportions. "Open up for me."

"Fuck!" The tip of the cock rubbed over a spot inside him that made his own dick jerk in response. He shuddered, his ass clenching down around the cock still sliding deeper into it, which only made the sensations more intense.

Mistress Julie moaned, also shuddering as she bottomed out, her body pressing against his, the leather base of the strap-on rubbing against his cheeks. Letting her hand slide down his happy trail, she reached his cock and wrapped her fingers around it, gripping him as she began to move.

"Oh fuck... fuck..." Connor nearly levitated off the bed as she began to both fuck and jerk him simultaneously, the rhythms flowing together. His back and ass tingled against the bed beneath him, adding to the sensation of full-body pleasure. He writhed helplessly, moving his hips to meet both her hand and her thrusts, caught in the give and take as waves of rapture battered his senses. "Fuck... please..."

"Hold on for me, Connor... don't cum yet..." Her voice was full of sensual need, her breath coming in gasps. He wasn't the only one highly aroused as she rode him, the dildo sliding back and forth inside him easily now. He was fully stretched open, his muscles clenched, making it burn a bit, but in a good way that had his toes curling.

He fought against the rising pleasure, shuddering and trying to distract himself. It was no easy task as she kept moving inside him, the cock sliding back and forth, pressing against his prostate. Her hand moved on his cock, precum sliding over her fingers, wetting his dick and adding to his growing ecstasy.

Panting, he strained, the headboard creaking as he gripped it tighter, feeling as if he was losing sensation in his fingers because he was holding on so tight.

"Please..." he begged, arching his back and closing his eyes against the sensual assault. Her fingers gripped, pulling on his cock as she filled him with hers. "Oh fuck, Mistress, please... I can't... I'm going to..."

"Come for me, Connor," she ordered with a gasp. "Come for me, good boy."

That was all it took. Her hand pumped, and he climaxed, his body shuddering with ecstasy as the build-up exploded through him, his cock pulsing against her fingers as jet after jet of cum finally released.

---

*J*ULIE

With her hand firmly wrapped around Connor's dick, she tilted it toward her. Warm liquid sprayed over her, streams of white cum spattering against her breasts and stomach, dripping down her. It was an utterly filthy sensation, and it tipped her over the edge as her clit rubbed against the inside of the strap-on. Her pussy clenched around the dildo inside her, and she cried out as his seed slid over her body, hot against her breasts and nipples, dripping down onto him.

She cried out, slamming hard into him, the waves of pleasure washing over her as she came.

It was hot, wet, and utterly satisfying.

Panting, she slumped over him, his cock softening in her hand. She reached up with her other hand to wipe her lightly damp hair from her forehead. Their gazes met, and she smiled down at him. Letting go of the headboard, he reached for her.

His hand cradled her head. She leaned forward, making him shudder. Their lips met in a kiss, gentle and sweet, his cum sliding across her body and onto his. It was perfect.

EPILOGUE

Z*ACH*

Reaching up to adjust his tie, Zach grimaced. He normally loved having an excuse to wear his tux. It was custom-tailored to him and fit him like a glove, yet right now, it felt too tight, even though he knew it wasn't. When he'd put it on earlier in the week to decide what vest and tie he was wearing with it, it had felt fine, so why did he suddenly feel like he was choking?

A large, warm hand came to rest on his thigh, and he felt the heat against his side as his boyfriend, Kincaid, leaned against him.

"Are you okay?" The question was asked quietly enough that no one would be able to hear it, even though the pews were tightly packed with wedding guests. At least Zach was at the very end of the pew, right next to the center aisle, so he didn't have anyone right beside him watching his discomfort other than Kincaid.

Letting his hand drop, he looked back at his boyfriend and did his best to give him a reassuring smile. Kincaid smiled back, though it didn't really reach his dark eyes, which were still full of concern. This was one of their first public outings, not just since getting back together after they took a break, but ever. Zach wasn't 'out' yet.

But it was Amy's wedding, and the only people they knew here were friends from Stronghold and Marquis... which were the only two places where Zach and Kincaid had previously been 'out'. Zach didn't consider the kink clubs to be public, though. Everything that happened there was still private.

The lack of public outings had been part of why he and Kincaid had broken up. That, along with the fact that Zach still wasn't out to his family. Every time he thought about telling his parents, fear choked him to the point of silence. He'd managed to tell his sister, and she was encouraging him to talk to their parents, but he just couldn't bring himself to do it yet. And it didn't matter that he'd fallen in love with Kincaid; he still couldn't tell his parents that he was bisexual.

Or, at least, that he wasn't straight. He'd never been attracted to any man other than Kincaid, so he also wasn't sure he could even say he was bisexual, but he wasn't straight.

Straight men didn't love getting railed by their boyfriend.

"I'm fine. I think I might have tied my tie too tight," he said, sliding his hand under Kincaid's to hold it. Immediately, Kincaid relaxed a little, looking down at their joined hands and smiling. Just that one little show of affection, the acceptance of Kincaid's hand on his and then joining them together, and Kincaid was thrilled.

That made Zach feel even shittier. It was a mark of how badly Kincaid craved that acknowledgment of their relationship, how badly he wanted to be able to treat Zach like his boyfriend, regardless of where they were and who was around them. He was working up to being able to tell his family.

The guests around them were getting restless, shifting in their seats the same way he was.

In front of him, Rick—another member of Stronghold and Marquis—leaned against his wife. Unlike Kincaid, he didn't keep his voice low enough to be unheard by those around him.

"What time is it? Isn't this supposed to have started already?"

Frowning, Zach shifted the hand Kincaid was holding to look at his watch. Yes, the wedding was supposed to have started five minutes ago. But the doors at the back were empty. No pastor, no groomsmen, no groom.

His heart started to beat a little faster in his chest.

Fuck, was something going wrong?

Do I want it to?

He was here for the bride, after all. The groom, in his opinion, didn't deserve her at all. But Amy loved Jeremy and would be devastated if something had happened. She had her heart set on this wedding, this marriage. As her friend and sometimes scene partner, Zach supported what she wanted.

As if Rick's question had been permission for everyone else to start questioning things, conversation rose in a murmur. Zach was hardly the only one twisting to look around, as if Jeremy or someone might pop out of hiding with an explanation as to what was going on.

The fact that he was turned around meant he saw Sam the moment she appeared in the doorway, looking stunning in a sage green bridesmaid dress that set off her blonde good looks and delightful curves perfectly. His heart started racing a little faster as she started coming down the aisle, her gaze scanning over the bride's side like she was looking for someone...

It felt as though it was going to leap right out of his chest when their gazes met, and she suddenly went from walking and looking to striding right for him. For a moment, he didn't believe it, but then she came to a halt right beside him. Everyone was staring, the conversation dropping off as quickly as it had started.

Bending down, she ignored everyone else, keeping her voice low, even though it wouldn't matter. Rick and Maria had turned around to see what was going on, and everyone was now straining to hear what she said.

"Amy needs you. *Now.*" Glancing up and past him, she looked at Kincaid. "You'd better come, too."

Zach leapt to his feet, Kincaid only a heartbeat behind him.

KINCAID, ZACH, AND AMY WILL RETURN IN THIRD WHEEL!

ACKNOWLEDGMENTS

I have a lot of people to thank for helping me with this book.

My amazing beta readers, who are invaluable in helping me catch mistakes, doing the initial grammar and word checks, identifying continuity issues, and working through problems with me. Marie, Candida, Karen, Marta, Rara, Piper and Katherine – you all make these books so much better!

Another extra special thank you to Katherine, who got me started down this career path and has been by my metaphorical side ever since.

Thank you to my husband for his continued loved and support. I could not do this without you.

And, as always, a big thank you to all of you for buying and reading my work... if you love it, please leave a review!

ABOUT THE AUTHOR

Golden Angel is a USA Today best-selling author of heart and bottom warming romance.

She is happily married, old enough to know better but still too young to care, and a big fan of happily-ever-afters, strong heroes and heroines, and sizzling chemistry.

When she's not writing, she can often be found on the couch reading, in front of her sewing machine making a new cosplay, hanging out with her friends, or wandering the Maryland Renaissance Fair.

www.goldenangelromance.com

BB bookbub.com/authors/golden-angel
g goodreads.com/goldeniangel
f facebook.com/GoldenAngelAuthor
instagram.com/goldeniangel

OTHER BOOKS BY GOLDEN ANGEL

Contemporary BDSM Romance

Venus Rising Series (MFM Romance)

The Venus School

Venus Aspiring

Venus Desiring

Venus Transcendent

Venus Wedding

Venus Rising Box Set

Stronghold Doms Series

The Sassy Submissive

Taming the Tease

Mastering Lexie

Pieces of Stronghold

Breaking the Chain

Bound to the Past

Stripping the Sub

Tempting the Domme

Hardcore Vanilla

Steamy Stocking Stuffers

A Sassy Christmas

Entering Stronghold Box Set

Nights at Stronghold Box Set

Stronghold: Closing Time Box Set

Masters of Marquis Series

Bondage Buddies

Master Chef

Law & Disorder

Switch Play

Legally Bound

Shallow Submission

Hidden Away

Secret Submission

Third Wheel

Dungeons & Doms Series

Dungeon Master

Dungeon Daddy

Dungeon Showdown

Dungeons & Doms Boxset

Daddies Everywhere

Chef Daddy

Foosball Daddies

Taco Daddy

Cheese Daddy

Garden Daddy

Little Villain

Historical Spanking Romance

Domestic Discipline Quartet

Birching His Bride

Dealing With Discipline

Punishing His Ward

Claiming His Wife

The Domestic Discipline Quartet Box Set

Bridal Discipline Series

Philip's Rules

Gabrielle's Discipline

Lydia's Penance

Benedict's Commands

Arabella's Taming

Pride and Punishment Box Set

Commands and Consequences Box Set

Deception and Discipline

A Season for Treason

A Season for Scandal

A Season for Smugglers

A Season for Spies

Desire and Discipline

A Season for Bliss

A Season for Desire

A Season for Christmas

Bridgewater Brides

Their Harlot Bride

Standalone

Marriage Training

The Duke's Pursuit

Rogue Booty

Sci-fi Romance

Tsenturion Masters Series with Lee Savino
Alien Captive
Alien Tribute
Alien Abduction

Standalone
Mated on Hades

Shifter Romance

Big Bad Bunnies Series
Chasing His Bunny
Chasing His Squirrel
Chasing His Puma
Chasing His Polar Bear
Chasing His Honey Badger
Chasing Her Lion
Night of the Wild Stags

Chasing Tail Box Set
Chasing Tail... Again Box Set